THE GRIMM SOCIETY

ALSO BY CHANDA HAHN

THE UNFORTUNATE FAIRY TALES

UnEnchanted

Fairest

Fable

Reign

Forever

THE IRON BUTTERFLY

The Iron Butterfly

The Steele Wolf

The Silver Siren

THE NEVERWOOD CHRONICLES

Lost Girl

Lost Boy

Lost Shadow

THE DAUGHTERS OF EVILLE

Of Beast and Beauty

Of Glass and Glamour

Of Sea and Song

Of Thorn and Thread

Of Mist and Murder

Of Gold and Greed

Of Secrets and Slippers

THE GRIMM SOCIETY

CHANDA HAHN

Thorns ripped at her arms and tore her clothes as she slid down the embankment, causing her to panic. She tried to slow her descent by digging her boot heel into the ground, but a protruding root snagged her ankle and sent her tumbling head over heels. She landed on her back, gasping for air as the wind was knocked out of her. Bright lights flashed across her vision before softening into the twinkling of actual stars. The tops of the evergreen trees pierced the sky like arrows, each pointing toward the moon. The encroaching clouds would soon cover its glowing face and cast her into utter darkness.

"No," she breathed out. She scrambled to her feet and limped away on a quickly swelling ankle.

Why had she agreed to this rendezvous? Why didn't she listen to her gut and return to the car when it got dark? Was it because she still had feelings for him and hoped to reconcile?

She followed the pin on her phone's map app until she encountered an abandoned cabin. The shutters over the window were nailed closed. Immediately she knew she had made a terrible mistake.

This was not the romantic meeting she had in mind.

A loud twig snapped. She turned to see red eyes reflecting

at her in the moonlight—cold, haunting eyes as if from a demon —and then a deep, guttural growl sounded.

She fled, away from the cabin into the thicket. Her terror caused the rational side of her brain to be blocked by the fight-or-flight response. The ground beneath her feet swam as she couldn't see through the terror and her tears. The branches of the trees reached like claws for her face, and warm blood ran down her cheeks.

She screamed and swatted at the attacking branches. Her heart raced as she mindlessly ran, then stumbled into the mud, her chin hitting the hard earth. Her soft sobs were the only thing that punctuated the quiet night. Even the crickets and owls had gone silent—as if they, too, could feel the approaching predator hunting her, staying just beyond the edge of her peripheral vision.

The growl came again.

"Go away!" she screamed as tears filled her vision. Grabbing a stick, she swung out at the shadows. The clouds started to cover the moon, the light quickly fading as the frantic beat of her heart grew louder in her ears.

A crack of a branch made her still, and she turned slightly to see the monster rush from the darkness toward her just as the clouds claimed the last of the moonlight.

CHAPTER 1

Fear raced through her as the steel handcuffs painfully bit into her wrists. She fought the panic that threatened to bubble up as the blindfold dulled her senses while highlighting the terror. The chill from the floor seeped into her body, stealing whatever warmth she had left, while the smell of must and dirt assailed her nose. Everly rocked her head until the sack that covered her face slid off. She blinked, trying to adjust to the semidarkness.

Everly took a deep breath to calm herself and focused on her immediate surroundings. Her feet were bound with duct tape, and her hands were cuffed behind her back. The room she was imprisoned in was dark with a damp smell, like a wet dog with a hint of bleach. It was a basement. Silent except for the ticking from a lime-green vintage clock on the wall, counting down the time until *he* promised to return.

Everly shuddered. She had little time left.

The far wall had a deep freezer big enough for a body. *Her body?* Why did her brain always go there? Above the freezer was a small padlocked hopper window with leaves piling up against the dirty pane. The window was big enough for her to squeeze through if she could break out of her bonds and then break the lock. To the right, stairs led to the main floor and an exit. On the left was a scratched and dented mismatched washer and dryer and a rust-stained laundry sink. Behind her was a dark corner with a water heater, an old furnace, and boxes of what looked like Christmas decorations.

By the stairs, a few metal storage shelves were stocked with old food cans—some missing their labels—stacks of bulk paper towels, laundry detergent, bleach, a rusted green toolbox, open tin cans, and dusty glass canning jars filled with odds and ends.

Everly rolled to her side and came face-to-face with a dead rat. It was mummified and stuck in the mousetrap. Its long teeth were even more prominent from decomposed remains and the hint of its skeleton. There wasn't much left; the maggots had long ago taken care of the rat.

She scooted farther from the carcass, hoping that was the only dead thing she would encounter down here. Pulling her knees up, Everly rolled and pressed her face into the floor, the cement crushing into her cheek. With a grunt, she pushed herself backward onto her knees and then struggled to stand. The duct tape was pinching into her ankles. She hopped over to the metal storage shelf, scanning the contents. She could knock the toolbox off the shelf, but the loud crash would alert others to her escape attempt. It could also provide a weapon to fight off her captor. Or it could be empty, and it was all for naught. No. Using the things in sight would be better, or searching the smaller containers. The glass jars were filled with thick nails and screws. *No use.* The screws were again too thick and not pliable enough.

Sweat trickled down her back as the clock drew closer to six. *The cans.* Using her chin, she gently knocked over the first tin can, and a bunch of bolts rolled out. One fell off the shelf and hit the floor, rolling under the freezer. She froze. She observed the stairs, listening for any creak in the floorboards above her.

On to the next can. This one was light and rolled toward the back of the shelf, stopping against the brick wall and turning to reveal the interior. *Empty*.

The third can fell over, and her eyes lit up when a clink of items tumbled out. More nails, lug nuts, the nub of a pencil, a half-used eraser, and *hope* in the shape of a paper clip.

The minute hand moved closer to the twelve.

Quickly, with ever-increasing numbing fingers, Everly took the paper clip in her lips and balanced it on the edge of the shelf. Turning back, she opened her palms and bumped the frame with her hip, knocking the paper clip into her open hands.

Her fingers tingled as she straightened the clip and felt along the cuff to orient herself, placing the wire into the top flag portion of the keyhole. She shoved it in and bent it at a forty-five-degree angle. Moving the locking bar on the handcuff, she rocked it toward her wrist until she felt it release.

From above, dust fell from the ceiling between the floor-boards as footsteps moved across the floor, heading toward the basement door.

She quickly worked the second lock and left the cuffs on the floor. She shoved her hands between her knees and broke the duct tape around her ankles using her upper body strength. She was free.

Just as the basement door swung open, light illuminated the hidden staircase in the darkened corner.

Everly spun, her heart pounding. Black heavy boots descended the stairs one at a time. Slow, methodical, the pace meant to instill fear.

It was working. She ducked behind the water heater and waited.

The man came to the bottom step of the stairs, surveying the empty floor where she had lain tied up only minutes before.

His voice was low, even, showing little emotion. "You escaped the cuffs and duct tape but failed to escape my clutches. You lose."

Everly's heart dropped.

He moved to the middle of the room and yanked the pull chain on the bulb light, illuminating the dreary interior. The man stood over six feet, and his dark gray overcoat almost reached the floor. A flat cap covered his reddish-brown hair, the silhouette accenting his intimidating build. He leaned down and picked up the duct tape, studying it, before turning over and grabbing the black cloth bag used to cover her face. He reached into his jacket and pulled out a silver pocket watch, flipping it open to gauge the time.

"Too late. You can come out now, Everly. You failed."

Everly stepped out from behind the water heater. Her eyes flashed in anger. "I didn't fail. You never said I had to escape the basement," she argued.

"Didn't I? I said you had six minutes to escape. I assumed you knew the endgame was to escape the house. Not just the binds." He held up his old-fashioned pocket watch to show her.

"Dad, this is messed up." Everly flung her hands in the air. "No one can do that in six minutes. Ten minutes maybe, but six?"

"Duct tape is child's play," her father said. "I gave you the easy way out."

Everly regarded her father, Everick Hart, homicide detective for Misty Creek Police Department. He was in his early forties but still handsome, with an angled chin and strong jaw. His hair had just begun to turn gray at the temples. The deep circles under his eyes attested to his latest case keeping him up at night and away from home most days.

Even though their town was beautiful, tucked against the mountains, it was always covered in fog and rain for most of the winter months, lending to its name, Misty Creek.

Misty Creek was the epicenter for all things weird and brought in plenty of tourists hoping to catch a peek of Bigfoot or search the caves for ghosts and lost souls. Not to mention the rumor of buried treasure. But it led to one of the highest rates of lost and missing people. It kept the police department and the park rangers always busy.

Everly rarely ever saw her dad anymore, and when she did, he always insisted on these training "games," as he called them. Though really, they were survival techniques. She knew it was his way to fight the demons of the past, the unsolved cases, the culprits that got away. He would ensure one less victim if he couldn't arrest them.

Everick Hart went to examine the cuffs Everly discarded.

"Paper clip. Good. Why not the nail?" Everick began the interrogation.

"Too strong. I could have maybe been able to bend a finishing nail, but there weren't any in there."

"Did you check the toolbox?" he asked.

"It was too much of a risk." Everly shifted her feet, keeping her arms behind her back.

"Why?" he pressed.

"It would have made too much noise if I knocked it off the shelf, alerting my captor. I would have gone for it after being free, but I ran out of time."

Everick moved to the shelf and opened the toolbox, dust sliding off the top to reveal it was empty. "That was a good assessment. The paper clip was the way to go, but you failed to notice the other weapon."

"You mean this one?" Everly pulled the crowbar from behind her leg. "I found it tucked behind the water heater. My escape plan would have been to stand on the freezer to reach the window and break the lock with the crowbar."

"Excellent!" Her father nodded, and the rare smile lit up his face.

Everly felt a moment of pride and wanted to stay in the moment. Hold onto it for a little longer. Maybe she played these morbid games because she wanted to prove to her father that she could care for herself. He wouldn't have to worry about her when the time came.

Everick started to cough, a deep, painful hack that attacked his lungs. He pulled a handkerchief out of his coat. Covering his mouth, folding the cloth, and tucking it away, he tried to hide the blood he had coughed up.

A sour feeling settled into the pit of Everly's stomach. She knew he was sick and would deny her allegations, just as he did all the other times. He was teaching her to be observant, but only on what he felt mattered. His health was not one of them.

"Rope would have been more of a challenge. Especially the constrictor or the double constrictor knot," Everly said, pretending ignorance as her father turned away. He took a few deep breaths as he tried to hide the evidence of his sickness.

Some families paid for escape experiences with generic puzzles, but her father set up real scenarios based on past cases, giving her a real-life look at life-or-death situations. A sixty-minute escape room had nothing on her father's challenges.

Everick nodded. His face was a little paler than before. He was looking at his watch. He frowned, gesturing to the stairs. "It's time."

He pulled the string on the light, plunging the basement back into near darkness.

She followed him up the stairs into their kitchen. It was

cozy with high off-white cabinets, an island, a giant retro stove, and an eat-in kitchen nook with two bench seats and two chairs. Beyond the kitchen was a solarium filled to the brim with plants, herbs, and white wicker furniture, all tended to by the eccentric Granny Hart, who everyone called Birdie. She was obsessed with all things plants, especially their medicinal uses. Everly was sure not all Birdie's plants were pretty flowers; she could have sworn she saw nightshade growing.

"So after dinner, we get to celebrate—"

"Mr. Plum, in the study, with what?" Everick loudly announced as he opened the cabinet and pulled out a glass.

"What?" Everly asked, heading to search the back of the fridge for a rogue Diet Coke and lime. They tended to get pushed behind the leftover containers.

"Mr. Plum," Everick repeated slowly. "In the study, with the... what?" He pulled out a glass for her drink.

"Another round?" Everly asked suspiciously.

Most girls' nightly discussions included sports, drama clubs, and boys, while Everly's frequently centered around cold cases, mortality rates, and murder games. It made her realize why Holland never wanted to spend the night at her house.

"Of course." Everick grinned. "Let's play a round of 'guess how they died.'"

"And I'm sure it was just as morbid then." Everly shook her head, popped the can, and poured it into her glass. "Can't we play a normal game like Monopoly?"

"Monopoly?" a high-pitched voice cried out in mock disgust. "Monopoly has been destroying families since 1935," Birdie interjected as she floated into the kitchen, dressed in a light blue shirt dress and pink slip-ons. Her once beautiful red-blonde hair had faded to a soft golden white and was pinned up in curls.

"Well then, how about Scrabble?" Everly tried to interject.

"Can you spell B-O-R-I-N-G?" Everick shook his head. "Just humor me. One round of 'guess how he died.'"

"I always loved the 'guess how he died' game," Birdie crooned as she played with the locket around her neck. "My George would have won in a heartbeat."

"That's because Grandpa was the county medical examiner, and you were his medical assistant. You two knew how everyone died." Everly stuck her thumb toward the white brick outbuilding near the alley attached to their property. You could see Grandpa Hart's old medical office through the glass sunroom, which her father used as his active case layout room. Why he wanted to work there with a senior medical table and trays with creepy drains in the floor was beyond her. But Everick spent many nights studying cases, working on missing person reports, and always locking them up before coming back inside.

Birdie's blue eyes zeroed in on Everick and his glass covered with condensation heading for the wood table.

Quickly, she pulled out a doily coaster before his glass touched the wood tabletop. "Really, Everick, use a coaster."

Everick chuckled and leaned over to kiss her head before reaching into the cookie jar and taking a few cookies.

Grandma Birdie was the heart of the home, and no one dared to argue with her... ever. She loved plants, being outside, and was obsessed with doilies, and she would cut you if you ever dared to remove one of those precious ornamental lace mats from the chair's armrests. Along with Birdie's preference for vintage was her disdain for paper plates and all things disposable.

"Get this," Everick continued with his game. "The victim's name was Mr. Plum. Like in the board game. The first officer on the scene called it an accidental death." He grinned before taking a bite; crumbs started to fall, and Birdie brought out another plate and put it under his cookie. "What with the knocked-over ladder and the broken tub of Christmas lights he was trying to put away in the garage. But after the autopsy, there was apparent significant blunt-force trauma to the back of the head. What do you think happened?"

"I know." Everly raised her hand. "He died from an over-dose of Christmas cheer," she said sarcastically.

"Use that beautiful brain of yours!" Everick tapped Everly on her forehead, and she blinked.

"Do you know that the average brain weighs six pounds?" Birdie called out over her shoulder. She had also taken a plate and a few chocolate chip cookies. "And a woman's brain shrinks when she's pregnant."

"Stop," Everly laughed. "No more random facts. If I play your stupid 'guess how he died' game, can we please have a normal night?"

Everick leaned back, pushed his spectacles up his nose, and crossed his arms. "Only if you win."

"What are the stakes," Birdie announced. She reached into the cabinet, pulled out a rose-colored teacup, and set the kettle on the stove.

"Stakes?" Everly laughed.

"No, no gambling." Everick waved his hands.

Birdie looked at her son in surprise. "Without stakes, there's no reason to play."

"All right." Everick cracked his knuckles and looked between his mother and daughter. "Loser has to do the dishes for the week."

"I already do the dishes," Everly stated.

"Fine. Then loser buys ice cream at Duke's after dinner."

"Fine. You're going down, and I'm getting the double-high monster strawberry sundae with extra strawberry sauce." Everly put her drink away and focused on her father. The gauntlet had been thrown. "Paint me a picture. What's in the garage? Where was the deceased found?"

Everick always had a flair for the dramatic. He leaned forward and began to rattle off information. "Storage shelf with plastic bins full of seasonal decorations. One wall was filled with garden equipment, a red toolbox with tools, a blue barrel full of sporting equipment, a mini fridge, and a snack cupboard."

"What's in the fridge?" Everly asked.

"Seltzer water and grape soda."

"Cupboard?"

"Animal crackers and peanuts." Everick held back a pinched smile.

"Any decor on the wall?" she asked.

"Cirque du Soleil poster, monthly *Sports Illustrated* calendar, St. Louis Cardinals poster, vintage neon Coca-Cola sign."

"Vehicles in the garage?"

"One 2019 BMW with black leather seats, two bicycles, a lawn mower, and a unicycle."

"Unicycle? What are you doing? Seltzer water, animal crackers, peanuts, and a unicycle. Are we investigating a clown?"

Everick shrugged, trying to hold back his laugh. "Humor me."

"I'm not falling for the clown stuff. That's all red herrings." She sighed and closed her eyes, trying to picture the scene. "What was around the body?"

"Besides the overturned stepladder? Nothing."

"Castoff?" Everly asked.

"Oh, good question. Did you know the first hit is considered a freebie and usually has no blood trail?" Birdie chimed in again as the whistle on her kettle went off.

"Yes, Grandpa taught me that too." Everly held back a smile.

"Oh, well." Birdie shrugged, added the tea bag into her cup, and poured hot water over it. An earthly, floral, and somewhat sweet scent filled the air, signifying Birdie was brewing a black tea over her favorite green tea's lighter grassy and lemon aroma.

"No castoff," Everick answered.

"Right, because if there were castoff, the first person on scene would have called it a homicide," Everly answered.

"Now, you're thinking." Everick clapped his hands.

Everly grinned. She was good at this when she wanted to be. "Describe the deceased."

"Man, late thirties, athletic."

"Describe the injury," Everly said.

"Took you long enough to get to this part. Blunt-force trauma to the head. The skull fracture." Everick leaned back and crossed his arms. She could tell from his body language that she was getting close.

"Any trace in the wound?" she asked.

His eyes twinkled. "One splinter. Wood. Maple."

Everly closed her eyes and tried to picture the scene again; car, tools, a barrel of sporting equipment.

"What was the size of the fracture in the skull?"

"It had a diameter of two and three-quarter inches." Everick's eyes narrowed. She was getting very close.

Everly chewed on her lip as her brain returned to the wall poster—baseball—and the tub of sporting equipment almost every family owned.

"Baseball bat."

"Ding. Ding. Ding." Everick twirled his finger in the air. "You are correct."

"I'm also getting double sprinkles." Everly grinned.

"I knew that," Birdie said, but her voice had gotten serious, and she was staring out the window toward the backyard and the path that headed to the mountains. "It sounded a lot like how Mr. Samuel Plum died in 2011 when the Cardinals won the World Series."

Everly couldn't understand her grandmother. She was the smartest while also the ditsiest person she knew. Her mind was a steel trap of nostalgia, and while she would almost always win at Trivial Pursuit, she couldn't find her glasses on her head.

"That's exactly the case I was referring to," Everick said.

Birdie headed into her sunroom and, a few minutes later, came out with some fresh cuttings. "I'll be out the rest of the night. Heading over to Elenore's for some late-night tea and gossip." She winked at the both of them.

Everly watched her grandma grab her shawl and head out the side door, crossing the yard to take the worn walking path into the woods. "She forgot."

"Yep," Everick mumbled.

"That's okay. I like having you to myself tonight." Her eyes followed her grandma's colorful scarf as she paused and seemed fixated on talking to a tree. An everyday occurrence in their house. "She's not going to Elenore's, is she?" Everly asked suspiciously.

Everick watched his mother go and shrugged. "I've learned long ago not to question her, but you noticed she cut out right when the dishes needed to be washed."

"I noticed." Everly stood, took her glass and Birdie's teacup and saucer, and put them in the sink, running the water to wash them. Their kitchen was far too old and small for an actual dishwasher. When the few dishes they used were washed and put away, Everick went to the hall closet and grabbed his jacket.

"You ready for dinner?" he asked.

"Of course," she said enthusiastically. "I'm starving."

Everly rarely got to see her father anymore, he was so busy with cases, and tonight was a special night. She wanted to cherish any time he had a night off, which was rare.

Everly's phone buzzed with a text message. It was her best friend, Holland Abernathy.

Can you come over? I'm bored.

How could Holland be bored? She lived on the other side of town and had a thousand amenities at her fingertips.

Can't. I'm with my dad.

Is he making you play detective again?

Maybe. I don't mind. We're about to get dinner to celebrate my—

Just then, her father's phone rang. He pulled his phone out of his jacket and moved into the sunroom for added privacy.

"Hello? Yes, Captain. I understand. But tonight's not a good night; I have my daughter. I see—victim. Female? Yes. I can be there shortly. Just let me take care of a few things."

Everly's heart dropped. She knew pizza night was about to be canceled. She picked up her phone.

Change of plans. Be over in 20. Can I stay over?

Of course. Stay forever. C U Soon.

"Hey, Everly." Her dad looked solemn. "Something came up. I need to cancel pizza night."

"What is it?" Everly asked. She could see that this wasn't a regular call out for him to be this worried. "Anything I should be worried about?"

"That missing hiker from Cedarville." He brushed his hand across his face. "They found her—" He didn't finish and didn't need to. She knew.

"Where?" Everly's heart sank.

"Near Mirkwood Falls trail."

Everly worried on her bottom lip. "Is she...?"

Everick sighed. "Yeah, forest rangers think a wild animal got her, but I won't know until... I may be a while, and Birdie is —you know, Birdie."

"Uh, not a problem." Everly tried to hide the disappointment and not glance at the wrapped present on the table. "I've been invited to go to Holland's."

Everick's relief was immediately evident in the tone of his voice. "Oh, good. I would prefer it if you weren't home alone."

A flash of light and crash of thunder shook the house, the lightning hitting close and making the power flicker out. They looked around and waited, the wiring just as old as the house. A few dreadfully long seconds later, the kitchen lights struggled to light up before gaining strength.

Angry rain began to pelt the house and hit against the glass windows of the sunroom. A chill raced through her knowing that her dad was heading out in that weather that took a dark turn.

"Will you be all right driving by yourself? Or maybe you could stay in, and I can call Nina to come over. It might be a long night. I might not even come home at all."

Nina Hastings, a dispatcher from the police station, had a crush on her father and would come and stay with Everly when her dad or Birdie was unavailable. Not that they didn't trust Birdie, but she tended to come and go without anyone noticing, and she frequently forgot appointments.

Everick didn't even offer to call her aunt since they both knew she wasn't that reliable. Everick's sister, Summer, was a hippie who found her brother's line of work too much. She lived in a city up north and spent most of her time bouncing between jobs and boyfriends. Her only contact with her niece was the occasional birthday card that always came a month late, with her name frequently misspelled.

"I'm *seventeen* and perfectly capable of caring for myself and driving in the rain." She glanced up from the corner of her eye to see his reaction.

"I know. I know. And I promise we will celebrate and eat all the ice cream when I return." He coughed again, and she winced at the sound. It was getting worse.

CHAPTER 2

"Finally, you made it." Holland rushed down the front steps, decked out in white slides, an oversized pink hoodie, and Lululemon leggings. Her luscious brown hair cascaded down her shoulders in waves, adorned with delicate highlights. She held up her iPhone. "I was tracking you."

Everly got out of the car and looked up at the effervescent Holland, who seemed to glow, surrounded by a halo of light from the foyer of her home. "Home" was a meager word for the Abernathy estate. Three stories of white brick, floor-to-ceiling windows, columns, and turrets made it seem more castle-like than home. Behind the main building was a six-car garage with a guest apartment above it, an in-ground pool, and tennis courts.

Holland's father, Abraham Abernathy, was a hotshot corporate attorney for the biggest companies in the state.

"The roads were getting slick with rain. I had to take it slow," Everly explained.

"But it doesn't mean you must drive like your grandma," Holland said.

Everly smiled. "You've never seen Birdie drive. She has more speeding tickets than Dale Earnhardt Jr."

"Who?" Holland asked, her forehead wrinkling.

"Never mind."

Holland looped her arm through Everly's and pulled her into the house.

The Abernathy home came from a Pottery Barn catalog, all white and cream furniture. The warm smell of clove and apples from oil diffusers perfumed the house.

Holland chattered like a mockingbird the whole way up the stairs to the second floor and into her bedroom. A crystal chandelier hung in the middle of the room over the white tufted king-size bed covered with a mountain of throw pillows. Everly knew from experience not to dive into that deadly mound, for some were merely decorative and had actual crystals sewn on for decor. Others were covered with beads and feathers, and when she spent the night, it usually took a good three minutes to transfer the pillows to the chaise lounge at the foot of the bed.

Holland's room was only kept picture-perfect and neat because of the constant attention of the housekeepers. Except for the bathroom vanity, which was an explosion of color and scents. Makeup from brands like Mac and Nars and French perfumes all littered the counter. Everly followed Holland, who stopped in front of a giant golden circular mirror and took out her phone, holding it aloft as she reversed the camera.

"Say, 'girl squad'!" she sang.

"What?" Everly couldn't register what was happening in time before the camera clicked on Holland's phone. A glance showed a perfect Holland pose, arched hip, full grin, and perfectly glossed lips. Everly was looking away from the camera like a stunned owl.

Holland was too busy typing, posting the photo for the world to see. "Hanging with my best friend, E. Hashtag, BFF. No boys allowed. And send."

Everly heard the slight sound of the photo being uploaded to one of Holland's many social media platforms and immediately wanted to cringe.

Everly always felt like the awkward teen next to the runway model. She couldn't help but compare herself to her friend. Holland was tall, five nine, and thin, with a perfect nose and a great smile. Everly was an average height of five feet and six inches with high cheekbones that tapered down to a small, pointed chin. Her hair was strawberry blonde, which complemented her pale skin. However, she wished for a more striking shade like deep red or platinum blonde. The soft color accentuated her big, inquisitive blue eyes, filled with unshed tears.

She had been holding back the disappointment of missing out on another night with her father. But tonight was special. It wasn't just because of pizza. It was more than that. Everly removed her vintage navy blue peacoat and hung it in the closet while Holland's discarded sheepskin fashion jacket was crumpled on the floor.

Holland began to rant about her current argument with her father and the state of her weekly allowance. "I'm seventeen. I should be getting closer to two hundred a week in allowance. A girl has needs. Right?"

Everly did what best friends do. Agree. Pretend shock and support Holland in her extremely reckless lifestyle. She wasn't sure exactly *why* they were friends. You could say that Holland had adopted Everly two and a half years ago when Everick was called in to investigate Pamela Abernathy's tragic passing.

Everly was with her dad that day when he got the call.

"Who are the Abernathys?" Everly had asked, sitting in the front seat of his unmarked police car. In a town as small as theirs, they knew everyone.

"Abraham Abernathy bought the Hershey estate. They moved in a few weeks ago. They were away on vacation when his wife, Pamela, came home early to take care of a million-dollar real estate deal on the verge of falling through. A maid found her at the bottom of the stairs this morning."

"Foul play?" Everly asked.

"That's what we're here to investigate." Everick turned onto the private drive and drove up the long tree-lined estate. She remembered him letting out a long whistle as the house appeared.

"Oh, the butler definitely did it," Everly said in awe when she saw the size of the house.

Everick's eyes widened as the staff lined up outside the house for interviews. "Yeah, but which one?" he said. "I heard they have three full-time paid staff plus ten part-timers." The medical examiner had already taken Mrs. Abernathy's body away, and they were there to conduct the interviews. He put the car in Park and turned to her. "I think it would be good if you got out of the car," her dad said.

"Why?" Everly asked.

"Well, their kids go to Gravemark."

"That fancy private school up in the mountains?"

"Yeah. I don't know if the Abernathy kids have a lot of friends. I think it would be nice if you were just there for them. Just listen."

"They're not going to open up to a complete stranger. They don't even know me. This type is going to close ranks and ask for a lawyer." Everly tossed a thumb at the mansion.

"Their dad *is* a lawyer."

"See what I mean." Everly shrugged.

"You're not conducting interviews. You're just a friend. All I want you to do is listen."

"Okay." Everly didn't think it would work. But Everly was directed around the back of the house toward the pool, where Holland was sitting on a lounge chair, a blanket wrapped around her shoulders, gold sunglasses covering her eyes.

"Who are you?" Holland asked warily.

"Everly. My dad is speaking to yours right now. I was in the car. He said it could be a while and for me to stretch my legs. Is it okay if I sit?"

Holland thrust her chin at the lounge chair next to her. Everly took the invitation and sat next to the girl who didn't even seem fazed that she lost her mother.

"I'm sorry," Everly said hesitantly. "About your mom."

"Everyone keeps saying that they're sorry. What are they sorry for? They didn't really *know* my mother. They worked for her. They were obligated to like her. It doesn't mean anything. That is what it means to be an Abernathy. You don't have friends. You have people who are *paid* to be your friends." Holland sighed and leaned back in the chaise. "It doesn't even feel like she's gone. I mean, she was gone more than she was home, but I half expect her to walk through those double doors any minute and yell at me and my brother."

"I had a mother like that," Everly said. "She couldn't handle my father's long hours or his job, and she got up and left when I was seven. I wouldn't even know if she's alive, except I get a birthday card each year. The postal address is always from a different city."

"Yeah, my mother sent a present from Tiffany & Co. overnight. It was always jewelry that she liked. Not me. It was never my taste. I think she always took overseas jobs to miss my birthday on purpose. She even left our family vacation early. It was Hunter's birthday. She left his party. The golden child. The favored one." Holland sighed long and turned her head to study the water. "I didn't even want to move here. It was her idea. She thought it would be safer here than in the big city. Ironic, isn't it."

Everly mirrored her and stared out at the blue sparkling pool and pink inflatable air mattress floating across the water and bumping into the side of the pool.

She didn't press for more information or ask questions but just listened as Holland began to lay out her life story, seeming to love the attention that Everly gave her.

When it came time for Holland to talk to Detective Hart, she asked Everly to sit with her during the interview. Everly sat in Mr. Abernathy's study, right next to Holland, holding her hand as she answered Detective Hart's questions. *What time did her mother leave the vacation home? When did they, as a family, get back? Was it usual for the staff to have the week off when the family was away?*

As they left the interview, Everly caught sight of Hunter and his father as they headed into the study.

Why was Holland allowed to answer questions without an attorney, but Mr. Abernathy was adamant about escorting his son for the interview?

After the initial investigation, Pamela Abernathy's death was ruled accidental. Everly thought Holland Abernathy would never talk to her again, but she was wrong. A week later, Holland texted and asked Everly to come over, and Everly did. Listening, providing moral support, and then the wall between them dropped. And they became friends. When school started, she thought Holland would move on to better friends at her private school. But one thing Holland was, was loyal. She came home every weekend and gravitated toward Everly. Everly was the designated wing girl. The token weird friend, but she was okay with that.

Holland was life, energy, always doing something or excited about a new project, show, or hobby. Everly never had time to be bored because Holland was constant fun. She spent more time at Holland's home on the weekends than her own because, at least at Holland's house, there were people, cooks, maids, gardeners, someone always bustling about working, giving the illusion of company. With her dad gone so much, it was usually just her grandma walking the mountain trails picking mushrooms and herbs.

In some ways, Everly admitted that they both started using each other for company. Everly needed Holland to pry her out of her shell, and Holland needed someone that was always there.

Holland got a text. "Oh, Hunter ordered pizza. Come on." They snuck down the back stairs that led right to the kitchen the size of Everly's whole first floor of her house. White Italian marble countertops, gold faucets, two islands, and an industrial gas stove that would make Chef Gordon Ramsay jealous. Not to mention the hidden pantry with a faux cabinet front that opened into a whole other room. Holland had spent plenty of time hiding in there and trying to scare Everly.

"Wait a second," Holland commanded, disappearing into their walk-in freezer.

Everly leaned over the open boxes and looked at the four pizzas—an excess for the number of people currently in residence. Abraham Abernathy was gone more than Everly's father, but they did have live-in help, so they were never truly alone and spent the weekdays at their school.

She peered at the boxes of Romano's pizza on the counter. There was a vegetarian pizza, sausage pizza, and supreme pizza with slices missing. Everly stilled at the last pizza box, which remained unopened. It had her name on the outside.

She opened the box to see her favorite pizza, a special order. Grilled honey chicken with hot sauce. The same one she always ordered with her dad. But this was different; someone had spelled out "happy birthday" in Sriracha.

"Hey, happy birthday, Everly." Hunter loped into the kitchen, giving her a lopsided grin.

Everly sucked in her breath, forgetting how handsome and extremely off-limits her best friend's brother was.

Hunter stood six feet tall with light brown hair styled in a trendy, slightly tousled look. It was hard to tell if it was a natural bedhead or if he had paid a stylist to achieve the look. His eyes were a striking green, which seemed to become even more intense when set against the olive-green army jacket he wore.

Hunter Abernathy was perfection manifested—tall, athletic, intelligent, and handsome. His only flaw, except for his personality, was the small white scar on his chin that Everly had given him a year ago during a game of lacrosse in the backyard that had turned into a heated competition that included name-calling. Half of the time, they got along. The other half, Hunter and Everly fought like cats and dogs.

Everly peeled her eyes away from Hunter's scar and tried to shove down the guilt that she was the one to ruin model perfection. Today, it seemed, he was offering an olive branch and being friendly. Tomorrow, he would probably call her a brat and push her into the pool.

Through the open kitchen, she could see the shoulder-length brown hair of Aimee Stillwell, who was snuggled into the white sofa in the family room watching some scary slasher movie.

Aimee was Hunter's longtime, on-again, off-again girlfriend. Their relationship was as tumultuous as a telenovela. Everly had seen them arguing over the last few months at the pool house and over dinner, and their stormy breakups were followed by their passionate reconciliations. The last Everly had heard they were "off again" weeks ago; she'd obviously been out of the loop.

He leaned over the marble countertop, his long, muscled arm holding out a lighter, and lit the white candle he placed in the center of the pizza. "Make a wish."

"How did you know it was my birthday?" she asked.

"*I* told him." Holland stood at the freezer door holding a giant tub of strawberry ice cream. "You were supposed to wait for me, dingus!" she yelled at her brother and dropped the tub of ice cream on the counter. "We were supposed to surprise her together!"

He shrugged. "I forgot."

"Whatever." Holland narrowed her eyes at her brother, knowing good and well he didn't forget but jumped the gun. She vehemently scooped out the ice cream into a bowl, giving her brother the stink eye, then slid it toward Everly by plopping a second birthday candle in the ice cream. "Now, you get two wishes."

Everly sat there staring at the white box with her favorite pizza and the bowl of strawberry ice cream. She then looked between the two Abernathy siblings. Her heart felt full. She half expected Holland to forget because she was not known to be organized, attentive, or punctual, which was endearing. It was a complete surprise that they both planned an impromptu birthday party for her. She glanced shyly at Hunter, who was grinning ear to ear, his adorable dimple appearing.

She blew out the candles, her wishes always a secret.

"That must suck that your dad had to work on your birthday," Holland said as she licked strawberry ice cream off her finger. Holland always spoke her mind. That is what Everly loved. She didn't have to guess Holland's feelings because she always told you.

Hunter elbowed his sister again, as he seemed overly focused on picking off a piece of pepperoni off his pizza. He was not hurrying to go back to the movie with his girlfriend.

Everly picked up her sriracha-covered piece of pizza. "Yeah, but I get the next best thing. I get to spend it with you two. But how did you know I was coming over today?"

"ESP." He winked.

"Uh, no, I told him you were coming over," Holland challenged and took the ice cream back into the freezer.

"But how did you know my favorite pizza?" Everly whispered.

Hunter shrugged. "I can't reveal my sources."

"I'm getting creepy stalker vibes," Everly teased.

"Takes one to know one. I mean, after all, look who your dad is. You are like a dog with a bone when you know someone is hiding something. But this is one secret you won't get an answer to."

"Want to bet?" Everly tapped her finger on the table.

This is how it had always been between them, friendly bickering, digs, and jabs. They were opposite sides of a coin, always disagreeing about something—even the most trivial things.

He gave her a nod. "Maybe next time. I've got a date with a hot girl." The scar on his chin appeared white as he ate his pizza and returned to the living room.

Aimee, who noticed her boyfriend's delay, called out, "Hunter, bring me a veggie slice."

Hunter turned, scooped up a slice of veggie without a plate, and carried it back to Aimee, but only after taking a bite.

Everly heard Aimee's mock anger and watched as she swatted his shoulder.

Everly stared at Hunter's retreating form, and Holland's head again dipped to stare intently at her phone. Everly closed the pizza box and ran her fingers over the outside, tracing her name. Her eyes welled with tears that she refused to shed.

That pizza was the perfect gift she got for her birthday.

They grabbed the two pizzas and cans of sparkling grapefruit water, headed back upstairs into Holland's room, and Everly settled onto the floor with her present. The underside of the box was still warm and comforting on her lap.

Holland frowned and started to scroll up on her phone. "Hey, did you see this?"

"See what?"

"The police are over at Mirkwood Falls. It's trending on TrendTok. It seems like they found a body. There's even a video!" Holland held out the phone, but the video was dark, and all that filled up the screen were the blue-and-red flashing lights of the police cruiser.

Everly grew quiet. She picked at the hem of her jean shorts.

"You knew," Holland accused, sensing her discomfort.

"I knew." Everly looked away.

"Is it the same as before?" Holland pressed, her eyes filled with worry. "An animal?"

Everly chewed and swallowed, not making eye contact. She nodded.

"I wonder if Hunter heard. I haven't gotten anything from my—" She looked at her phone and then put it away as if about to reveal another gossip thread. "What has your dad told you?"

"Nothing much other than it looks like another animal attack near Mirkwood Falls."

Holland grew contemplative. She went through her phone and started texting someone. This went on for a few minutes, and Everly had to assume it was someone on one of the school Discord servers spreading more gossip about the tragedy.

She tucked her phone away and then sighed dramatically. "I forgot. I have a mandatory summer school trip I have to go on tomorrow. Are you doing anything fun for the last two weeks of summer?"

Of course, how lucky were Holland and Hunter? They

were some of the fortunate few who attended Gravemark, the very prestigious private school about twenty minutes from town. While the rest of the ordinary populace attended public school

Everly chewed and swallowed. "I plan to devour a whole box of Cheez-Its and have a *Murder in DeGuise* marathon."

Holland wrinkled her nose.

"And watch *Gossip Queens*," Everly quickly added Holland's favorite show about girls rating their dates on an app.

"Yes, I would do anything to switch places with you. I would love to see if Amber and Jose meet again," Holland said dreamily.

The conversation turned to more reality shows and European vacations.

"Hey, Everly," Holland said, putting her half-eaten pizza back in the box.

"What?"

"How come you aren't at Gravemark?"

"You know I can't afford the tuition."

"But what if I said that there's like a special scholarship that you could get? That it's not about money but getting accepted to like... a secret club."

Everly put her pizza down and gave Holland her full attention. A secret club sounded interesting. "Really?"

Holland leaned forward as if sharing a secret. "But not everyone can pass the entrance requirement."

"What's the requirement to join?" Everly asked, feeling a moment of intrigue. Her competitive nature kicked in. If there was a way to go, she wanted to go.

Holland didn't meet her eyes but ran her finger over the edge of the bed. "It's a tragedy. You have to have lost something and gain something at the same time."

"You're talking in riddles." Everly hated that Holland knew

something she didn't.

"And once you get in... well, the assignments can be dangerous." She wrapped her arms around her bent knees and rested her chin on the top.

"What kind of danger?" Everly asked warily. "Are we talking about streaking across campus dangerous or life-threatening?"

"Does it matter?" Holland asked.

"Yes, it does." Everly reached for Holland's hand.

Holland looked uncomfortable. "I'm not supposed to talk about it outside of school. There are rules."

"I'm always suspicious of anything dealing with keeping secrets and rules."

"That's what being a teenager is all about... and giving parents mini heart attacks. I'm just surprised that, you know... with your family history. You're not a student there."

"What family history?" Everly pressed.

"Nothing. I just... forget it." Holland looked sad. "Truthfully, I don't know how long I can stay enrolled. I'm not really doing that great. I'm not that talented."

"You're brilliant," Everly said. "Plus, you have me as a friend."

"You're the only one who believes in me."

"Always," Everly said.

Holland flipped back over on her stomach and gave Everly a serious look. "I don't know what I would do without you, Everly. I think I would literally die."

Everly's heart thumped in her chest. She hated when people used extremes. "No, you wouldn't."

Despite them being a floor up, Everly heard a scream from the surround sound below as one of the side characters met their untimely demise. The rumble of music came through the floor, and her happiness turned to unease.

CHAPTER 3

EVERLY DROVE HOME THE FOLLOWING AFTERNOON. HER brain was working overtime. She was angry and filled with guilt at the same time. The anger was aimed at her dad for putting his work first, and then the guilt followed for being selfish. She pulled onto the familiar street. They lived in the historic district; most houses, like hers, were over a hundred years old. Unlike the pure white stone of Holland's house, Everly's home was a two-story Victorian with a deep red turret, brown shingles, a wraparound front porch, and spindles everywhere. The deep colors of the old house, in style for the day, made it seem dark and foreboding. Their home was on the edge of town, and it backed up to the forest preserve, where her grandmother loved to go and forage for herbs and plants—always bringing back injured animals to nurse back to health.

She ran up the back steps and used her key to let herself in, sweating when she crossed into the kitchen. She turned the dial on the old thermostat down a few degrees, waiting for the AC to kick in.

Then her father burst through the back door. His face seemed thinner in the kitchen light, his cough more pronounced as he ranted about his current case.

"I don't understand it. What am I missing?" Everick rushed out, frantic as he paced their tiny kitchen.

"Dad?" Everly called out hesitantly.

"Everly, there's something you should know, but I didn't want to tell you yet." He coughed. "There are things you can't see. The case is grim," he struggled to speak. "It's grim." Then he fell to his knees, coughing up blood. He clutched his side before sliding to the tile floor in a heap.

He didn't respond. He muttered something but was struggling to breathe.

Everly called an ambulance and waited desperately, holding his hand until she heard the sirens grow louder and stop in front of their house. Loud boots and voices rushed up the stairs, and their small kitchen was soon filled with emergency personnel. She stood shocked as she watched her father get loaded up onto a stretcher and taken down the stairs into the waiting ambulance.

"Dad!"

Everly sat by her father's bedside. He looked even older in the white polka-dot hospital gown—a breathing tube in his nose, IV in his arm.

When did his hand get so slim? How much weight had he lost and hid behind oversized jackets and coats?

His skin was jaundiced as his liver was giving out.

"Pancreatic cancer," Dr. Sykes said, looking over his notes. "He was diagnosed in the spring. He didn't tell you?" the doctor asked in disbelief.

Everly shook her head as she tried to process the news. How could her father keep something like that from her?

Why had she not seen the signs sooner?

Because she didn't want to.

Everly didn't want to confront the fact that she would soon be without her father. That her rock, her stability, was going to disappear. They were both excellent at pretending not to notice. To play a part in a Shakespearean play that they knew would end in tragedy. To look the other way, hoping for a different ending or outcome, but it was written in the stars.

"I knew he was sick, but not what or how serious," Everly said. "He was not one for showing weakness or letting others know when he needed help." She had tried to snoop through the mail when she saw the letter from Mayfair Memorial Hospital. Her father had caught her. He then redirected all the mail to his work. Everyone gave her the cold shoulder and pitying looks when she asked around at the station. They had been instructed not to tell her anything. Even Nina refused to say. Once, she had opened her mouth as if to reveal a secret but then promptly closed it again as if she couldn't be the one to bear the bad news.

All her father was doing was delaying the inevitable and trying to take down the enormous monster. For that was what he was and always would be to her, a shining brave knight who, with his last breath, was still trying to protect her from monsters.

"Is there anything we can do?" Everly asked hopefully.

Dr. Sykes was solemn. "It seems that your father had prepared for this moment. He signed all the paperwork for his end-of-life care to spare you or Birdie from making the decision. There's a DNR and a hospice plan in place, but Everly, I don't think he is strong enough to transfer to palliative care. He should have entered the facility weeks ago. Truthfully, I don't know how he could keep working for so long; he must have been in immense pain."

Everly turned toward Birdie, who sat in the corner chair, her head low, eyes glistening with unshed tears. Silently.

"You knew!" Everly accused.

She nodded gravely. "When my George was in hospice care, it was..." She swallowed. "... difficult. Your father and I decided this was for the best."

Everly's heart was heavy with mixed feelings—bitter at being lied to for months and simultaneously grateful.

"I would notify next of kin and prepare for funeral arrangements," Dr. Sykes said.

"I'll call Aunt Summer," Everly said, knowing Birdie and her daughter didn't always see eye to eye.

"I'll call Nina at the station. Stay by his side, Everly. Don't leave him alone." Birdie stood up and stepped out of the room.

Neither of them mentioned Everly's mother. She took off one night and never returned. Divorce papers arrived in the mail a week later. And her family removed her from their life, wedding pictures, clothes, and mementos, pretending she never existed. No one even brought up her name except for the ring. Her dad never removed his wedding ring.

Everly scrolled through her phone book and pressed the number for her aunt Summer. Her dad's sister.

The phone rang. Each piercing ring, she whispered, "Pick up. Pick up." And on the last one, she almost yelled into the phone as it went to voicemail. It was just like her aunt to avoid a call.

"Hey, it's me. Dad's really sick. He's at the Mayfair Hospital. Can you come? He needs you." Everly didn't say she needed her because it was a lie.

She placed the cell phone on the hospital table and waited for her aunt to call back. She never did.

Everly sat helplessly staring at the floor when a tapping noise drew her attention to the window. A giant raven was pecking on the glass with its beak, his wings flapping against the pane.

Was it sick? Why was it trying to get in? Goose bumps ran up her arms at the foreboding omen of a raven appearing right after her dad's diagnosis. They were an omen of death.

"Go away!" Everly hissed, standing up and waving toward the bird, trying to scare it off. But the bird was not easily intimidated and continued to cause a ruckus until Grandma Birdie noticed and entered the room.

At four foot ten, she never seemed more intimidating than when she stormed over to the window and snapped at the bird. "Not now!"

As if obeying Granny Birdie, the raven stopped attacking the glass pane and flew away.

"Crazy old coot," she muttered and then moved to sit by her son's bedside.

———

Over the next few days, Everick Hart slowly deteriorated. Holland didn't call or text during this time, which was surprising and also not surprising since she was on a school trip and updating plenty of Instagram photos. To Holland, posting a picture was communicating, but Everly didn't have the heart to ruin her friend's summer school trip by messaging her. She only had the energy to hit the heart button on all pictures.

Everick fought valiantly for each breath, his lungs rattling. Everly squeezed his hand tight between hers, as if by her strength and willpower alone, she could keep him by her side.

"I promise to be good," Everly whispered. "I promise I will do everything you ask if you stay by my side a little longer."

Tears formed in her eyes as she knew it was childish to try bribing her father into living longer for her. But for a brief moment, that's all she wanted to do, to crawl back to her childhood, as if it was a tunnel, and then she could rewind time. Give them a few more years.

She let her mind wander briefly back to a younger Everly and her father playing games with her; they were walking downtown past a pet store. They were always observation games. "I spy with my little eye. Something blue."

"The sky," she had said.

"Nope." He smiled. "Guess again."

"The flag."

"Nope."

She frowned. "The mailbox, the door, the dog's leash, the newspaper stand."

All of them were nos. Everly was becoming impatient, and then her father leaned down and lifted her chin and turned her toward the storefront window so she could see her reflection.

"Your eyes," he said, smiling.

"But I can't see my eyes," she whined, pouting like only a five-year-old can.

"Exactly. Just because you can't see something doesn't mean it's not there. You are too close to the problem and must look at it differently."

"These games are dumb. You cheat," Everly had sulked.

Everick roared with laughter, his face full and tanned. He was healthy and happy. "Someday, you will understand what I'm preparing you for. Someday you'll thank me... or you will curse me."

Everly gently sat next to her father's bed, rubbing the back of his wrist. She leaned forward and whispered into his ear. "I spy with my little eye. Someone... I love very dearly."

She wasn't sure but thought she momentarily saw his eyelids twitch. Was that a tear in the corner? It could just be her imagination.

"It's okay, Dad. I can take care of myself. You've taught me well."

She leaned over and kissed his cheek.

"I will be fine. You don't have to fight anymore."

There was a deep sigh, his hand slackened in hers, and a long tone from the monitor filled the silence.

CHAPTER 4

"That was a beautiful goodbye," Birdie said. She walked around to the other side of the bed and leaned over to kiss him on the forehead. "Goodbye, sweet boy. She won't be alone. I'll take care of her." Birdie gripped her handkerchief tightly in her tiny hands as she tried to stay stoic.

Finally, Birdie took a deep breath and gathered her inner strength.

"I will notify the hospital staff," she whispered. "Do you want to try your aunt again?"

Everly picked up the hospital landline phone and tried to call her aunt Summer again from a different number in case she was screening her calls. But like before, it went to voicemail.

"Dad is... gone." Everly didn't know what else to say, so she left another message in a sea of unanswered voicemails.

Her hands trembled as she started to text Holland.

Hey, something happened.

Delete.

My Dad died.

Delete.

Everly struggled to put into words her circumstances. Before she could hit Send, the phone slipped from her fingers as more tears filled her eyes. She cried until Birdie entered the room and scooped her into a hug.

"Shh, bug. It will be fine."

Everly didn't realize how much she needed a hug and clung onto her grandma for dear life.

Birdie picked up the phone. "Let's get you home."

Everly didn't remember the ride home, Birdie helping her into her room, crashing on her bed, or falling asleep with her clothes on.

———

Two days later, a pounding on the front door awoke Everly. She got up and headed downstairs to the foyer.

Birdie came from the back hall armed with a toilet plunger. "Is someone trying to kick in the door?"

"I don't know." Everly reached for the handle.

"Wait!" Birdie stepped behind the door and held the toilet plunger high. Everly looked through the sidelight and let out a long sigh as she unlocked the door. A bedraggled Summer holding a taped-up box full of clothes and a can of Pringles was trying to take another kick at the door.

"There *is* a doorbell." Everly pointed at the white button and then down at the scuffed door from Aunt Summer's boots.

"Can't reach it with my foot. There's more stuff in the Uber. I need help." Summer ignored her niece and pushed into the front room. Summer had dyed, permed red hair pulled up on her head, held back with a rainbow scarf. She wore a blue tank top, boho skirt, a zillion bracelets, jade, health beads, and various crystals hung from her neck. She fingered a crystal and gave Everly a carefree grin. "Come on. You're young and strong, and the driver doesn't have all day." She took off down the front steps again.

Birdie only slightly lowered and hid the plunger behind the door. "I can call Murphy and tell him we had a break-in," Birdie whispered conspiratorially.

"She's *your* daughter," Everly exclaimed.

"Not by choice. That one came out backward, I swear. The whole town breathed a sigh of relief when Summer moved out of Misty Creek." Birdie looked wide-eyed toward her daughter, who burst through the door again with a guitar case and a mini ukulele. "I should give earplugs to the neighbors."

"What are you doing?" Everly asked as her aunt pushed her way into the front room.

"I'm moving in with you. You know this is what my brother would have wanted. You both need a caretaker."

"Where have you been the last week when we needed you?" Birdie fumed.

Summer brushed her red bangs out of her face. It was frustrating to see how much Summer looked like Everick. Everly felt it was because of Summer's lifestyle that Everick went into the field he did. Everick had a savior complex, and Summer constantly needed saving. Now, Everly realized how wrong she was. Her aunt didn't need saving. She needed a babysitter.

"Mom, you know how delicate I am. I can't handle sick people and all that. It's because I'm an empath. I get all sad and stuff." Summer fingered her necklace with a moon crystal on it.

"That's what happens when people are on their deathbed," Birdie chastised.

"No." Summer waved her finger, cutting her off. "No, Everick literally sought it out. It was his job—to hunt down killers. Not to mention you and Dad working with dead people. I mean, who does that? Only our family has this obsession with death. Everick would have wanted me to stay away for my mental health."

Mental was right, Everly thought to herself.

"Plus, you don't understand how inconvenient it was for me to move across the state to care for you two. You should be grateful, not snarky." Summer dusted off her hands and looked around the house. "Now. Where's my room? Same as before?"

"No." Birdie smirked. "I turned your bedroom into my sewing room. You get the attic."

"But it's so hot! No one can stand living up there."

"Exactly," Birdie muttered.

The following week flew by as the force known as Hurricane Summer went through the house, claiming every spare piece of furniture as hers with either a lost or dirty sock, bra, or colorful scarf. Incense was the new air freshener, and Everly had to sleep with her window open to keep from getting headaches.

But through it all was the saving grace of Granny Birdie sticking to her guns against her daughter, who she swore was put on this earth to test her as a punishment for her own reckless youth.

Then it came down to planning the funeral, and Summer was against a big service because of cost and said Everick should just be cremated. But Birdie and the police department pulled rank and announced that wouldn't do. Everick Hart needed to be honored.

Summer almost had a fit because of the amount of food needed to feed everyone. "They don't expect me to cook, do they?"

Birdie, who had remained quiet and solemn through the last few days, turned on her daughter and folded her hands in prayer, her eyes reaching toward heaven. "Children should be seen and not heard."

"So archaic." Summer sighed.

Birdie opened one eye at Summer, and she zipped her lips.

Somehow, despite Summer, and only because of the love and support of the police department, the small funeral turned into a regal one meant to honor one of their fallen members. It was a beautiful ceremony at St. Mary's, and Summer stayed outside waiting in the car the whole time. Everly stood alone in the receiving line, welcoming and thanking each of her father's friends. She greeted Captain Harris—the one who had called Everick Hart away on her birthday.

He seemed distant, his cold blue eyes rimmed with lack of sleep. He mumbled his condolences and then turned to run his hand along the casket.

Nina, who was tall, tanned, and blonde, couldn't stop bawling and hovering by Everly's side. Birdie was tense, her eyes darting here and there. Not a single tear was shed, and instead, she seemed scared. Everly was thankful for her support because there was no way she could have gotten through this without Birdie.

Standing by the casket, Everly got a distinct feeling of being watched. The hair on the back of her neck rose, and a sick feeling knotted in her stomach. She glanced down the line of people before gazing at the choir balcony, where a lone figure stood staring down at her. Dressed in a long overcoat and hat pulled low, their gaze was most certainly directed at her. She quickly tried to place all her father's closest friends, and he didn't meet any of the profiles of the ones not in attendance.

Sergeant Garret was tall and round. Murphy was of medium build and in his thirties. Lee was Asian, and Mitchell was the heartbreaker of the bunch, a tan and tattooed body-builder. The person on the balcony was definitely a stranger to her, but that didn't mean anything when one's father was a well-known profiling detective. It could be anyone from the courthouse, like the District Attorney or judge. But how they stood, half hiding in the shadows, watching from afar, told her they probably weren't any of the above.

Their build was thin, and they wore dark sunglasses inside the church.

"I'm sorry about your father," Officer Stevens said, drawing Everly's attention away from the stranger. The sandy-haired young officer was tan with golden brown eyes; he was the youngest on the force, having just graduated. "I looked up to him. He was a good man," he said.

"Thank you. He spoke highly of you too. Hey, Stevens, who's that?" Everly pointed back to the choir loft, but the stranger was gone.

"Who?" Stevens asked.

"Never mind."

But that prickly feeling of danger never left. In fact, it followed Everly all the way to the cemetery. Birdie got into the driver's seat of her Subaru, Everly crawled into the back seat, and Summer continued to lament how this whole day was negatively affecting her and that she couldn't possibly go to the cemetery.

"Seeing my brother put into the ground is too traumatizing for such a sensitive soul as I."

"Oh, shut it!" Birdie snapped, gripping the steering wheel. "It's not about you. Today you need to be here for Everly. If you so much as open your mouth again, I will duct-tape it shut and throw you in the trunk. Do you hear me? I've done it before with..." She trailed off and mumbled something incoherent.

Summer grew silent. Birdie chuffed. Everly held back her laugh.

Birdie followed the hearse and pulled into Shady Elm Cemetery. The crowds were gathering, and the sky turned dark. It looked like a rainstorm was coming. She put the car in

Park and gave Everly a solemn look. "It's time, sweetie. To say our final goodbyes."

Everly stepped out of the car, not even remotely prepared for this moment. Everything had seemed like a dream until now, one that she had hoped to wake up from. The graveside ceremony was short, sweet, and plagued by a tree full of birds. More ravens. Each one sits quietly as if there to attend the funeral. None of them made a sound.

Everly made a note to point them out to Birdie. "Look at all the ravens. Why are they here?"

Birdie didn't even turn her head. "Unkindness."

"What?" Everly asked.

"A group of ravens is called an unkindness, and they're here to pay their respect to your father."

"Respect?" Everly gazed at the birds warily.

Everly could have continued to quiz her grandma but instead let it go. That was just one of the many odd things she had grown used to about her family over the years. The way Birdie spoke in puzzles. Born Evelyn Ganere, she was often seen talking to birds and had been ever since childhood. The townspeople had started calling her "bird brain" or "crazy bird lady" behind her back.

Then one day, she took on the moniker and started calling herself Birdie before anyone else could, and as she aged, it seemed less and less weird to be talking to birds.

As they turned away from the gravesite and started walking back to the car, a lone raven split off from the group and flew toward them, swooping low and dropping a single black raven feather. It fluttered in the wind, and as if on cue, Everly held out her hand, and it nestled into her palm. The feather was beautiful.

"Ew, drop it," Summer admonished. "It's probably covered

in germs and who knows what kind of diseases." She started walking toward the car a few steps ahead of them.

But Everly didn't think so. It felt more like a gift. She picked the feather up by the shaft and gently turned it here and there, watching the color change, the hint of blue, green, and purple. But then the feather turned red, flashing before her eyes, and then it was ash that brushed against the underside of her wrist and in its place was a mark. The shape of a raven appeared in a triangle before fading away.

She rubbed at her wrist, but nothing was there, just skin.

"What just happened?" Everly asked, wondering if she imagined it.

Birdie looked at Everly, her eyes narrowing before turning back to the tree full of ravens. Her voice was low and filled with worry. "So it begins."

CHAPTER 5

THE BED WAS SAFE. SO SAFE, EVERLY DECIDED SHE WOULD never, ever leave it. Cocooned under her dark comforter, she could close her eyes and pretend that her father was still alive, downstairs preparing for the next test or "guess how he died" game. That they were still going out for pizza and ice cream. She huddled under her covers for days crying, her heart aching, her chest feeling like it was squeezed in a vice, and her breathing shallow.

And then one day, she woke up and the tears were gone; her heart didn't hurt as much. It felt wrong, a betrayal to her dad that she couldn't feel sad forever, but Birdie told her it would be like this, that "one day it'll hurt less, but it never means you'll forget."

She looked over at her dresser and the unopened present from her dad. It was a beautiful pink-striped package with a polka-dot bow. The wrapping was uneven, and the tape job was haphazard, but it was the last gift her father gave her, and she was unable to bring herself to open it. Opening it meant that it would be over. Saving it was like keeping a memory alive. So it stayed there, like a monument, next to the movie theater gift cards, teal hoodie, and matching socks Birdie got her for her seventeenth birthday. Why did grandparents always buy socks? Was it written in the grandparent rule books of how to embarrass teens?

Everly's phone buzzed, and finally she had the energy to look at the missed message from Holland, who had returned from her trip two days after the funeral. When she had heard the news of her father's passing, there was a flood of messages:

Why didn't you tell me?

I would have come back sooner.

How are you?

Do you need anything?

Want me to come over?

Everly?

Are you okay?

And at the time, she wasn't.

Everly *wasn't* okay, and it was fine to *not* be okay for a short while. But that wasn't a state one could perpetually live in. She had to move from okay, and the first step was to get out of bed and face the day.

Everly pulled the covers down and looked around her room. Her room wasn't messy if you knew how to navigate the books and clean laundry piles. One of the many problems with older homes was their minimal closet space; some rooms had zero closets, and they had wardrobes instead. Everly's closet was the size of a broom closet, with clothes and feather boas spilling out onto the floor like a creature from the black lagoon trying to escape. It wasn't her fault that Everly loved to make and sew her own costumes. The collage of pictures on her wall wearing all them proved it. Eleven-year-old Everly was a vampire with wax teeth and blood, twelve-year-old as a were-wolf, where she had painstakingly sewn on fur to all her clothes from one of Grandma's mink stoles, head and all. And another as Frankenstein's monster. She had formed the nuts from polymer clay and glued them to her neck.

While everyone else at school had dressed in something feminine, Everly had always gone for the macabre costumes that were original to their movies and stayed true to form.

Her one bookshelf was filled to the brim, and then there were piles around the sides of the room with even more books in order of how often she read them or would reread them. They were like old friends that she wanted to visit again frequently. Putting a book in a cardboard box was like breaking up with your boyfriend. No, she wanted them where she could see them. She didn't have her own bathroom like Holland, but she did have a full-length mirror and a small side table that held her hairbrush, dryer, and curling iron. Her only makeup could fit in a pencil case.

On top of the bookshelf were all her Taekwondo tourna-ment trophies and her third dan black belt. Something that she had also not wanted to do, but her overprotective father had insisted.

Everly moved from the bed to the bench seat in the turret bay window, grabbed a blanket, and settled in to watch the street below. People were coming by at all hours to drop off frozen casseroles, desserts, and condolences, so she had retreated to her room. She didn't feel like pretending.

A shadow passed over her, and she glanced up to see another raven fly overhead and then sit on the fence in her yard, staring up at her.

"Go away!" Everly rapped against the glass, but the bird didn't move. She proceeded to open the window and yell again. The raven ruffled its feathers and turned its head to look at her out of the side of his eye. Feeling frustrated, she took one of her shoes and tossed it out the window. It hit the side of the fence with a thud, and the raven flew off.

Everly slammed the window shut, muttering angrily, before getting dressed and heading downstairs. Without her father's presence, the kitchen felt bigger. His seat was empty, and the newspaper was no longer spread across the table as he proudly showed off any article regarding him and cases he had worked on.

Birdie was puttering around the kitchen, making eggs and burnt toast. For some reason, she always burned the toast and blamed it on the confusing toaster settings. Everly had gotten her a new toaster for Christmas that had foolproof nobs. The following day, burnt toast accompanied the scrambled eggs.

"It's how Grandpa made his toast," Everick whispered to her. "Since he passed away, she always serves burnt toast."

Everly just took it, scraped off the burnt edges, and slathered it with jelly to cover the charcoal taste.

Birdie poured a glass of orange juice, put it on the table next to Everly without a coaster, and returned to her cooking. Everly reached for the crocheted coaster to find the whole box of coasters missing from the dining table.

"Birdie, um, where are the coasters?" Everly asked.

Birdie shrugged. "How should I know?"

"Should I use a paper napkin?" Everly reached for one, but Birdie snatched the napkin dispenser off the table and tossed it on the microwave stand.

Then she understood. *This is how Birdie chose to honor her son.*

Sorrow tugged at Everly's chest, and she struggled to

swallow her emotions, but then the pain passed. She looked at her burnt toast and the coasterless glass and could almost imagine her grandpa and dad sitting beside her. Everly smiled.

It was good.

She could get used to this.

Near Everick's chair was the folded-up Misty Creek newspaper. Her mouth went dry when she read the front page.

ANOTHER HIKER KILLED.

She couldn't help but pull it toward her, unfold the paper, and read the article. "Rocky Cordon fell victim to what appears to be a cougar attack, Wednesday, September 1, near Mirkwood Falls National Park. Cordon is the second victim of a wild animal roaming the reserve. The first victim was Shelly Miller, a twenty-seven-year-old dental hygienist. Sergeant Mitchell, who has served Misty Creek County for twenty years, says he's never seen an attack like this. It looks to be the work of a large cougar."

"Another hiker was killed," Everly said out loud.

"Hmmph." Birdie made a noise in her throat, then walked her pan over to Everly and scooped eggs onto her empty plate. "And what do you think you should do about it?"

"What can I do?" Everly asked in confusion. "I'm not a cop or a detective."

"You are much more than that," Birdie muttered. "You have a natural g—"

Everly didn't know what else Birdie would have said because Summer came moping into the kitchen, moaning and groaning, her hair wrapped in socks, her face covered in a charcoal mud mask with gold under-eye stickers for wrinkles.

"So hungry," Summer groaned and flopped into the seat next to Everly.

"Speaking of monsters," Birdie grumbled. "Summer, what have you got all over you? It smells like my compost heap, and you're leaving a trail." She pointed with a spatula toward the trail of glopping mud that was coming down the hall.

"It's the latest in facial detoxifying masks. Proven to take years off your face." As she said, "off your face," another glob of mud plopped right into Everly's cup.

Everly pushed her glass of orange juice away.

"Well, if you're going to impersonate the blob, then you should carry around a mop and clean up after yourself," Birdie chastised.

As grandmother and daughter got into another argument, Everly took her burnt toast and headed into the backyard through the side kitchen door, letting the screen door slam behind her. The sun was out, the morning humid as Everly made her way to the bench that faced the preserve.

Everly tossed the bread crumbs over by the gravel walk for the birds, who she knew would easily scoop up the feast.

She loved watching the squirrels race across the branches and store their nuts for the winter. Except this morning, there was no chittering of squirrels. The birds were eerily silent. Nothing moved in the stillness of the woods except for the wind that blew a few scattered leaves over the walking path.

And a single raven that watched her from her grandma's garden fence.

"Go away!" she yelled and motioned with her hands, but the raven didn't move. Instead, she could have sworn it laughed at her.

A cry of pain from the woods drew Everly's attention. It sounded like a wounded animal. She dropped her toast on the bench and followed the sound. The woods were dense, and very little light filtered through the treetops despite it being morning. This made it perfect for cultivating moss and mushrooms and Birdie's more exotic herbs.

Her shoes made little to no sound on the well-worn path as she walked along the earth. Just off the trail by an outcropping of rock covered in moss, Everly heard another whimper.

"Oh, you poor thing." Everly detoured from the path and crawled up the incline through the brush to get to the rocky wall, kneeling to look for the animal.

But the rock started to shift as pebbles fell. No, not fell, but moved and formed to reveal a creature made of stone, with black beady eyes and snarling teeth like pointed shards. Moss clung to its body like fur, and it lunged for Everly, and she screamed, falling backward.

"Grie-e-ver!" its voice like gravel in a rock tumbler called out. Its strong hands grasped her ankle, and with unimaginable strength, it began to drag her to a cave that it had been hiding with its body.

"No!" Everly screamed, turning over to claw at the tree roots to fight as the creature tried to drag her into its lair. Everly's heart raced. *What is this thing?* She focused her attention and aimed a snap kick at its face, but her foot connected with solid rock, and she felt the resounding jolt of pain up her leg. The creature didn't even flinch from her attack. She swung her leg and tried a crescent kick to knock it off-balance, but it was like hitting a tree trunk. Everly couldn't fight with pure strength. Her fingers dug into the root, and she could feel her grip loosen. With a tug, the creature pulled her free, and she felt the root slip from her fingers as she was dragged another two feet until she wrapped her arm around another tree.

Its grip tightened around her ankle, and Everly cried out in pain.

A flurry of black feathers came from the sky as the raven who was just at her house flew into the stone creature's face, pecking incessantly at where its eyes were. But it was only a minor distraction, and with a meaty fist, it swatted the raven away, never releasing Everly.

"Not my granddaughter!" A scream exploded, and a ball of fire erupted near Everly's foot, almost burning her in the process.

Standing over her was Birdie, her face filled with utter ferociousness. She had a utility lighter and a can of hair spray in her hands as she yelled and lit up the ground with a stream of fire. The creature screamed and released Everly, seeming to fade into the woods, but Everly could still see it as it waited, just along the shadows.

"Where is it?" Birdie cried out, turning in full circles as if blind.

"There!" Everly pointed.

Birdie turned, aiming her makeshift blowtorch at the creature and sending another fire spray but missing it entirely.

She heard a chuckle as the creature turned to charge, knowing it was invisible. The crunching of leaves was the only sound it made as it raced to attack Birdie from the side. Its mouth opened impossibly wide.

"Four o'clock!" A voice called out instructions.

Birdie swung to her right and blasted the stone creature straight in the face. The mossy hair and beard ignited, creating an outline of fire and smoke that made it visible to Birdie.

"What is it?" Birdie snapped out.

"How should I know?" Everly answered.

"Moss golem," a different voice answered.

"Is it the only one?" Birdie asked, her eyes searching the rocky outcrop.

The moss golem continued to cry as the moss burned away and it shrank.

"Yes."

"Who are you talking to?" Everly cried out.

"Not you, sweetie," Birdie answered, going over to the trail of smoke left by the shrinking creature. She kicked around in the dirt, searching.

"What just happened?" Everly asked.

Birdie looked worn out. She leaned down and picked up a small rock the size of her fist and tested the weight in the palm of her hand. "That was your first grimm encounter."

"My what?" Everly asked in shock.

Birdie looked around fearfully. "I will explain more, but I need to drop this down a well or stream before it awakens again. Go inside where it's safe. Corvis will watch over you. I'll explain everything when I get back."

"Who?"

But Birdie was gone, slipping into the woods as she had done many times before. She had always thought her grandmother odd, but now she had many questions. *Like, what was that thing? And how was her grandmother so cool? She looked like a superhero.*

CHAPTER 6

Everly dusted herself off, her ankle only slightly swollen and bruised, and made her way back to the path that led home, but as she did, she passed her grandfather's old medical office and felt a pull as if drawn to the building. The building had been off-limits for so long and held so many secrets her family had kept from her.

No longer.

As she walked toward the peeling white outbuilding, she couldn't help but run her hands over the metal commemorative plate. Dr. G. Hart, Dr. E. Hart, County Medical Examiners.

Her aunt Summer was right. Her family was in the business of death. Before Grandpa George, his father was the county undertaker like his father before him. The old crematorium was still sealed off just behind the medical office building. It was considered a historic site—protected by the city, before he became the county medical examiner until he retired. Birdie did as well, not wanting to continue working without her husband. It didn't feel right. Her dad broke the medical tradition when he became a detective.

She had only been in the outbuilding once, and that was when she had followed her grandpa inside when he accidentally left the door open. She passed the small two-chair waiting area and headed into the back room. It was a long room with a tile floor and medical tables. All she remembered was the white sheet covering half the room, the bright lights coming from the other side of the curtain, and the voices. She remembered hearing two voices when she pulled the curtain aside. All there was, was her grandpa. Alone, with a dead body on the table, covered in a white cloth, and a stuffed owl on his desk.

"What are you doing here, Everly?" He quickly chastised her and led her out of the room.

"I heard you talking. Who are you talking to?"

"No one," Grandpa said. "It was just the radio." He led her out and closed the door, locking her on the other side.

She approached the door with trepidation, her hand reaching for the knob, giving it a turn.

Locked.

It was always locked. Everly didn't know what else she expected.

"Behind the nameplate."

Everly spun. Her heart raced at the sudden voice. Her eyes searched the shadows, but she was alone.

"Who's there?"

Silence again. Why did she keep hearing voices?

Maybe she was going crazy.

But now the thought was in her head. She followed the instructions of the mysterious voice and examined the metal plate, running her fingers along the edge. Even though it looked like it was screwed to the wall, it was a decoy. She lifted the plate, which swung out, revealing a small crack in the wall, and wedged between two bricks—a key.

Everly took the key, put it into the lock, and held her breath as she turned. There was resistance, and then she felt the bolt slide. The door opened inward with the slightest creaking noise. She entered, her hand sliding along the cold brick wall, searching for the electrical box and the switch.

She flicked the light on, and the room came to life. At first, it looked like any old medical office. Waiting room chairs, a rack of magazines, and an old tube television hung in the corner of the room. A small reception desk that Grandma used to man. Then behind the desk was a door that led to the examination room and the other, her dad's private office.

She felt five years old again, and the room felt smaller, like it was shrinking, but she looked at everything at a different height. Everything felt normal, but why did she think she had to come here?

Ghosts?

She entered his office first. Tall bookshelves lined one wall, a metal desk in the center of the room, and metal cabinets on the other. Behind his desk was a locked wardrobe. She made her way to the desk and slid open the bottom drawer. Inside were journals, some newer moleskin, others old and falling apart with leather. She opened the first one and almost dropped it when a horrendous monster looked back at her. She flipped the page and saw another monster: half man, half beast with long fingers and a tail.

"Knew you would eventually make it here. All your family does. Except for your aunt. She's broken."

"What?" Everly stood up, the journal falling out of her hands. She backed up and bumped into the wooden wardrobe as a black form flew through the room and landed on her dad's desk.

It was the raven. The same one who had knocked on the hospital window. However, it seemed larger than a normal raven by six inches. The raven hopped onto a wooden perch that was on the desk and gave her a curious gaze.

"Did you speak?" Everly knew she was going crazy.

"Of course I speak. This is just the first time you can actually hear me. No one ever listens to me, but I have plenty to say." The raven's mouth opened, and even though the beak only moved once, Everly heard him clearly in her head.

"What is going on?" Everly touched her forehead. "I must be hallucinating or dreaming." She pinched herself to make sure she was indeed awake.

"You're not dreaming. Although for some, it can feel like a nightmare. But you've been preparing for this your whole life."

"I don't understand. Who are you?"

"I'm Corvis. I'm an omen."

"What's an omen?"

"A protector." He puffed out his chest.

"From what?" Everly asked.

"From the things in those journals." Corvis shook his head and nodded toward the bottom drawer.

"They're just pictures." Everly's stomach dropped, and a sour feeling of uncertainty rose. "Right?"

"Yeah, just a harmless murdering golem that enjoys eating toes like candy. They're grimms, and they are very, very real."

"Grimms?"

"Creatures, monsters, shapechangers that live among us. They were nicknamed grimms because they were first documented by two German librarians, Jacob and Wilhelm Grimm. Very few humans become grievers and can see them for what they really are or survive their first encounters."

"I don't like the sound of this." Everly plopped down into the desk chair and watched as the raven hopped around and continued to talk.

"You have a choice. You don't have to become a griever, but let me tell you, it is in your blood. And once you have the sight, you can't stop seeing those things." Corvis flew to another bird stand, and Everly followed him as he proudly fluffed his feathers.

Along the wall were black-and-white photos.

"That's your great-great-uncle Jonathon Hart. He was a griever. Look at the first photo."

The photo was of a man standing over a bear carcass, a shotgun over his shoulder.

"I've seen it. We have a duplicate one in our house."

"Look at it again."

At first, it seemed ordinary until she looked closer at the details in the photo.

Then the picture shifted. It changed, like those magic eye optical illusions. If she focused hard enough, she could see beyond the photo. It was never a bear but a creature of similar size with antlers and long ears.

"That's not a bear!" Everly said in shock. "I've seen this photo a hundred times but never noticed the antlers and long ears."

"See, you do have the sight." Corvis seemed pleased. "That is called a bugbear. They are nasty creatures, powerful. Their weak spot is the eyes. Now the next photo."

The following photo was in a black frame and of two men standing in the woods, a tall rocky outcrop behind them. On the ground in front of them was a group of puddles.

Everly squinted her eyes and focused. Like before, the picture shifted slightly, and the puddles changed from many into one as big as a car, in the shape of a human foot.

"Giant," she breathed out. "How come I couldn't see this before?"

"You couldn't because your brain wouldn't allow you to see them. Most humans can't. Only those that have seen death close up have the *sight*. Because you have grieved death, you're a griever. And you can see grimms, and they can most definitely see you. It's like you will have a permanent neon sign that follows you everywhere, making grimms drawn to you. Hence the moss golem. Although, they are more a nuisance when you understand their main weaknesses are fire and water."

"I feel I'm a little lost," Everly said.

"Corvis!" a sharp voice interjected. "What are you doing?" Birdie stood in the doorway to the office, her hands on her hips. "I came out to investigate why Everick's office was open. I should have known you were behind this. You're a rascal. Starting her training already, I see."

The raven winced and tucked his body into a position of shame. "Sorry, Birdie. I just thought she should know. Since the unkindness marked her, the grimms are already targeting her."

Birdie sighed. "You're right. It's no longer safe for her here. I had hoped to give her more time, maybe even another year, but that would have been selfish of me to deny her gift."

"Grandma," Everly spoke her name and pointed to the trunk and the photos on the wall. "Is all this real?"

Birdie nodded. "It is, darling. Look at your wrist. And press your thumb like you are taking your pulse."

Everly turned her right wrist over, and she did as instructed. A faint mark appeared and then disappeared. A raven inside a triangle.

"That is the mark of the sight. It allows you to see grimms, like your father, George, me, and our family before us. But it isn't forever. One day that mark will fade, and you will lose your sight."

"Fade, do you mean you couldn't see that thing attacking me out there?" Everly asked.

Birdie shook her head. "No, and that is why it's dangerous for us to continue to be grievers. I'm a liability, but I still do my part with the help of Corvis and the other omens. I can still patrol the woods. Even though it is against the Grimm Society's rules."

"But why not tell me sooner?"

"It is strictly forbidden to speak of the society before one has been marked as having the sight or becomes eligible to be a griever."

"Why does it need to be a secret?"

"Bug, do you think the world is ready for goat-eating trolls or Bigfoot?"

"They're real too?" Everly asked.

"Of course. Our sworn duty is to protect the innocent while keeping the grimms in check. And my son has done his best to train and protect you, but he didn't want you to walk down this path. No one wants their child to suffer or see death at a young age, but that is what it takes to give you the sight, and then an omen will mark you as a potential griever."

"I still can't believe all this."

"Hello, anyone here?" A nervous voice came from the front room. Summer stepped hesitantly into the office doorway. She winced as she looked around the room as if it made her uneasy. "So, um, I was thinking of going out shopping. Do you want anything?"

"No," Birdie said, moving to stand before Corvis.

"I'm good," Everly answered quickly.

Summer was wearing an orange dress and cowboy boots. She looked at the surroundings with contempt.

"I always hated this place. It has a bad"—Summer waved her fingers around—"aura. I should bring in some sage and clean it out. With some new wallpaper and carpet, it has the potential for a cute little apartment." Summer wrinkled her nose at Corvis, who was pretending to be a taxidermic bird. "Except for that. It's nasty. Here, I'll throw it out right now."

Everly thought she saw Corvis's feathers ruffle just the slightest in annoyance.

"No!" Birdie interjected. "Why don't you pick up a frozen lasagna from the grocery store and salad for dinner tonight? You can take my car."

Summer perked up and held out her hands for the keys. Birdie handed over the keys to her Subaru, but Aunt Summer didn't move until the money dropped in her hands. She gave a wave, and when she left, everyone sighed in relief.

Birdie turned to Everly. "Spend the day, think about your future, and know that your father has prepared you for this your whole life. But the choice is yours and yours alone. We can't make it for you. Just like Summer had no desire or interest or even natural talent for becoming a griever. She couldn't find her way out of a clearance rack let alone follow the trails of a grimm." Birdie reached out and gave Everly a pat on her shoulder.

"What if I choose wrong?" Everly asked.

"There is no right or wrong choice regarding your future," Birdie said solemnly. "It's your path, and only you know the route."

They left the medical office, and Birdie locked it back up, tucking the key in her pocket, and Corvis flew away to a nearby tree.

"Is he gone?" Everly asked, feeling sad that he had left.

"No, he has gone to join the others. He is, after all, nick-named the prince of ravens."

"Others?"

"The other omens. Omens are a griever's magnifier. They amplify your griever abilities. Cats are great for sensing the unseen. Bats amplify one's hearing." She smiled proudly. "And it seems the ravens, particularly, are drawn to you."

"Did Dad have one?" Everly asked and looked around the sky, hoping to catch a glimpse.

Birdie's smile fell. "Orly, his owl, passed away years ago."

"But I never saw my father with an owl. I've only ever seen *you* talk to birds."

"That's because they grew apart when he could no longer hear or speak to Orly. One doesn't have their griever gifts forever. As you age, you lose your gift. In the same way a child who believes in the tooth fairy will someday stop believing." She opened the screen door, and they headed into the kitchen and down the hall. Birdie tapped a picture of her father leaning against the fence in the backyard. He was young, in his teens, and Birdie pointed to the hollow of a tree over his shoulder where a brown ball of fluff was hiding away.

"That's Orly." She smiled sadly.

"What about you? What was your omen?"

Birdie wiped at the corner of her eye. "Why do you think I got my name? I was always talking to a cuckoo bird."

Everly bit her lip and chuckled.

Birdie grew solemn. "My omen died years ago. This way is better than for a griever to die first, causing the bond to be severed suddenly. It is quite painful for an omen. Many of them don't survive the death of their bonded griever. The few that do... tend to go mad."

"But you can still talk to Corvis?"

"That's because I'm a child at heart. I'm one of the few who can talk to omens after our griever gifts fade. That's why all grievers are teens. And now that you have fully come into your gift, you will soon be contacted by the Grimm Society. If you pass your test, you'll get to enroll."

"Enroll for what?" Everly asked.

"Why, for school."

"But I already go to Misty Creek High School."

Birdie made a noise in her throat. "Regular school can't teach you what you need to survive as a griever."

This was what she had been afraid of. That somebody would suddenly yank away the rug from under her. The fragile foundation she had rebuilt was already sinking with the threat of change.

"You're sending me away. No. I won't have it. You can't send me away to a far-off school like in one of those stupid teen movies to get rid of me. I won't leave you. We're family." Everly stood up, making a very moving speech. "Family sticks together."

Birdie's eyebrows rose in surprise, and then she laughed. "Oh, bug, you won't have to go far. It's just up the road."

"Up the road?"

"Yeah, Gravemark Academy. It's only twenty minutes away. They train grievers and their siblings there."

Gravemark? *The fancy private school that Hunter and Holland go to? Did that mean that they were grievers?* But a certain thrill ran through her at the thought of going to the same school as her best friend.

"But you have to pass the entrance test."

"Test, what test?" Everly asked eagerly.

"Patience, bug." Birdie smiled. "You'll learn soon enough. Now, go wash the dishes."

———

Now that her sight had been opened, Everly could reflect back on her childhood and start to see things that weren't there before, clues, muffled conversations that her dad had with Birdie late at night. When he trained her to fight, escape, and use her wits, it was always against physical threats. Now she realized her fight would be against a different kind of monster.

Grimms.

Why couldn't they tell her sooner, train her to become a griever? Because to become a griever, she would have to see someone die. That was traumatizing in itself. What if her dad had told her about grimms, but then she never became a griever? She would have thought he was mad. She hated to admit that they were right. It was better this way.

Everly sighed, turned off her light, and crawled into her bed. The moon had come out, illuminating the floral pattern on her wallpaper, but as a cloud passed over the design, it seemed to shift and change from flowers to skulls.

A tapping at the window drew Everly's attention. When she saw the bird outside her window this time, she didn't shoo it away. Instead, she opened it and stood back as a raven flew inside and landed on the footboard of her bed. A thick white vellum envelope with a red wax seal was in its long beak.

"Corvis?" Everly asked hesitantly.

The bird shook its head, dropped the envelope, and flew out the window.

"Thank you," Everly called out, but the bird was gone.

She turned her light back on and picked up the white envelope. The red wax was imprinted with a monogram of G. She ran her finger under the wax seal, breaking it, and pulled out the single folded white paper inside.

It was blank.

Was this a joke?

She lifted the paper and looked at it carefully, flipping it over to look at both sides and even holding it up to the nightstand light. Still blank.

"Weird?" Everly muttered. Why would someone send her a blank piece of paper? Unless it wasn't empty.

She took a deep breath, relaxed her eyes, and tried to open

the part of her mind that housed her imagination. Just like the wallpaper, there had to be something there—a test.

When Everly opened her eyes again, gold ink was scrawled across the paper.

Greetings, Everly Hart.
We at the Grimm Society invite you to join us at
Gravemark for testing.
To enter...
Speak your heart's death.

Everly's heart raced in her chest. There was something overwhelmingly addictive to solving a riddle and catching a bad guy. Her aunt Summer was right, their family had a habit of searching out death, and now she knew why. It was in their blood.

But could she follow in her father's footsteps?

CHAPTER 7

"Creepy," Everly said aloud as she drove up to wrought iron gates that marked the entrance to Gravemark Academy. Dead trees stood like foreboding sentinels on either side of the winding drive, and an unnatural misty fog obscured her view beyond the metal bars.

She parked her car and looked for a speaker box or a keypad to unlock the gate. Stone gargoyles with snarling gaping mouths and claws digging into a shield with the Gravemark crest stood on either side of the drive.

Everly leaned out the window and spoke toward a gargoyle's open mouth, expecting it to hide a speaker box within. "Hello? I'm Everly Hart. A new student."

Nothing.

"Open sesame.... Abracadabra."

Still nothing.

She inched her car closer to the gate, hoping her bumper would trigger a motion sensor. Everly sighed and leaned over to grab the letter from the school and reread it.

It didn't make any sense, but then Everly thought about it. What had sent her on this track to become a griever? The death of her father.

Her throat swelled, and her mouth went dry as she tried to say the name, "E-Everick H-Hart."

The gates opened inward with a long, haunting whine. Everly eased her car through, nervous that the great gates would swing shut and trap her. Past the entrance was more fog and woods, and she drove for five minutes before the road went higher up the mountain, clearing the mist, and the school came into view.

School was a loose term. A creepy castle that could pass as a Tim Burton movie set rose before her. And she half expected Helena Bonham Carter to come waltzing down the front steps in a crazy costume.

Yep, there goes her wild imagination again.

Her fingers tightened on the steering wheel as she contemplated turning the car around and heading home. But she remembered being here meant she could continue her father's work. She could make him proud.

Everly pulled into an empty parking space next to a Fiat.

Did being a griever mean a big, fat paycheck? She didn't think it brought in that kind of money. Suddenly, she became self-conscious of her vehicle.

Her white Mini Cooper convertible had seen better days— the leather top had been repaired multiple times with duct tape, and the parking brake didn't work. It wasn't even worth locking the car because anyone with a wire hanger could easily jimmy the leather soft top, unlock the door, and steal anything. But it was wheels, and wheels meant freedom to go places, and when the weather was nice, riding down the highway with the top down was the most freeing thing about living on the coast.

Everly opened her door and stepped out. "It's okay, Sheldon," Everly mumbled to her car. "Don't be intimidated by their shiny exteriors and expensive insurance premiums. You've got something they don't have."

"What's that... rust?" a teasing voice called from behind.

Everly turned to see the smirking face of Hunter Abernathy.

She patted the top of her car. "Shh, you'll hurt Sheldon's feelings." Everly pretended to pout.

"I can't believe that car is still running." Hunter slipped past her and moved to the front of her car. He brushed his hand across the hood. "I had to jump-start this thing like what—three times?"

"Four," Everly corrected. "The last time was during a snowstorm, but since then, I've had the starter replaced. Holland still won't let me drive her anywhere for fear of getting stranded."

Hunter's smile fell when she mentioned his sister; he looked around in confusion. "What are you doing here, Ev?" He used his nickname for her. "Does Holland know you're here?"

Everly didn't know what to say. "No. I'm not here to see her."

"Are you here to see me?" He touched his chest and almost sounded hopeful.

"Uh, no, we both know my taste excludes creepy older brothers," she teased.

Hunter made a playful stab to his chest. "You try to wound me, but you miss."

"Easy to miss when you don't have a heart." Everly grinned.

"Yeah, well, my taste doesn't include scrawny little sister types," Hunter countered, raising his chin.

That stung more than it should. It hit home as Everly was very self-conscious of her lack of curves.

"That's because you prefer people without brains." Everly was unable to hide the bitterness in her voice.

Hunter winced. "Ouch! Noted. But really, why are you at Gravemark? How did you get through the gates?"

Everly slammed her driver's door and confronted Hunter. "Maybe I'm going to start attending here?"

Hunter shook his head in disbelief. "No. This school is... It's not a normal school for normal girls like you."

Normal felt like a punch in the gut.

"What is normal anyway?" She shrugged.

Hunter stared at her. "I just know how much you despise Gravemark students. You've made fun of our school for years, calling us upper-crust, stale bread."

"Hey, you should take that as a compliment," Everly countered. "Everybody loves carbs."

Hunter laughed. His green eyes disappeared, and his dimple made her heart flutter.

"Plus, maybe I had a change of heart?" She fidgeted with her car keys. "Since my dad passed away—"

The color drained from Hunter's face, and his shoulders slumped in empathy. He leaned forward as if to rest a hand on her shoulder but then pulled it back. "Oh, Ev—I'm such a jerk. I was so surprised to see you here. I forgot about your dad. Holland and I were away and couldn't return to the funeral. We didn't even know he was sick." He gave her a pointed look. "Why didn't you tell us?" His voice turned to one of accusation. "You know we would have been there for you."

"It's not that simple." Everly shrugged. "I didn't want to burden you."

"A burden? Everly, you forget," Hunter said softly. "You're not the only one to have lost a parent. You were there for us. You should have let us return the favor."

Everly's head dropped, and she stared at the crack in the pavement. He was right, but she wasn't going to admit it.

"So you're officially a griever now?" Hunter asked.

She nodded and held out the white envelope with the remains of the red wax seal. "I got this shortly after my dad's funeral."

"Yeah, Gravemark." He ran his hands through his hair. "The only school where seeing death is a prerequisite for enrollment. You know, it's not too late to leave," Hunter said and gently took her shoulder, pushing her toward her car door. "You can turn around and go home. The sight will eventually fade. You can pretend you never stepped foot inside those gates. I won't say anything."

Everly was hurt that he was pressuring her to go when this was the first time she felt she belonged somewhere. She pulled her arm out of his grasp and rubbed it gingerly. "I don't want to leave."

"Everly." Hunter reached for her shoulder again, but she backed away. "Not all of us make it to graduation—if you know what I mean?"

Everly raised her eyebrows in confusion. "The tests are that hard?"

His face was grim. His voice dropped to a harsh whisper. "Walking across the stage is hard if you're dead."

She sucked in her breath in shock and looked up into Hunter's eyes, which were a turbulent green. He was serious.

"Is that a threat?"

"It's the statistics for what we do. There's a reason the students nicknamed the school the Graveyard."

He tried to scare her into leaving, but she wouldn't be intimidated. Not when every word he said excited her at the thought of danger. *There really was something wrong with her.*

Everly's jaw clenched, and Hunter crossed his arms and glared at her. They were staring at each other in one of their famous showdowns—each too bullheaded to admit defeat.

Everly let out a sigh of frustration. Moving around to the trunk, she pulled it open and grabbed her laundry basket filled with bedding and a pillow. She hoped Hunter would ignore the obvious signs of her hastily packed car—the folded-down back seat with her duffel; the box filled with instant ramen cups, a box of granola, shampoo, and conditioner; and her cardboard box of keepsakes and framed photo of her and her dad. She didn't know what to bring, so she brought everything.

Hunter sighed in resignation. "Here, let me help you." Hunter reached into the tiny back seat for her duffel in a show of remorse and trying to be helpful.

"I've got it." Walking to the side of the car, Everly slapped his hand away and pulled the duffel to the ground.

"No, really, I can help." Hunter reached for the box inside.

"First, you tell me to leave. Then you want to be nice, carry my things in, and help me stay." Everly slammed the door quickly, almost costing him his fingers. Her heart was beating wildly in her chest. Angry tears threatened to spill forth because one minute he was kind, the following mean. She looked him dead in the eye. "Make up your mind, Hunter. Either you want me here or you don't."

Her heart was in her throat, and she looked at him pleadingly, wishing he could see her as an equal and not a little sibling he wanted to protect. She saw the indecisiveness in him and the moment he made his decision.

"I *don't* want you here." His green eyes met hers, and she could see he meant it. "But it won't matter what I say. You've always done what you wanted anyway."

Everly expected that. She pushed past him roughly, checking him hard on the shoulder as she stormed around to the car's passenger side. "Glad to know that I'm once again a disappointment to the great Hunter Abernathy. But I don't need your permission to be here."

Hunter raised his hands in surrender. "Okay, I get you loud and clear, Everly. It's been fun. Enjoy class. Don't come running to me when you get in over your head." He gave Everly a two-fingered salute and walked away. He was leaving her to carry her stuff in by herself.

She reopened the passenger door and pulled out the last small bag, adding it to the top of the basket and then slinging her duffel strap over her shoulder. Everly couldn't help but stare at him as he left, memorizing his strong shoulders, the confidence he exuded. No matter how much she tried to deny it, she had a crush on him. Holland had repeatedly lamented to her how so many girls had only pretended to be friends with her to get close to her older brother. It had deeply hurt Holland, and Everly promised she wasn't like them. She would *never* date Hunter and would purposely pick fights to prove it. But somehow, over the last few months, she found it harder to keep her defenses up.

Everly frowned. She needed to get Hunter out of her head and focus on her studies.

Just then, an older Ford Bronco blaring rock music almost ran her over as it recklessly pulled into the spot next to her car.

Everly had to jump back and drop her laundry basket of items. The driver cut the engine and stepped out of the vehicle.

He was young with a striking appearance. He was tall and had a lean build, with wavy blond hair and piercing blue eyes. He was dressed in dark clothing and a black jacket and even had a pleasant scent. Everything about him spelled trouble.

"You almost hit me!" Everly cried out in exasperation as she leaned down to throw her items back into the basket.

"Didn't see you." The young man turned to lean across the seat and grab his duffel bag.

"I was standing right in the open."

"Maybe *you* shouldn't stand there," he said, still not looking at her.

"Maybe *you* could at least say sorry," Everly said heatedly. Her words were bitter because her emotions continued after her confrontation with Hunter.

He sighed and leaned against his car. "Look, newbie. Maybe you should get back in that car that seems to be held together with duct tape and glue and drive off into the sunset. I don't think you'll survive long here. You're nothing but grimm bait." He slammed the car door, put in earbuds, and headed into the school.

Everly grumbled as she picked up her clothes, shoved them back into the basket, and then put the rest of her dumped belongings in with them. He was the second person who told her to leave, and she hadn't even graced the school's front steps yet. *Should she take it as a sign?* No. She would follow in her father's footsteps. She wouldn't let two people's opinions dissuade her from continuing her family's legacy. Resolute in her decision, she gathered up what she could hold, frustrated that her pride hadn't let her accept Hunter's help.

Arms burning from holding onto her belongings, she headed toward the entrance.

CHAPTER 8

"Whoa!" Everly breathed out when she stepped into the main foyer of the academy and was met with a sweeping grand staircase. "Birdie did not do this place justice in her description."

The academy's entrance was grand, with white tiles and walls of polished dark oak adorned with decorative trim. High stained-glass windows in various patterns illuminated the space, creating a colorful kaleidoscope on the floor. Despite the darkness, the atmosphere felt inviting and not at all frightening.

"You must be Everly Hart?" a dry voice intoned.

Everly turned to be greeted by a teacher whose blonde hair was cut short into a bob; a single strand of pearls adorned her neck and was complementary to her blue pencil skirt and white top. Everly recognized Ms. Bellcamp from the online staff directory. She was the school's guidance counselor, journalism teacher, and one of the school's staff resident advisors. Currently, her gaze was focused intently on her iPad.

"Yes, I am."

Ms. Bellcamp barely looked up. "Welcome to Gravemark, where you will put your mark on history," she said blandly, like a waitress reciting the daily specials. She beckoned with a polished nail for Everly to follow her along the carpeted runner that lined the floor up the stairs. She spoke as she walked, giving a mini tour in a monotone voice. "Gravemark is a unique school, as you know, with rigorous entrance requirements. Just because you have the sight does not mean you have what it takes to become a griever or a Grimm Society member. Have you any other gifts?"

"Not that I know of?" Everly hedged.

"What about an omen? Has one chosen you yet?"

Everly shook her head.

"Pity, one will certainly help you in your training. Come along. There are a total of thirty students on campus. They are divided into four halls, plus the primary and secondary wings. These students are now your family. You sleep, eat, and live together because your lives will depend on how well you function as a team. You must learn to trust one another. There is an opening, so I'm putting you in Serenity Hall."

Everly listened intently, praying, hoping she was in the same hall as Holland. She didn't want to interrupt Ms. Bellcamp as she didn't seem intent on answering as her pace was brisk.

"Each hall has a staff resident advisor, and I'm Serenity's. My apartment is here." She waved at a wooden door with a gold nameplate on the side. It read, "Serenity Hall" and underneath "Bellcamp" in block letters.

As they walked through a pair of double doors, they arrived at the main living area of their residence hall. They were greeted by three couches arranged in a U shape, facing a magnificent fireplace and a flat-screen TV mounted above it. On a nearby shelf, Everly noticed an Xbox and PlayStation console. Continuing, they passed by a sizable dining table crafted from solid wood and featuring a natural cut and a fully functional kitchen with a granite island.

"Halls are coed. The boys' rooms are to the left of the living room, and the girls' rooms are on the right. They shall not commingle after hours." She gave Everly a stern gaze, and Everly shrank under Ms. Bellcamp's warning. "Lights out is ten sharp unless you are on reaper assignment, and then you are under the care of your GTL, but you must always check in afterward with me. Do you have any questions?"

"When do I go on my first reaping assignment?" Everly asked, feeling the urge to go out and prove her worth.

Ms. Bellcamp stopped walking and looked at her. "You don't. Not until you pass your reaper tests or are specially selected by one of the GTLs, griever team leads, but..." She trailed off and returned to reading her iPad. "They don't take new students on reaping assignments."

Everly kept her eyes on the doors as she passed. The second door was open, but the interior was dark; all the window shades were pulled closed. A girl with elbow-length, fuchsia-dyed hair, dark, winged eyeliner, and deep pink eyeshadow stepped out of the room directly in Ms. Bellcamp's path. She wore pink cat headphones over her ears and bright purple nail polish.

"Ms. Dorn," Ms. Bellcamp addressed the student respectfully but received nothing from the teen except for a dramatic eye roll. "Will you be willing to show Ms. Hart around?"

"It's Kat." The girl looked around at the people in the hall suspiciously as she popped bubble gum in her mouth. "And uh, no. I'm busy." She retreated into the darkness to escape and slammed the door.

Ms. Bellcamp didn't seem fazed by the introverted nature of the elusive Ms. Kat, who did not seem like one of Grave-mark's model pupils but more like the black sheep.

"Are all the dorms occupied?" Everly asked.

Ms. Bellcamp seemed hesitant to answer but could find no reason not to. "No, there haven't been as many new students enrolling as we hoped." She stopped at the room on the end, closest to the emergency stairwell. "Here you are, Ms. Hart."

"Oh, murder central," Everly quipped.

"What?" Ms. Bellcamp's head snapped up from the iPad, the color draining from her already pale face.

"You know." Everly pointed to the emergency exit sign. "Last room on the end of the hall, easy entrance for"—Everly dropped her voice—"murderers." Her attempt to ease the tension was falling flat.

"I can assure you that no such thing has happened here," Ms. Bellcamp stressed, her voice rising in pitch.

Everly pushed open the door to the dorm room, brushing aside the teacher's paranoia. "Relax. I don't plan on being murdered anytime soon," she said.

Ms. Bellcamp's mouth dropped open, and she averted her eyes. "It is a dangerous job, and we know it is a lot to ask of you. Your school uniforms are in the wardrobe, collected from your submitted sizes, and your schedule and room key are on the desk. You will be assigned a griever mentor to help catch you up." Her voice was low, sad.

"Thank you, Ms. Bellcamp," Everly said, feeling guilty for teasing her advisor.

Once inside the room, Everly dropped her duffel on the dresser and the basket on the floor. She tossed her pillow on the bed and returned to her car for the rest of her belongings.

It only took two trips and fifteen minutes for Everly to unpack all her things. The room had a four-poster bed with twisted mahogany posts resembling vines overlapping with intricate leaves. A built-in bookshelf was already filled with books, primarily fairy tales. She had an empty desk with a study lamp and an overstuffed chair.

She took out the photo of her dad and her sitting on the front step of their very unique red house. Everick was laughing, and Everly was looking up at her dad. Behind them was the front door and the house number.

Her heart felt a little numb as she put the photo down. Then she clipped her room key with the Gravemark crest onto her car keys.

Everly opened her wardrobe and saw the multiple green blazers, plaid skirts, sweater-vests, white shirts, and the green tracksuit for gym. She reached out to touch the green sleeve of the blazer, pulling the front out to see the Gravemark crest.

"I can't believe you didn't tell me!" A feminine voice echoed loudly from the hall.

Everly's door was open, and Holland stood there in shock. Her dark hair was pulled back into a braid, and she wore jeans and an oversized shirt.

Everly's head dropped toward the floor, and she waited for her friend to rant and rave at her for not telling her that she was coming here.

Instead, she picked up the conversation as if no time had passed. "And you're in Serenity Hall. Lucky. I'm in Liberty Hall with Mr. Halsey as my advisor. He's such a weirdo and is never in his apartment." Holland crossed the floor and wrapped her arms around Everly in the biggest hug, her words coming a mile a minute. "I'm so glad you're here. I don't have to lie or keep secrets from you anymore. Although, I'm sorry for the circumstances under which you came. Oh, Everly, you must think I'm horrible."

Everly's walls crumbled, bit by bit. The emotions she was holding in check, hiding, fell under the gentle hug of her friend.

After Everly cried, Holland led her to the bed, and they sat down. "I'm sure you have a hundred questions."

"I don't know—a few. I guess. Like, were you really on a school field trip?"

Holland's mouth pinched tight, and her nose wrinkled.

"No, I was on a reaping mission in Cedarville. Bagged a level-two boggart. Nasty things tend to throw their heads at people to scare them. But it was easy once we gave it a box of rare wood. They hate the light and prefer to hide in anything coffin-like."

"But the photos on your Instagram?" Everly asked. "They keep refreshing."

"Oh, you'll have to do it too. It's part of our cover. We take tons of photos on a fake set or use Photoshop to create cover stories anytime we are away on assignment. Our extended families aren't allowed to know what we do. Kat is the best at computers and does most of the research for your hall. You're lucky. I'm in the same hall as Aimee Stillwell and always hear her rave about my brother. But you will be the envy of all the girls—"

"So we don't have classes together?" Everly interrupted, feeling a moment of dread at trying to stay afloat in this new school.

"Oh, we have generals together in the lecture hall. But when we break out for training, we might get paired with different teams depending on your skill set."

"So you're a griever?" Everly asked, looking down and picking at a stray thread on her bedspread.

"I'm not. Not officially. I'm a sib."

"Sib?" Everly hadn't heard that word yet.

"An unmarked griever who doesn't have sight. Usually a sibling of another griever." Holland tucked her hair behind her ear. "Sometimes it happens in families where one gets all the gifts and the other not so much. Like a copy of the original isn't as good."

"What do you do?"

"I'm backup support for reaping assignments, as grievers call it." Holland tried to show pride, but there was pain and disappointment she was hiding.

"How long?"

Holland let out a long breath as she steadied herself to explain. "Three years ago, I was in a car accident, and one of our friends died. We don't like to talk about it, and I don't remember anything from that night, which is probably why I don't have the sight. But I could still develop gifts... one day. It happens." It sounded like she was trying to convince herself, not Everly. "I'm not gifted like Hunter. I don't bring much, even as a sib of a griever, but I want to try. After all, it was a grimm that killed my mom." Holland's hands curled into angry fists.

"What? I thought she fell down the stairs."

Holland shook her head. "No. Your dad knew it wasn't an accident. After he talked with my brother, who was still new to being a griever, his suspicions were confirmed. He was the one who helped cover it up. Even though he no longer had the sight, he was still a liaison to the Grimm Society. They need people in high places, like the government, police departments, and medical examiners' offices, to hide the cause of death. People with power and deep pocketbooks."

Everly shook her head, feeling like the person she grew up with was a stranger. "I didn't know."

"One of the first things we learned was the legacy of the Hart family. I was surprised you weren't already a student here."

Everly looked at the photo on her dresser. "Me too."

"But then I think about what it takes to become one...." Holland shivered. "To do what we do. I had hoped that you would never grace those doors."

Everly had mixed feelings. She was the most prepared and the least prepared for Gravemark Academy. Her dad had taught her everything needed to navigate the real world, but nothing about grimms. Could she survive in this one, where monsters were real?

"But finally, you're here!" Holland grabbed her hands and shook them in excitement. "Welcome to the *Graveyard*."

———

Everly had never had to wear a uniform before and wasn't sure it was for her.

She stood in front of her mirror, adjusted the tie, and then slipped on the green blazer with the school crest on the breast. A green-and-gold half-oval emblem with a sword and ax criss-crossed behind the letter G. It did look like a headstone.

"Look like I'm going to a funeral, hopefully not mine," Everly sighed and fluffed her strawberry blonde hair before grabbing a notebook and pen and heading to her first class, leaving the map and schedule Ms. Bellcamp gave her on her dresser. She didn't need it. She had already memorized the layout of the school.

As she left her hall, she noticed Kat's door open and her room empty. She must have headed to the lecture hall. Everly didn't see anyone else come out of the girls' wing, so she assumed she was the last to leave. She had spent hours talking with Holland the previous night and never got out to meet anyone else in her hall.

Everly swiped a banana out of the fruit bowl on the communal kitchen counter, half expecting it to be wax. When it wasn't, she quickly ate it while walking to class. She didn't assume Holland would walk her to lessons, knowing she was always late to everything and her hall was in another school wing.

Gravemark's classes ran in blocks, and instead of having eight classes a day, there were two to three classes with longer blocks of time. She had a free period today. But first, she had to get through history in the main lecture hall.

The lecture hall had theater seating with long tables in front and wheeled leather chairs. She grabbed an empty seat on the end third from the back. She craned her neck down the row to see if she could spot Hunter or Holland, but all she could see were the backs of heads.

"Hey, you look familiar!" a voice cut in cheerfully.

Everly glanced up to see a brunette with big, sparkling brown eyes and a grin that revealed the cutest dimple. She tapped a painted nail against her cheek. "Don't tell me." Her dark eyes narrowed in thought before she jumped back in surprise. "You're Holland's friend. I've seen your picture on her Instagram."

"That's right. I'm Everly Hart."

"Lacie Duvall, from Lupine Hall." The exuberant girl waved her hand excitedly, and an expensive bracelet with a charm swung in the air. "If you're a friend of Holland's, then you're a friend of mine." She half sat on the table next to Everly.

Duvall. Everly knew who Lacie Duvall was from Holland. She was the great-great-great-granddaughter of one of the founding members of Gravemark. Everly would never have expected Lacie to try and befriend her.

"You and Holland are close?" Everly asked as she spotted Hunter enter the classroom over Lacie's shoulder. He turned his body, searched the hall, and stopped when he saw her. He frowned.

"Well, everyone here at Gravemark tends to grow close. I was Holland's mentor when she first came here. Unlike her brother, who excelled in every subject, she was lost and hopeless."

Hunter walked across the room with an energy drink and made a beeline for them.

"Speak of the Abernathy devil," Lacie whispered under her breath, flashing her brightest smile toward him.

Hunter pulled out the chair in the row below Everly and sat down. She noticed he wasn't wearing his school blazer.

"Lacie," Hunter said, turning to the heiress. "I don't usually see you mingling with the new students."

"I came to make a new friend and maybe say hello to an old friend." She leaned close to him, twirling her hair around her finger, waiting for a response. Hunter ignored her, focusing his gaze on Everly. His hand clutched an energy drink, and he was not saying anything.

Lacie noticed the tension in the air between them, and she quickly excused herself. "It was nice meeting you, Everly. I'm sure we will have plenty of time to talk later." She gave a little wave, and the girl, all bubbles and smiles, waltzed away.

"You could have been nicer," Everly chastised. "Lacie seems sweet."

Hunter took a sip from his drink and almost choked. "Too perfect and sweet for my taste. I've always been more of a sour person." His eyes flickered to her briefly.

Everly made a face at him, and Hunter smirked. "That's the girl I know." He put the can down and leaned forward. The muscle in Hunter's jaw clenched, and his hand tightened into a fist on the table. "Everly, have you considered what I said about leaving?"

"I heard you the first time. I'm not going anywhere. Besides, you're not my father." When Everly said "father," there was a hitch in her voice, and she clutched the pen so hard her hand shook. She dropped her head and tried to take a few deep breaths to calm herself.

"Everly." Hunter's voice became soothing. "I'm sorry... about everything. About your dad."

Everly shook her head and quickly wiped at her eyes. "It's fine. It's not like you knew him. Why do you care?"

"I do care," he said softly.

"But not enough to let me stay."

"Everly, this school is not for you. Look at what happened to my..." He looked up as Aimee Stillwell came into the room, and he trailed off.

Everly glared at Hunter. "What happened?" she pressed.

Hunter sighed, rubbing his temples. "Never mind."

Just then, Aimee Stillwell sidled up to Hunter. "Hey, hon!" Aimee leaned down and kissed Hunter on his cheek, though his gaze never left Everly's, making her uncomfortable. Aimee turned to see who had caught his attention, and her eyes widened in surprise at seeing a familiar face. "Since when is Holland's little friend a griever?"

"She's not staying," Hunter said. "She'll drop out soon."

"Will not," Everly challenged.

"You'll leave as soon as you realize you don't belong here," he added.

A side door slammed from the front of the class, announcing Professor Stubbs's entrance. He was tall, at least six foot eight, and the word that came to Everly's mind was spindly, despite his short-statured name. He looked like he spent the nights burning the midnight oil, solving complex math problems as his peppered hair stuck up at all angles from running his hands through it multiple times. Professor Stubbs put his lecture books on the podium and then patted his pocket, looking for his reading glasses that were on his head. He turned around to search his leather briefcase. Just as Holland tiptoed into the hall without a sound, she slid into the empty seat next to Everly and wiped her forehead in relief.

"You're late, Ms. Abernathy," Professor Stubbs intoned, still searching his briefcase.

"How *does* he do that?" Holland grumbled and flopped her head on the table. "He has eyes in the back of his head, I swear."

Professor Stubbs turned around, his smile sly. "Or I'm just very observant. As they say, the observant one gets the worm."

Everly chuckled at the misquote, but it made her narrow her eyes to study him closer. Suddenly, he seemed to transform into a bark-like figure with root-like fingers and moss gathering under his long T-shirt, resembling a bearded tree human.

Everly inhaled and gripped Holland's arm. "Do you see that?" she hissed, staring at their professor, who looked like a walking tree. She blinked a few times, and then she saw Professor Stubbs again.

"See what?" Holland squinted and looked at the front of the classroom.

"The professor, he's a—"

"Dryad, Ms. Hart. I'm what is known as a dryad." His smile was slow, and she could almost hear the creaking of the bark around his face, even though she couldn't see it.

A tittering of laughter followed at Everly's expense, and she felt her cheeks burn.

Holland, on the other hand, looked nonplussed. She pouted. "What? You can see him. No fair."

"It seems that our newest griever has a strong gift of sight." Professor Stubbs gave a clap. "I was not even projecting, and you picked up on my aura. Well done. It usually takes years for a student to get that good."

Another murmur followed, and this time it wasn't laughter. She could feel the slight undertone of jealousy.

"And for those needing a reminder or not having the gift of

sight. Grimms cannot be seen unless they want to be by doing what we call projecting. Which can happen in extreme circumstances of fear, anger"—he wiggled his eyebrows—"or even passion."

Everly raised her hand, feeling unsure. "So not everyone can see what I see?" she asked.

"Let me demonstrate." Professor Stubbs relaxed his body and dropped his head back, and it was a better effect than what happened before. Everly had caught a passing glimmer of his true self that lasted only a few seconds. Now, the dryad before her was ethereal, his presence filling the room. The girls that could see him sighed. A few boys shifted in their chairs and tried to keep their faces neutral. But some, like Holland, continued to squint and lean forward, trying to see beyond the scruffy sweater-vest.

"Who here can see me?"

Everyone raised their hand.

Professor Stubbs shook his head. "No, I mean, what color is my beard? Let's take a poll. If you think it is brown, raise your hand." About 30 percent of the students raised their hands. "White?" Ten. Professor Stubbs looked right at Everly. "What color do you see?"

Everly licked her lips. "I see a beautiful moss green with a hint of brown, but I think it is just a bird's nest."

Professor Stubbs's smile lit up the room, and now Everly swore she heard birds sing. "Correct, you are ever as talented as your father before you. I had the pleasure of teaching Everick Hart as well."

Everly felt her chest tighten.

The students instantly murmured when Professor Stubbs said her father's name.

"As in *the* Harts?"

"A legacy?"

Everly looked over at Professor Stubbs for help when the class wasn't seeming to die down.

"Why is this a big deal?" she whispered to Holland.

"Because most grievers don't live long enough to get married, let alone have as many grievers from the same family. You're like famous here," Holland said. "And you're my bestie, even better."

Professor Stubbs clapped his hands to get the class to settle down again. He began by writing on the whiteboard the word "rules." "Everly, since you are new, I need to reiterate that there are two main rules that grievers live and die by. One, always hunt in pairs. Grimms can sense grievers the same way grievers can sense grimms. And two, grimms can never be trusted." He underlined the word "trusted." "They survive by trickery, deception, and lack of regard for human life. That is the way it has been for hundreds of years. I know from firsthand experience that when the first explorers came to my grove on Roanoke Island, they fell victim to a group of naiads. A whole new colony lost... forever." His voice trailed off, and he looked into the distance. "I was but a sapling unable to move my roots or speak, but I've watched and learned."

"But what about you?" Everly spoke up, confused by the fact that a grimm was teaching. "You're a grimm."

Professor Stubbs's voice was deep and brittle, and he spoke with years of wisdom. "That I am. Some grimms are considered pax—er, uh, peaceful. Do you expect a human with such a short lifespan to know the history of grimms? As fond as I am of your kind, my love of teaching far outweighs the necessary evil. For I have found that both species, grimm and human alike, have the capacity for great good and even greater evil."

Captivated. That's the word Everly had for her class with Professor Stubbs.

It was clear that most of the class had heard the introductory griever spiel multiple times and used this time to zone out. They were leaning back in their chairs, playing on their phones, or doodling. Everly was surprised to see that in the front row was a group of twelve younger kids between eight and thirteen years old.

Everly leaned over to whisper to Holland. "Who are they?"

"We call them foundlings, orphans with the sight but deemed too young to be grievers. They can't survive in a normal school with their gifts, so they come here to learn until the Grimm Society deems them old enough to start training. It's tricky because the younger you are when you get the sight, the stronger your gift is, but it also tends to wreak havoc"—she tapped her head—"up here. Most lose their sight before reaching griever status. Except for him." Holland covered her mouth with her hand and turned to point out a boy sitting two rows behind them by himself—the *Mad Max* driver.

"Ian Holmes," she whispered.

Ian's eyes were half closed, like he was sleeping. He had reclined in his chair, his black shoes resting on the desk. Or like a king observing his subjects.

"He was ten when he became a reaper. The youngest ever in the history of our school. Makes him the best, but he's a bit intimidating."

Everly looked at Ian long and frowned. Ian caught her staring. His gaze met hers, and he lifted an eyebrow in question. She instantly turned away, and she heard his deep chuckle.

She turned and glanced again; this time, Ian was leaning forward in his seat and taking a drink out of a silver flask. *Was it alcohol? Was he drinking during school hours?* His lips curled into a knowing smile as if he knew she couldn't resist another glance. He lifted the flask in her direction to offer her a sip.

She snapped back around so fast.

Her cheeks went red, and she swore she heard the slightest whisper of insult.

"Grimm bait."

There was another prickly feeling as she could feel the eyes boring into the back of her skull. She turned to see a girl with dark braided hair and olive skin glaring at her, with a look of utter disgust and even ... could she say? Hatred?

"Who's that?" Everly pointed with her pencil over her shoulder at a girl who was staring.

Holland turned and looked in the direction. "Oh, Gemma Kane, top female griever in the school. Please don't get on her or the tweedles' bad side. Killer instinct. Short temper, but cr-a-zy," she said, drawing a finger in a circle around her temple.

Everly frowned. "Tweedles?"

Holland brushed a speck of lint off her jacket. "Yeah, her two goons on the side of her. Deenah and Dom. We call them Tweedle Dee and Tweedle Dom. They like to do whatever Gemma tells them to and have sent more grievers to the hospital wing than anyone else."

"Why are they still here then?" Everly whispered, feeling the burning sensation still being directed toward her.

"Because they don't hesitate to attack in the face of danger. They run toward it, not away."

Everly bristled; that sounded a bit like her. She turned to focus on Professor Stubbs's lecture as it moved onto their lesson, and her pen flew across her paper. She took notes on the various types of grimms. It appeared that "grimm" was the general term the United States used for fairy-tale or mythological creatures. Other countries had different terms for them—kaiju, fae, oni, and sidhe—and had their own societies that managed and kept them in check. Humans couldn't see grimms; only those with sight could. But there were other gifts that a griever could develop besides sight, one being the ability to hear omens other than your own.

Everly thought of Birdie and her gift of being able to talk to birds. Were they all potential omens?

No one knew where the grimms came from, but they appeared near epicenters and in groups, which was why so many showed up at Misty Creek. Some philosophers believed that many were put under a cursed sleep, and over the last two hundred years, more and more of them had begun to surface. But with the age of modern medicine, there had been fewer and fewer grievers, but more and more grimms.

After class, as Everly slid out of her chair, she was blocked by Gemma Kane. She was tall and athletic, and Everly could feel her anger and strong perfume rolling off her. The scent triggered a memory that Everly would rather forget.

"What?" Everly asked when the girl didn't immediately move out of her way.

"Nothing." Gemma snapped her gum at Everly. "I see absolutely nothing. Just a waste of space." She laughed and headed up the stairs.

CHAPTER 9

THE DINING HALL WAS AN ENCLOSED DOMED COURTYARD in the center of the four wings. The sun's rays created a watery effect on the floor, making it feel like a glass snow globe, and they were underwater. She knew she had to be dreaming when she realized the dining hall served edible food, not a reheated frozen meat substitute or hash made from the previous day's leftovers. There was actual, honest-to-goodness meat, honey ham, steak, cod, and vegan, gluten-free, and dairy-free options. It was like eating in a restaurant with three Michelin stars.

Everly loaded her plate with steak and a whole serving of mashed potatoes and gravy, taking way more hot rolls than she could eat. She knew if this was how it would be every day, she was going to pack on a few pounds happily.

With her plate filled high, Everly sucked a gravy drip off her thumb as she scanned the long tables. Immediately she headed toward an empty table. Holland came, sat beside her with a salad, and Everly was surprised when Kat joined them. Kat spent the whole lunch break downing cookies and licking the frosting off cinnamon rolls while watching her phone intently.

After twenty minutes, Kat left her plate, grabbed her phone, and headed off without looking back.

"Is she always so talkative?" Everly asked, confused.

"Oh, Kat?" Holland said, using her fork to point at Kat's retreating head. "She's always like that. Lost in her online world."

"Won't she get in trouble?" Everly asked.

"No, she is a prodigy," Lacie cut in on their conversation, sitting in Kat's vacated seat. "She has the highest IQ in the school. She's already heading to Yale on a full-ride scholarship when she graduates in two years..." Her voice lowered. "If she survives till graduation."

Lacie leaned in close to Everly. Her eyes twinkled with mischief. "Truthfully, I think she is secretly in an online relationship with a guy and can't bear to be offline from him."

"That could be." Holland's mouth dropped open in surprise.

"I think it's weird," Lacie added, her nose wrinkling. "You never know who could be on the other side of that screen or even what country they're from. What if you fall in love with someone, and they turn out to be a catfish? It's probably some middle-aged married guy that drives a Mini Cooper."

Everly choked and was able to recover and hide her mouth.

Holland piped up, "Hey, Everly, don't you drive a min—"

"But isn't that what social media is?" Everly cut in. "With all the filters and editing. It's selling a lie. Life isn't what people see on the outside. It's really about what's on the inside."

"Exactly, Everly Hart. That is exactly why I hunt grimms." Lacie's hands gripped her plastic water bottle that was now empty, crushing it. "The grimms need to be exterminated. They pretend to be something they're not." Her voice became stern.

"Chill out, Terminator." Holland rolled her eyes. "It's not a competition."

"It is," Lacie spat back. "They are ruining our society, and I feel like another legacy would understand. After all, our families have dedicated their lives to the annihilation of this race, and they keep spawning like flies on garbage. I've lost countless family members to the grimms."

There was the gist. Lacie grew up hating grimms. She had a lifetime of resentment and built-in prejudice against all grimms. In comparison, Everly was trained but raised with a different bias. She had come to extend an olive branch of friendship to gain another member of her agenda.

"I guess I will have to wait to form my own opinion. I've only encountered one."

Lacie's eyes were still heated when she grabbed her bottle, standing up to leave. "You will, and then you'll understand." She tossed her cup in the trash and left the dining hall.

Hunter and Aimee came into the lunchroom. When his eyes met hers, he looked away. Even after he got his plate, Holland waved her brother over to sit with them, but he turned away, giving them the cold shoulder.

"That's fine," Holland pouted out the side of her mouth. "I didn't want to sit with you either... even though I *need* to know where Aimee got that cute purse. Excuse me." Holland swung her legs from under the table and picked up her tray. Like a bee going in for a pretty flower, Holland fluttered between the tables until she reached Aimee's side and pointed to her cute little purse with a gold shoulder chain.

Everly suddenly felt alone. She tried to take another bite but couldn't when she realized she was being watched. Even though he wouldn't eat with her, Hunter didn't stop staring at her. As his girlfriend and Holland gabbed about shops, he was oblivious. A permanent frown appeared across his handsome face, making Everly uncomfortable.

She couldn't finish her lunch. Her appetite was gone. She dumped the rest of the food off her plate and left her tray on the cart. Maybe it was better to avoid Hunter at all costs. Take her meals somewhere else for a while.

Man, but she shouldn't have to avoid him. Gravemark was her school too. She was invited. She had every right to be here, same as anyone else.

Thinking about Hunter, she grunted and slammed her palm into the exit door. She wasn't prepared for the repercussions of the door being oiled so well that it swung back and hit something hard. A surprised cry followed as Everly heard the clatter and then the crack of glass as it spilled.

"I'm so sorry!" Everly cried out as she saw the dark liquid stain her victim's white shirt. She followed the color up the muscled chest and gazed into the surprised ice-cold eyes of Ian Holmes.

Ian looked down at his ruined uniform shirt. "Just great." His voice was deep, gravelly.

Caught off guard, Everly had no control over the nervous word vomit that came spewing forth.

"Yeah, that shirt had it coming. I think you would look better without it." Everly gasped and slapped a hand to cover her face.

"Uh, thanks." Ian smirked, pulling the wet shirt away from his skin. He ran his hand over the back of his neck. "But I think I would prefer to stay clothed."

Everly gripped her hands together. "Yeah, I mean, you definitely should keep covered. Not that I'm saying you wouldn't look good without a shirt on, because you obviously would... I mean only if you want. And I'm going to stop talking now."

He snorted and gave her another appraising look. Everly

felt herself shrink under his gaze. She stood there awkwardly, trying to figure out where to look. Not Ian's handsome face or those blue eyes. His feet. She would look at his shoes. Except the black shoes had a dark stain. She was a moron.

"Relax, Everly. I'm not going to melt from getting water dumped on me. I'm not a witch, as some would lead you to believe."

"How do you know my name?" Everly dropped her arm.

He frowned at her. "I was in class."

"I'm sorry." She closed her eyes, took a deep breath, and tried again. She looked down at the floor and desperately wished to melt into a puddle and disappear into the cracks of the tile. Never before had her brain been unable to compute or speak. He must think her an idiot.

Ian sighed, finally letting his frustration show. His patience for the new kid had run out. He stepped around her and headed into a side closet next to the kitchen. She stood there staring at the puddle, unsure what to do next or who to tell when Ian returned with a rolling bucket and mop.

"Here you go, grimm bait. Your first lesson in surviving Gravemark. Clean up your own messes." With a push of his foot, he slid it across the floor to her.

Her cheeks burned in embarrassment. She knelt and picked up a few stray ice cubes. She tucked her strawberry blonde hair behind her ear. She was proud that she could hold her tongue and not say anything dumb for the next two minutes while she cleaned and Ian supervised, which made her feel insignificant.

"You missed a spot." He pointed with his shoe.

Everly's teeth gritted in shame and anger, but she cleaned it up without a comeback.

"Done," Everly said as she wrung the mop out and saw the

empty hall. Ian had disappeared, leaving her to clean up her mess alone.

A soft tone signaled the end of the lunch period.

Everly headed across the outdoor courtyard into another building that looked like it used to be a church, with double arched doors. As soon as she entered the building, it took her breath away. On either side of the library were stained-glass windows of giant sunflowers, daffodils, and peonies lining both walls. Each window showcased different genus of flowers.

The front desk was unmanned. A placard read the name "Professor Halsey," but no professor was in sight. She decided to explore the library and head to the back.

The floor had old rug liners to muffle the sound of footsteps but did nothing to mask the scent of must, dust, and book glue. A central staircase led to the second floor, which housed a restricted section and smaller side spiral staircases that led to private study rooms. Study tables lined the hall. Further back were the rows of books along two floors and even some alcoves with smaller tables nestled with what looked like fake gas lamps.

Everly heard soft snoring. She walked through the main stacks to find someone sitting in one of the two high-back chairs before a crackling fireplace.

In one of the chairs, sleeping, was a gentleman in his seventies, with gold-rimmed glasses and pale skin as if he always spent time indoors reading. He had a long white beard and a mustache that tapered into little curls, like the villain in a cartoon.

"Excuse me. Mr. Halsey?" Everly came to stand next to the sleeping professor.

His eyes opened suddenly, wholly aware, and they were a golden brown.

He only gave her a cursory glance before pointing to his left to a study table with a golden lamp.

"Go ahead and sit at the table behind me," he instructed as he picked up a pipe and lit it with a match, taking a few puffs before the pipe ignited. A stream of smoke followed.

Everly batted at the air as the smell from the pipe wasn't pleasant. It had a slightly sulfurous aroma. How unsafe was it for the head librarian to smoke in the library? Much less have an open fire. He must always be cold in his old age.

After putting the pipe in his mouth, Mr. Halsey reached for one of the books on a side table, opened it, and began reading.

Everly put her bag on the table, pulled out a chair, and waited for the other students to arrive. Five minutes passed, and she was the only one in the library. Everly kept checking her phone and looking at Mr. Halsey, but he was still reading his book.

"Excuse me, Mr. Halsey?" Everly called his name. "What am I supposed to be doing?"

"It's a library," he answered without looking up. "You read."

"But..."

Mr. Halsey turned on her. "There are five levels of grimms, starting at the lowest. Level ones—the tricksters—pixies, fairies, gnomes. For the most part harmless if left alone. Followed by level twos—haunters. Your basic ghost, boggart, apparition-type grimms. Level threes are called lures—mermaids, sirens, kelpies, ones that lure people to their death. Level fours are the titans—giants, cyclopes, and minotaurs. Their biggest asset is their strength but not necessarily their minds. Level fives are the most dangerous. They are the hunters—cold-blooded killers, like werewolves and vampires. And how you fight each one is different based on the circumstance. So your assignment is to read." He pointed to the stack of journals in front of her.

Everly glanced to the middle of the table and picked up the first, a soft moleskin cover. She flipped to the first few pages.

September 21, 1999

A level three almost lured Melanie to her death. I must remember that level-three grimms survive by enticing, tempting, and trapping their prey. The each-uisge has many similarities to a kelpie, gentle at first until they get their first smell of water, which can trigger their murderous rage...

November 8, 1999

Encountered my first level-five grimm today—a vampire. I stumbled into its lair and almost became grimm bait. My team lead swooped in and saved the day by opening the shades. I learned a valuable lesson. Always check the windows of a house before entering. A boarded house with many heavy curtains usually means a creature with a weakness to sunlight.

November 30, 1999

A manticore, a great lion-like beast with a scorpion's tail and human-like head, hid among a pack of lions at the nearby wildlife sanctuary. Never would have suspected it, except it kept escaping to hunt its prey and then returned every night to its enclosure. A manticore has three ways of killing, teeth, claws, and venomous tail. He never killed the same way twice. I wonder how many other grimms hide in plain sight.

· · ·

Everly fell into the stories, the journals, the heartache as the griever recounted their first few hard-learned lessons. They were highly educational.

After thirty minutes, Everly looked up from her journal and glanced around the room to find she was still the only student.

"Mr. Halsey," Everly addressed the back of his head, "why am I the only one here?"

"Because you are the only one worth my time." He closed his book and turned to look at her. Those golden eyes met hers for the first time. "The others don't care about my research." He rubbed his eyes, and they came away glassy with unshed tears. "But your father, Everick Hart, did." Mr. Halsey got up from his chair and came to stand next to Everly. "He was my friend. He saw me, understood my quirks and desire for knowledge." As he talked, he reached out and straightened the stack of books.

Everly realized that he wasn't odd but brilliant with ASD.

"Everick was special. He brought me books...." He trailed off and cleared his throat, overcome with emotion. "I had tried to be there for him at the end when his sight faded, but he pushed me away." He pushed his glasses up his nose and gave her a small hopeful smile. "So, because of your father, I will finish what he started in your education—I will fill in the gaps. You are teachable, others not so much."

That wasn't the answer she was expecting. She sat there, mouth agape in confusion, her hand on the book.

"Thank you," she said halfheartedly.

"As grievers, you are encouraged to keep a journal and write down everything that happened after every reaping. I'm the guardian of that knowledge, and most students couldn't care less about our history. They only care about dealing with the quickest solution to a problem. But not every grimm has the same weakness. There are oddities among all races. It's rare, but I've seen it here." He tapped the journals. "But no one cares." He slumped back into his chair, and he seemed tired. He waved her off. "You can go for the day."

Feeling uncomfortable, Everly started to restack the journals.

"No, wait. Take that one with you. It should stay in the family." He pointed to the one she was reading.

"Whose is it?"

"Have you not figured it out or recognized the handwriting?" His eyes seemed to fill with delight.

"Wait, do you mean these are my..." She couldn't finish as tears filled her eyes.

He nodded. "I hope reading them brings you peace and comfort and eases your heart."

"Thank you so much!" Everly took the journals and raced back to her room.

CHAPTER 10

The afternoon was free, and Everly read her dad's journals. They were eye-opening, full of knowledge and tricks that weren't in the general textbooks. She knew because she kept quizzing Holland on them, who had no idea. But maybe Holland wasn't the best litmus for her testing. She didn't usually retain information.

Everly hid in her room during dinner, eating one of her Shin instant ramen bowls and avoiding the dining hall crowd. She had thought it would bring her peace. Instead, it made her feel even more alone. How could being at a school with her best friend feel so lonely?

October 10, 2001

I was griever team lead, tracking a werewolf in the smoky mountains. This beast had evaded the best of them for too long, taking too many victims. Last night would be its last. I assembled the best grievers, Carol, Eugene, and myself, chosen because of our strength and teamwork.

Carol was dangerous with any weapon, swift on her feet, and I'd once seen her take down a full vampire with one blow. There was an untamed wildness about her that was almost frightening. Eugene was the survivalist. He knew every plant, herb, and way to survive off the land. If there was a weakness in a grimm, Eugene knew it.

We did it—a success. I tracked down the human alias of the werewolf. During the day, he worked at an auto mechanic shop. He would profile his victims and any out-of-towners who came in for work on their vehicles. He would sabotage them. Make them pick up their car right before closing, causing a slow leak in their power steering fluid as they drove home. He would follow them into the mountains.

I quiver, knowing that there are grimms that kill so ruthlessly that live among us—posing as one of us. The werewolf had been able to keep his killing under control for years, but it was as he aged that he found himself unable to resist the call of his wolf.

The three of us did a stakeout. Carol, Eugene, and I followed in my truck.

We almost didn't get there in time, the grimm having shifted before it was dark; it dragged the man from his vehicle into the woods to finish him off. But Eugene saw the tracks. His griever sight led the way through the dark. He drove the truck into the werewolf, hoping to pin him to the tree. The werewolf escaped. My truck didn't.

It was a ruthless fight. The werewolf's strength far exceeded anything we had ever encountered before. I was pinned in the passenger seat, the front dashboard collapsing into my legs. Carol confronted the werewolf but was thrown against a tree and blacked out. I was losing blood and consciousness and trapped inside the truck. I would have died if it wasn't for Eugene, who killed the werewolf, but not without taking severe injury.

He saved us, but at what cost?

I had failed as a team leader.

. . .

A pecking came at her window. Everly looked up from her journal and wiped her mouth from a dribble of broth. Another raven was trying to get in.

"'Kay, be there soon." She lifted the bowl and drank the rest of the ramen broth before getting up. She opened the window, and the raven swooped in a circle, dropping the white envelope on her bed before flying out the window without saying a word.

"I guess other ravens aren't as talkative as Corvis."

The envelope was the same as her first one. She broke the wax seal and read the simple line.

Entrance Griever Test

11:00 p.m.

"I didn't know they had classes this late?" Everly looked at her phone. It was after six, and she knew there wasn't anything on the schedule. What kind of testing was this going to be?

At 10:45 p.m., a knock came at her door, and Everly opened it to see Maddie Eerie from Liberty hall.

"It's time," Maddie stated. Her dark blonde hair was the same length as Everly's but a brighter shade and pulled into a braid. She wore a long green cloak. "Follow me."

"Where are we going?" Everly grabbed her jacket. Since officially class was over for the day, she had changed out of her uniform and wore black sweatpants and an oversized sweatshirt with sneakers.

"To your first test," Maddie whispered as they walked down the hall. Most of the lamps and lights had been turned down low.

"What kind of test is it going to be?" Everly asked.

"Not the pen and paper kind," Maddie added cryptically. "This is going to test your instinct."

"Is this a 'we don't talk about fight club' kind of thing?"

"Maybe," Maddie answered. As they walked, Everly saw Holland head down a different hall on the left toward her room.

"Hey, Holland," Everly called out.

"No." Maddie turned and put her hand over Everly's. "Sibs and non-grievers aren't allowed to come. She shouldn't even be wandering around at this time of night."

Everly felt horrible at not including Holland, but she was still new and didn't know the rules.

Maddie walked behind a set of stairs and paused by an enormous grandfather clock. She looked at her watch and waited to ensure no one was around. Maddie opened the glass cabinet and stopped the giant pendulum, making the clock freeze at a particular time. Reaching up, she adjusted the hands on the clock like a dial, turning the hour hand right and the minute hand left like a combination lock.

Everly's eyes followed the combination carefully.

A soft click followed, and the clock base swung outward without a sound, revealing a dark corridor behind it.

"Where does it go?"

Maddie wouldn't say. Her eyes just twinkled mischievously. "Narnia."

"Well, I don't know anyone that wants to walk down a creepy staircase."

Maddie pressed the light on her phone, and the passageway lit up. "After you, legacy." She waved her hand, and Everly reached for her phone and turned the flashlight on. She tentatively took the first step and followed the narrow passageway. It turned suddenly, and Everly had to brace her hand on the top of the passage. It was getting to be a tight squeeze. She had to take a break and focus on her breathing.

This was nothing. Everly told herself to pretend it was a test by her dad. She could escape.

Soon the steps stopped, and the floor leveled out, and they were in what looked like a giant dungeon with tall ceilings and cement buttresses. A fluttering of shadows near the top told her that bats were probably living in the crevices but also that it wasn't entirely underground, for there had to be air ducts for the bats to come and go.

Along the far wall were weapon racks with spears, swords, and shields. She wasn't sure if they were there for a purpose or display.

Torches flickered, making it feel even more creepy, revealing the row of prison cells. Some looked to be occupied. Above the cells was a balcony filled with people in long hooded green robes; most had their faces hidden in the shadow of their hoods. A few wore white raven masks, distinguishing them from the others. In a separate section of the balcony were what Everly assumed to be the leaders of the Grimm Society, for they wore silver raven masks with one in a golden mask. She couldn't tell if they were male or female.

She moved to the center of the room and the black-and-white-patterned floor that spiraled out from the center like a vortex. A stone table stood in the center.

It looked like it had once been used for torture or sacrifices because restraints were on the side. Except these restraints were too large for human wrists. And next to the bonds were particular objects.

"What is going on?" Everly turned to address Maddie, but she was alone.

One of the white raven masks separated from the others and moved to stand in the center near a podium box and levers.

They were shorter than the others and had a raven brooch whose head had a big, fat, red-jeweled eye. "I'm the Master of Ceremonies for tonight's gathering. We're here for your initiation. The unkindness has marked you."

The MC pointed toward Everly's wrist, and as she spoke and her eyes adjusted, Everly saw the raven mark appear on her wrist and then disappear.

"The ravens are the official watchers for the Grimm Society. They mark those that have the sight. But before you can officially train to be a griever, you have to pass the first initiation."

"Isn't this a little early for a test? It's only my first day," Everly tried to joke.

"Grimms don't wait until we are ready. They strike as soon as they smell a griever."

A thud hit the closest cell, and Everly jumped in terror as something rammed the metal door. She could hear a deep, throaty chuckle of amusement from the creature within.

She heard something scratch at the cement floor from the second cell as if trying to escape. "Hungry!" yelled the voice within.

Everly walked along the edge and looked into each of the cells, squinting, trying to figure out the grimm within, taking stock of what these grimms had to do with her test.

The third cell held the most significant and scariest threat. Everly could almost feel their anger, and she didn't want to tangle with the occupant within. Everly paused and sniffed the air, confirming her suspicions.

She returned to the stone table in the center of the room set with various items: a net, silver knife, bo staff, T-bone steak, wooden box, and iron chains.

"What do you think of our collection?" the MC asked Everly.

"It's okay." Everly looked up at the speaker and shrugged.

"Are you not afraid?" The MC seemed confused.

"Not particularly."

Her answer seemed to displease the MC. "Then let the testing begin." They reached over to a control box on the balcony and pulled a lever.

A metal whine sounded as a cell door swung open. Everly turned, counting the prison cells to find which creature had been released.

"Can you defeat the grimm?" the MC said.

There was a cacophony of voices from the balcony. "Run!" "Fight!"

"Choose, griever," the MC said, pointing to the table. "What item will save your life?"

Everly grabbed the steak and tossed it into the second cell as the black shaggy beast neared the entrance. The creature darted and grabbed the steak bone, dragging it back into the darkness. A loud huffing and chewing noise followed.

"Mmm, good," the omen said and continued to chew noisily.

Laughter filled the balcony.

"I'm not scared of an omen," Everly answered.

"And how did you know it wasn't a shapeshifter?"

"I didn't."

That confused them. But Everly wasn't going to tell them that she could hear the giant wolf's thoughts, which meant it was an omen. Since not everyone had that griever ability, she thought she would keep it to herself. She didn't want to spoil the fun.

A second cell door opened, and Everly turned, her heart racing as her focus turned to the ethereal creature within the first prison cell. This thing had rammed the door to try and startle Everly. This was most definitely a grimm.

The boggart floated out of the cell and tossed a round object her way. She ducked, and it hit the far wall and then rolled across the floor, coming to land by her foot. It was a head. Round, with a broad nose and dark black eyes. The boggart head grinned at her and winked before cackling and rolling back to its body.

The boggart was dressed in rags with a scarf around its neck, probably to keep its head when it wasn't tossing it at people as a joke. It reached down to pick up its head, and Everly ran to the table, grabbed the African blackwood box, and opened it. Kneeling like she was going to play shuffleboard, Everly slid the box across the floor, and when it reached the foot of the boggart, he giggled happily and dove into the box and closed the lid on itself.

Everly went over, picked up the box, and used the hook latch to lock the lid.

More murmuring of surprise came from the gallery. Everly pinched her lips together. She was silently thanking Holland for having given her the answer yesterday. She was the one who had told her about bagging a boggart and how they loved throwing their heads as jokes until they could hide in a coffin box made of rare wood. The boggart was probably the same one her team had caught.

Applause followed from the gallery, but she knew the final cell held her biggest rival, and she wouldn't wait to be surprised. This creature didn't follow the rules.

Everly walked straight to the table and grabbed the staff. She picked it up and tested its weight in her hands. She had been trained to fight only in a life-or-death situation. Her instructor wouldn't be proud, but this was how the game was played. If this was the final test, she didn't want to fail.

The cell door swung open, and Everly gripped the staff, her

knuckles white, and she shifted her weight from foot to foot and stared at the darkness within.

"Let's go, Gemma," Everly said as a hooded person came out of the final cell.

"How did you know?" Gemma pulled her hood back and glared at Everly with that same hatred.

"Your perfume," Everly answered. "I've only known two people who wear that particular brand called Lux. I'm not fond of either person. You and my mother."

"You think you're so smart with these tests because you're a legacy," Gemma sneered. "Let's see how you do against a real griever."

Gemma grabbed a weapon that Everly had never seen before. It was like an escrima stick but thinner and painted black.

Everly took a deep breath, waiting for Gemma to make the first move.

Gemma attacked. Her strikes were quick, silent, and filled with power. Everly was surprised because this wasn't like a sparring match in the gym, where her partner pulled his punches. This was full of attack, and she had to adjust her thinking.

She waited, blocking each strike with her staff, watching how Gemma fought. Everyone had a pattern in the way they attacked—a rhythm. No one was truly random. Starting with how they were trained, they usually leaned on strikes they were most comfortable with before switching to a harder one.

Everly ducked as the black blade swiped at her head. She also knew that the more tired her opponent became, the quicker their strikes and attacks would come, in their desperation to end the fight and win.

Everly grinned as she continued to block strike after strike, only dancing around the circle as she wore out Gemma.

"What's wrong, scared to fight me?" Gemma taunted.

Everly jumped to avoid the strike aimed to take her out at the knees.

"This isn't fighting," Everly answered and spun under another attack. Still refusing to fight. "This is like watching paint dry." She purposely baited Gemma, trying to make the much more experienced fighter make a mistake.

There was a chuckle from the gallery at her comment, and she glanced upward and saw that one of the members had removed his hood. Everly saw Hunter. He had pushed through the crowd and now leaned forward, both hands resting on the balcony railing, his face filled with worry.

Great! Now that Everly saw Hunter, no matter where she moved, she was aware of him. The way he flinched when she blocked a hit. He bit his lip when she didn't duck, and the weapon grazed her shoulder. It hurt. It was solid metal. She would have a bruise later. But once she knew Hunter was there, it was like the only thing she could focus on was him.

Not the angry griever intent on taking off her head.

She heard him suck in his breath, and she lost focus.

She lowered her staff a split second and never saw the hit coming—a jab to her gut. She gasped, the wind knocked out of her lungs, and she fell to her knees. Her mouth opened and closed as she struggled to take that first breath.

Gemma threw up her hands in victory, and only Deenah and a few others slowly clapped for her. Not as many as she had hoped because she started to yell up at the other grievers. "What?"

"Focus!" a cold voice growled out, and Everly saw Ian standing to the left of Hunter. Now that her eyes had adjusted to the dungeon's darkness, she could easily make out his strong jaw and stony expression.

Everly pushed herself up to her feet, her stomach feeling

like it would eject her ramen on the floor. But she couldn't quit. She readied herself, trying to ignore Hunter attempting to push his way down the stairs to stop the fight, but grievers were blocking him, holding him back from interfering.

"You can't go down there!" Dom pushed Hunter back. "It's against the rules."

She couldn't pull her gaze away. The second blow came from nowhere, behind the knees. Everly fell and smacked the floor, her cheek brushing against the cold stone. Her ragged breaths caused puffs of dirt to rise into the air.

"You're getting distracted," Ian reprimanded.

What would happen if she just laid down and didn't get back up?

Gemma thought it was over and was already speaking to Deenah, leaning over the balcony. "That's one less legacy going to be strutting around here." She turned and made a face.

"Get up!" Ian yelled. It wasn't an encouragement but an order. "Don't you understand what will happen if you give up?"

She didn't. *What was the worst that could happen?*

Ian glanced over to the far side of the balcony where there was a separate viewing box, and within were six other hooded members, all with silver raven masks, watching her, their robes a little nicer, their movements more regal. They weren't cheering or clapping but observing, taking notes. One had a gold mask and a three-inch thick silver and emerald-studded livery collar that marked their status as more important than the others. *Was this the leader of the Grimm Society?* Did they come here to watch her get bullied and made fun of? This wasn't a joke or a hazing ritual. Were they going to expel her if she failed?

Seeing the society observing her made her all the angrier. She wasn't in the mood to be someone's entertainment.

Everly got to her feet. Her eyes focused on the gold mask in the middle. This was their fault. She turned and cast one final glance to the griever gallery; she saw Ian nod, then back away into the crowd.

She was tired of playing the game. Now she wanted to end it. When Gemma saw Everly rise to her feet, she cursed under her breath.

"Haven't you learned your lesson?" she hissed. "Stay down."

"Maybe it's because you're not a very good teacher." Everly favored her sore stomach. She turned her body to telegraph her movements loud and clear. Baiting Gemma. Pretending to cover her right side as if it was weaker than the other.

Gemma attacked, going right for the weak side, but Everly was faster. She dropped her staff, grabbed Gemma's wrist, and, using the girl's momentum, turned, flipped her over her back, and tossed her onto the floor. Everly didn't wait. She grabbed that wrist, twisted it, and put her foot right over Gemma's neck, applying enough pressure to make her lie back down and not move.

"Do you concede?" Everly spoke.

"No." Gemma struggled and tried to push her up.

Everly twisted her wrist and heard a whimper. "How about now?"

"You don't know what you've just done," Gemma threatened. "No one makes a fool out of me. I'm going to make your life a living hell for this."

"You were out to get me the moment I stepped foot in this school. Why?" Everly asked.

Gemma shook her head and only looked up at the person in the silver collar. She bit her lip and wouldn't say. Everly followed her gaze, and the leader of the Grimm Society got up and left as if disappointed in Gemma.

She felt the girl crumple under the abandonment.

"Concede," Everly repeated.

"I concede," Gemma said softly as a tear ran down her cheek.

Everly released Gemma and stepped back. Gemma was wiping the dirt from her face. She looked to the gallery and made a motion with her hand.

Deenah, standing close to the control levers, seemed to fall backward and bump a lever with a silver raven handle.

Suddenly, the ground beneath her trembled and shook, causing the stone table to split in half. In the center, a seemingly bottomless dark pit was revealed, with a staircase leading down into the darkness.

"Who opened the oubliette?" shouted the speaker with the gold raven mask. "Close it now, before something escapes!"

Too late.

An enormous gray hand reached from beyond the depths of the pit and gripped the arena floor, pulling its large body out of the oubliette.

A humanoid creature with a bald head, large teeth, and thick fists like boulders emerged from the pit. Its huge eyes were dark, red-rimmed, and filled with fury. When the beast rose, it directed its murderous gaze toward Everly.

"Ogre!" Gemma screamed.

"Everly, run!" Hunter yelled.

Everly heard a roar and saw the ogre towering over her. The creature effortlessly lifted the stone table, turned it, and swung it down in an arc toward her head. Everly dove and rolled out of the way, noticing that Gemma had already left the floor and was climbing up to the safety of the upper-level gallery with the help of Dom and Deenah.

Everly raced toward the balcony and Hunter's outstretched hand. He was already reaching down, as low as he could, to pull her to safety. She jumped and grabbed his wrists, but she felt someone else hold the back of her shirt as they started to lift her in the air.

They weren't fast enough as the ogre tore a round shield off the wall like it was made of plastic and tossed it at Hunter like a frisbee. The sequence felt like it was in slow motion; she saw Hunter's eyes widen as he calculated the angle. She knew when he made the decision and dropped her. He grabbed the other grievers by their cloaks and pushed them below the stone barrier as the shield skittered across the half wall, sending sparks, and embedded in the wall behind them. It would have cut them in two.

Everly fell and dropped back into the testing arena. Her head smacked the stone floor, and stars flickered across her vision.

Out of the side of her vision, she saw Ian jump down from the gallery, grab a spear from the rack of weapons that had been knocked over, and throw it.

It soared through the air and lodged into the ogre's side, but it did not slow him.

She could feel herself start to black out as she looked up at the meaty heel of an ogre's foot coming down toward her head. Hunter had made it to the stairs and ran across the arena but was blocked by the open pit.

A tentative question touched the back of her mind, asking permission to help.

"Yes!" Everly called back, knowing that help would be too late. She reached toward the thought. "Help me," she begged.

"Mine," a high-pitched voice echoed throughout, and then a colorful explosion, like fireworks, started going off in her mind, overwhelming all her senses at once. A bouquet of smells, flashes of colors, and echoes of sounds continued to rise in pitch.

A raven swiftly descended and attacked the ogre's eye, preventing it from delivering a fatal blow. The ogre cried out in pain as it lost sight in one eye. It attempted to strike the raven with its claw but was met with another dangerous creature.

The wolf omen joined in the fight, skillfully dodging the ogre's blows by jumping. It launched in the air, the wolf's powerful jaws locking onto the ogre's forearm. The two omen protectors were locked in battle with the giant ogre as someone reached her side and picked her up. Her vision faded as her head dropped into her rescuer's chest. His grip tightened as he carried her away.

CHAPTER 11

"Well, I've never seen that before," Ms. March muttered.

Everly was drifting in and out of a hazy sleep. *Did she pass out?* Under half-closed lids, she saw Ms. March, the headmistress, for the first time in person. She was plump, in her late fifties. Her thin, pastel-painted lips wavered into a frown of compassion. A glimmer on her shirt revealed the same raven brooch as the speaker in the ceremony.

"Headmistress March, what happened?" A female voice she didn't recognize seemed to be interrogating Ms. March. The second speaker was standing behind the lamp just out of sight, disguised by a blurry halo of green robe and silver collar.

"I don't know. Never in the history of our griever tests has that ever happened."

"We ask you to oversee the first test because of the safety precautions you put in place. Tonight was a disaster. Not only was that Kane girl out of line, but who in their right mind would open the oubliette, releasing the ogre?"

"I know." Ms. March dipped her head. "A student admitted to falling into the lever."

"Did you check the oubliette? Are there any escapees?"

"No, but I will check again."

"Enough, find out the answer. The society was very displeased with the proctoring of tonight's test."

Everly was lying on an unfamiliar bed in the medical wing and watched the two women discussing her as if she wasn't there.

"Last night was not a sacred ceremony. It was a madhouse. And during the midst of battle, she bonded with an omen, without any training," the leader of the Grimm Society continued. "That shows her mental strength and fortitude."

Ms. March's lips pinched, her lipstick disappearing. "That particular raven is not like other omens. He is highly unusual."

"And these are highly unusual times, wouldn't you agree?" the woman countered. "Or have you forgotten the increase in all grimm attacks nationwide? I fear without Detective Hart, we are fighting too many enemies blind. We need his inside information. We can't send grievers out unprepared. I don't want to lose any more students to senseless deaths. I will not have what happened to Crypthaven Academy happen here."

"I haven't forgotten," Ms. March said firmly. "We won't let you down, madam."

There was a scratch of a wooden chair moving backward across the floor, the heavy falls of footsteps. Everly heard the door open and close.

The room fell silent.

"You can stop pretending to sleep," a wry voice called. "They're gone now."

Everly's eyes flew open, and she saw that the medical wing was empty. Both the head of the Grimm Society and the headmistress had left. Corvis was sitting on top of the curtain divide, watching over her. With a swift hop and a swoop, he landed on the nightstand next to her bed.

Everly dropped her head on her pillow and covered her face with her hands. "That was an absolute nightmare."

"I don't know. I thought it was fun."

Everly rolled over and propped herself onto her elbow. "Fun? It was terrifying. Why were you there?"

"Birdie sent me to watch over you," Corvis said softly. "She thought you might need some help."

"She knew this would happen?"

Corvis bobbed his head. "There's always an entrance test within the first few days of a new griever coming to Gravemark. No use training a griever if they faint at the first sight of a headless boggart. Or if they don't have any survival instincts. Usually, it's a harmless boggart, omen, and a fellow griever. The only one you are physically allowed to fight is the human griever. Believe it or not, they don't want to put children in the face of danger or monsters. This is how they test them. That was your real entrance exam. And you passed. And as a bonus, you got me."

"Yay, me." Everly pulled the blanket over her head.

"It wasn't that bad." Corvis plucked at her blanket with his beak and pulled it back. "You passed with flying colors. The ogre attack was just a fluke."

"I'd be dead if it wasn't for you and the other omen."

Corvis shuffled his feathers as if fluffing himself up. "That was Shadow. We make a good team. But it seems you had more than one protector tonight."

"What do you mean?" Everly asked.

"The boy."

"What boy?"

"There was a boy that risked his life to cross the ogre's path; he jumped the oubliette and carried you away," Corvis answered. "Brave that one; if a human falls in, they almost never come out."

Everly racked the fuzziness and the memories, trying to remember who was there. But her head was still throbbing, and she could feel her eyes start to want to close again. "Hunter?"

Corvis cocked his head and looked at her. "I don't know his name. You humans all look alike."

"Liar." Everly felt herself smile, her eyelids heavy. "Ravens have excellent eyesight."

"You know nothing," Corvis said, pretending to groom his feathers. "Get some sleep. I'll watch over you."

CHAPTER 12

Everly was struggling to focus. Since being bonded to Corvis, she realized her sight and hearing had grown considerably. All of a sudden, she could hear the other omens across campus. Her griever ability to talk to omens now included super hearing.

"Shh, Corvis, why are you thinking at me so loud?" Everly muttered, brushing her hair, wincing when she bumped the bruised spot on her head. She was thankful it wasn't a concussion.

"It will get easier. It's only loud now until you get used to it. This connection is how you call me." Corvis was dancing on her dresser, looking at himself in the mirror.

"Call you?" Everly pulled her hair back and braided it into a fishtail.

"I can fly very fast," he bragged. "You call me; I will come to rescue you."

Everly bit her lip to hold back a smile.

The omens were banned from attending classes, as they were usually a distraction. Everly learned there were only a dozen omens on campus, and most preferred to spend their days in the vivarium, their omen sanctuary.

Except for hers. Corvis had an addiction to TV. When she headed to class, he sat on the coatrack in the central commons and begged her to let him stay and watch.

"What do you want to watch?" she asked, flipping through the channels.

"The omen cartoon," Corvis answered.

"There are no cartoons about omens," Everly corrected.

"Yes, yes. Yes. I choose you, Pikachu!" he crowed happily, almost mimicking the voice.

"That's not about...." She trailed off, thinking about the cartoon animals traveling in little balls and protecting their trainer. "Okay." It took a bit for her to find a channel, but she left it on, and Corvis flew to the end table and put a claw on the remote. He was obsessed with TV shows, and now she understood where he got his witty quotes.

Everly headed toward the lecture hall and sat next to Holland.

Ms. Bellcamp was going through her iPad, preparing to project the lesson on the screen.

Holland was confused at all the odd looks and fingers pointing Everly's way.

"What's going on?" Holland whispered to Everly. "Why do I feel like I have something in my teeth?"

"It's not you. It's me. I had my griever test last night and was almost dinner to an ogre."

Holland's eyes went as big as saucers. "What the grimm—" Everly clasped her hand over Holland's mouth.

"Shhh." Everly pressed her finger to her lips. "You weren't supposed to know."

Her eyes flashed angrily. "It's because I'm a sibling. An unmarked griever-in-training with no abilities. They are so stuck up here about true grievers that I don't know if I would even want to deal with the mess."

"At 11:00 p.m. I called out to you in the hall."

Holland frowned. "But last night I wasn't—"

"Everly, are you okay?" Hunter interrupted, reaching to touch her shoulder. "I went to the medical wing this morning, and you were gone."

Everly turned to give him her full attention and saw the red bruise on his cheekbone, and she couldn't ignore the fresh bandage along his collarbone, half hidden by his uniform.

Did this all happen last night? she wondered. *Because of her?*

She tried to quell her feelings from last night. "I'm fine, just a bump the size of a goose egg on my head and a bruised rib. Dr. Madsen cleared me for class. But are you okay? What happened? I don't remember much."

Hunter's jaw clenched. "It was an ogre. They're tough but not invincible, and we had a room full of grievers. He is contained again. But are you sure you're fine?"

Everly saw the evidence of the attack on Hunter, and her heart started to race again.

"Not fine. Smell fear," a grumble came from the front of the classroom by the podium.

Everly's brows rose, and she leaned to the side to get a better view. She would never have seen it, except after her pairing with Corvis, her sight had improved, and she could see the wolf hiding in the shadows on the floor below the podium; no, he was the shadows. He blended in perfectly; one could see right through him except for a faint outline. This was Shadow— the omen from her testing who helped save her from the ogre.

"I'm fine!" Everly said again, this time directing her answer toward the wolf. "And thank you."

Hunter looked toward the podium and the omen to see what had caught her attention.

"You can see him?" Hunter asked in surprise.

"See, hear, smell." Everly rubbed her forehead; she was feeling pressure there. Probably a hangover feeling after the firework show of being bonded last night.

"That's Ms. Bellcamp's omen, Shadow. No one except me has ever been able to spot Shadow when he doesn't want to be seen. You see him?" he asked again.

"He's right there!" Everly pointed, but he was gone. Shadow had moved. Frustrated that he had made a liar out of her, she spun around and quickly began to scan the hall. Now she had something to prove.

She turned to the Grecian urn and saw him blending in with the wood floor; his back hackles had turned white, and he was hidden against the clay.

"There he is." Everly pointed at the wolf.

"Drat!"

"He's not too happy that I keep finding him," Everly said.

"Amazing that you can hear him as well. You're lucky." Hunter grinned while giving her an appraising look. "I can only see him."

Holland cupped her hands around her eyes like binoculars and was focused on the area they were searching. She threw her hands in the air. "I give up. I got nothing."

"Take care, and it will happen one day, sis," Hunter encouraged.

"Thank you for saving me," Everly whispered, knowing that every eye in the room was still upon her, judging her. "You got me out of there."

Hunter rubbed the back of his head. "I tried, but Ian got there first."

"Ian?" Everly's mouth dropped open, and she looked around the room to see that he was absent. Was he okay? Did he get injured?

Just then, Ms. March appeared at the front of the classroom. She was again wearing the raven brooch, this time with a navy suit-dress. She rapped her knuckles on the podium until the class settled down. "Excuse me, students. I regret to inform you that all teacher-led classes for today have been canceled. Everything else is still running as scheduled."

"What happened?" Lacie called out and took a sip from her frappe.

"Nothing that needs to concern you at this moment. Just an in-house investigation."

"Does this have to do with the recent attacks?" Kat held up her purple phone. "It's all over the news."

Ms. March's face paled, and her hand went to her heart. "The news... but how?"

"It went live this morning. It seems Misty Creek PD and Park Ranger Raglan busted a staged big game hunting ring," Kat said. "Poachers bringing in illegal animals from the north and doing staged wild hunts for money. The article said one escaped, and they're still looking for the last cougar."

Ms. March's face relaxed. "Oh, that. Well, good. It turns out it's not grimm related after all."

"But do we believe that?" Kat asked.

"Since we no longer have a liaison with the police department, we are in the dark. But we must assume that if the park rangers caught the animal, it was not, in fact, a grimm."

Liaison? Everly dug her fingernails into her palms, and her breath hitched. *That was her father.* She now understood the importance of his job once his gifts were gone.

"That will be all." Ms. March cleared her throat and stepped out of the side of the classroom.

"Hey!" Lacie spun around in her seat. "What are you doing later tonight?" Lacie asked coyly, using her straw to scoop out the whipped topping of her drink.

"Probably sleeping or studying... no wait. After last night. Sleeping."

"No, you're coming to my party," Lacie said.

"What party?"

"Yeah, what party?" Holland mimicked Everly.

"The one that we throw for new grievers."

"We've never thrown parties for new grievers." Holland crossed her arms and challenged Lacie.

"Well, we do now. I know just the place, near the bluffs. It's on Hollow Lake."

"Can I come?" Holland asked. "Or is this a sibless party?"

Lacie pursed her lips and furrowed her brows in thought. "Of course. Hunter's sister is always welcome. Be there at 9:00 p.m."

Lacie walked away, sucking on the straw.

Holland dropped her head onto the table. "Look, now I'm reduced to Hunter's sister. There was a time when I was popular at my old school, way back when Kerrigan was still around. Before she went off to start her own online company." Holland seemed to drown in her sorrows, and then her head shot up. "I need to go pick out my outfit!" Quickly forgetting her previous heartache, she jumped up from her chair and turned to Everly. "You coming?"

"No, I'm going to head back and study." Everly parted ways with Holland and headed up the stairs to the back of the class-room. She was passing the last row when Ian stepped in front of her.

"Just where are you going?"

His hair was slightly damp, making his blond hair darker and his eyes more ice blue than usual. Or maybe it was her newly amplified sight that was making him seem even more noticeable.

"Heading to my room to study. I have a lot to catch up on."

"No. You're mine." Ian's voice dropped low.

Her heart did a little flutter at how deep his voice was when he called her mine, but she pushed it aside. "Excuse me?"

"We're training in ten minutes."

"Training?"

Ian crossed his arms over his chest and glared at her. "You heard Ms. March, all teacher-led classes are canceled. I'm not a teacher. After last night's attack, Ms. Bellcamp assigned me to be your mentor."

"Mentor?"

"Yes," he said. "We have lessons."

"Lessons?"

"Why do you keep repeating everything I say? Are you sure your new omen isn't a parrot?" Ian frowned.

Everly was flustered. "No, I didn't. I'm just..."

"Ten minutes, Training Hall." He was gone. As quiet as he came, Ian Holmes disappeared.

———

Everly let out a whistle when she entered the training room. It reminded her of Mr. Lee's dojo. Blue mats lined the floor with practice dummies, punching bags, and martial art weapons.

The other half of the training gym had a track around the second floor. There was a climbing rock wall, balance beams, and through glass doors, a weight room. Ian was free-climbing the rock wall with a self-belay system. He reached into his chalk bag and dusted his fingers before he jumped to make an almost impossible grab. Ian hung there briefly before swinging his right foot to the next foothold. When he reached the top, he kicked out and came down the wall. He grabbed a white towel to wipe off his hands and stepped out of his climbing harness.

"You're late," Ian said without looking at her. "If you can't be on time, don't bother showing up."

Ian had already changed out of his school uniform and was in his green workout pants and tight white shirt, his arms were crossed, and his muscles bulged. Either he was flexing on purpose, or he was irritated at her.

Everly looked down at the skirt she wore. "I'm right on time." She held up her watch, which read 9:00 a.m.

"On time is late... You can't show up at nine when coordinating with your reaping team. You must be there and ready to go before the stroke of nine."

"I will strive to do better next time," she said through gritted teeth.

Ian's eyebrow rose at her tone. "If you haven't figured it out, I don't like to be kept waiting."

"I think I would prefer someone else to be my mentor, maybe anyone with manners." Everly didn't budge.

Ian scoffed. He shook his head. "I'm the best. That's why they gave me you."

"So *they* say. I've yet to see anything impressive about you."

Ian's eyes darkened, and she could see the tick in his jaw.

"You've got a mouth on you, grimm bait. But do you have the talent to back it up? Last night was pure luck. You might have impressed the society, but I saw your weaknesses. You were too distracted by a pretty face and would have been grimm bait if not for me."

Everly's cheeks burned in embarrassment. Ian was right. His coaching from the balcony got her through her fight with Gemma. She couldn't even remember what happened after the ogre attack.

"What happened with the ogre?" Everly started.

"It was subdued."

"But how?"

He gave her an exasperated look. "There was a room full of grievers; we can care for a meager ogre."

"I just thought I saw you jump the pit. It was at least a twelve-foot jump, impossible for a—"

"What will you do when faced with a level-one grimm?" Ian interrupted.

He was testing her, avoiding the subject, or, more likely, both. Everly decided to let it slide.

"Check my shoes and pockets."

"Why would you do that?" Ian challenged.

"Level-one grimm constitutes a nonthreatening fae type; fairy, sprite, changeling puck. Known for stealing and causing mischief more than harm. Most break-in reports are the cause of low-level grimm activity."

"All right, smarty pants. What does a changeling like?"

"Um..." She had to rack her brain.

"Sweets," Ian answered.

"I was getting there. You didn't give me time to answer."

"Level four," he pressed, showing no emotion or reaction to her knowledge.

"I don't know."

"Typical." Ian seemed pleased to have stumped her.

"Am I downwind or upwind?" Everly asked, holding back a smile. "Level fours are the titans, mostly giants and cyclopes, with excellent senses when it comes to hearing and smell. One must stay downwind in hopes of catching them by surprise. Their strength is far superior, but they are impulsive creatures that lack common sense. Your best bet is to outsmart them rather than a full-scale attack. If you are upwind, the best bet is to stay where you are, disguise your scent, and not move."

Ian seemed confused. "How do you know all this? It took me years to learn, and that's not even in our textbooks."

"Reading is my superpower. Mr. Halsey gave me access to old griever journals."

"He's never given me griever journals." Ian's jaw clenched. "But there are other talents besides just knowing things."

"I have other talents," she argued.

"Prove it to me. Right now."

"It's not that simple." Everly sighed. "I can read people, profile them."

Ian scoffed. "Okay, profile this: you come upon an injured griever, and they're not moving. What do you do?"

"Render first aid." Everly thought the answer was an obvious one.

"Wrong." Ian made a motion to slash his throat. "You're dead. You check your surroundings first," Ian said. "Because grimms never leave an injured griever *ever*. They kill them on the spot. Unless it's a trap. See how well your profiling worked there? It didn't."

Everly sucked in her breath at the intensity and anger he spoke with. She could read it in his body language. The way he held his head and avoided looking at her, in the flicker of his hands, curling and uncurling. He spoke with conviction and undeniable firsthand knowledge. He was belittling her, making her want to push and challenge him back.

"I see. That's what happened to you," Everly stated, her voice softly filled with empathy. "Who was it?"

Ian's head snapped up, his eyes meeting hers in surprise. "What? How did—" He stepped back and bumped into the belay rope. "You're just guessing."

"You asked me to prove it. I can read it in your body language, clear as day. The evidence is here." She stepped forward and pointed to his face. Ian tried to move but was trapped by her. "I can hear it in your voice, how you avoid looking at me. Your body movements are telling me what I need to know."

"You don't know anything," he growled, his fingers curled into a fist.

"The hitch in your shoulder and the timbre of your voice is telling me that you don't believe a word you just said."

Ian looked down at the ground and held his breath, not making eye contact.

His expression told her that he felt guilty about something.

Everly backed up into the wall. "It wasn't your fault."

"Stop it." Ian's voice was weak, and he tried to turn away from her.

"Not until you stop carrying the guilt for what happened."

"You weren't there." Ian spun on her. "You don't know what happened."

Everly listened to her gut, what this situation was telling her. She hated to be the one to turn the table on Ian, especially her mentor. "You were not grimm bait," Everly said, her voice filled with conviction.

Ian's eyes were like fire as his fist pulled back, and she could see the muscles in his arm, the anger building in his eyes. She read the situation, closed her eyes, and felt the wall shake as his fist connected with the rock behind her.

Ian was leaning over her when she opened her eyes, his body quivering with emotion. Whether it was anger or sorrow remained to be seen. His punch had landed centimeters from her cheek, and she could feel his shame radiating off him. His head lowered, and she could smell his shampoo; there was the barest pressure as his head dropped to her shoulder.

They stayed like that for a few seconds. He was not moving. Ian trembled and backed away, his head low as he tried to hide his pain. His voice was grim. "You proved your point. That's all for today."

His eyes were unfocused as he reached for his flask. His hands trembled as he screwed the top off and took a long drink. His eyes seemed to flash in anger, and his face grimaced.

"You shouldn't drink at school," Everly said, deciding to call him out.

"You would know." He wiped his mouth. "You would cause a man to drink."

Everly released the breath she had been holding. It was a gamble for sure, reading people and the situation, but she felt right on the nose, and it was the only way to turn the situation around. She may have made a greater enemy out of her mentor. Everly looked at her shirt and saw the slightest tear stain—evidence of his pain.

Over her shoulder, the wall was caved in where his fist connected.

Evidence of his power.

CHAPTER 13

Everly returned to her room, feeling horrible.

She had used her training to injure and manipulate another. It's what a profiler would do, what her father would do, but it felt like an invasion of privacy.

She dropped onto her bed and stared up at the ceiling. What had made her confront Ian like that? It was her gut. She knew she was right, but at what cost? And was it worth it?

"You were right, you know." Corvis interrupted her thoughts. He had flown into her room through the open window she had left ajar for him.

"I know."

"But you didn't know if he would hit you?" Corvis was starting to lecture her.

"He wasn't going to."

"You couldn't be sure."

"I was sure."

"How did you know?" Corvis asked.

"Because I hit a nerve. Ian was in pain. I could see it in his eyes. He wanted to feel pain elsewhere instead of here." She touched her heart. "It is not the healthiest way to attain that, but I read the situation. Plus, if he hurt me, I would have blamed you."

"Me!" Corvis was affronted.

"Aren't you supposed to protect me?" Everly asked.

"From grimms, not your own stupidity." If a raven could have snorted, he would have.

This was news to Everly. "So you really would have let him hit me?"

His shiny black head tilted, and he looked at her out of the side of his eye. "You will never know."

"Gah!" She flung her hands at him. "Go away."

"Gladly, I think I found someone cute in the other hall to flirt with."

"You are despicable."

"Of course."

Everly spent the rest of the afternoon studying. She didn't want to be behind in classes, but she didn't open her textbooks, opting instead for another of the journals Mr. Halsey had given her.

———

A notice on her phone brought Everly out of her reverie. She looked at the phone. It was past nine. She initially thought Lacie must have forgotten her or changed her mind. She swiped on her phone and saw a text from a number she didn't recognize and a pin location outside in what looked like the middle of the woods.

Clothes!

She needed something to wear. Flinging open her closet, she felt a sense of unease. There were two extra uniforms; skirts, shirts, vests, a few soft cotton T-shirts, tons of hooded sweaters, jeans, sneakers, black army boots, and not much else.

"What you see is what you get." Everly pulled on a pair of jeans, a gray T-shirt, and black army boots. Finally, she pulled out a black denim jacket.

She slipped her phone into her outer pocket. Next, she opened the bedside drawer. Other girls wouldn't leave the house without makeup. Everly never left the house without protection... of the pepper spray kind. She clipped the personal-sized pink pepper spray onto her keys.

Coming?

Everly texted Holland.

Running late. Meet you there!

That was normal with Holland. Always late for everything.

Everly was surprised at the lack of security as she left the school; there wasn't anyone to stop her as she pulled out of the parking lot and headed toward the location on the map. It was a ways away and close to the national parks and where the hikers had gone missing, but it was near an old boat dock. Or so it seemed. She turned down a dirt road and found a line of cars parked at odd angles.

Two girls were piling out of a red coupe and giggling loudly.

"This way!"

"It's so cold. Why do we torture ourselves and do this?"

"Because there are boys from Gravemark coming here."

"They are so hot and mysterious," the second girl added.

When they exited their car, they seemed lost as they held up their phone and turned in circles, trying to get a bearing on the pin.

Everly came up behind them and looked over their shoulders. It was the exact pin location she was heading to.

"It's left." Everly held up her phone to show them. Despite being still September, with the sun going down, it was cold, and the girls wore short dresses and heels that seemed more fashion-forward than worthy of trekking through the woods.

Immediately the scene from *Jurassic World* popped into her head where Bryce Dallas Howard was running in heels the whole movie from dinosaurs. She looked at the two girls, holding each other in their heels, trying not to slip on the muddy gravel. They definitely wouldn't outrun a T. rex in those. Or a zombie apocalypse. Yeah, the twins would be the first to go.

Everly started walking along the path and veered off the sidewalk onto the trail. She didn't look to see if they were following but instead heard the crunch of leaves and a yelp as one girl almost fell. Her heel sank deep into the wet earth.

"Wait for us! We don't want to get lost," the first called, and then her legs split out at awkward angles, and her hands flew in the air, resembling Bambi learning to walk.

"You can follow me if you like, or just follow the tracks." Everly pointed out the sets of fresh footprints in the mud toward the woods.

"She's so smart."

"Or just sensible," Everly said. Everly was used to saying what people wanted to hear. She had learned all her people-pleasing skills from Holland.

The girls slowed their pace while Everly trudged further into the woods. No sooner did she enter into the darkness and pass the first line of trees when someone lunged at her.

"Boo!"

Everly's hand reached for the spray but stilled on the

trigger when she recognized Holland. Her hair was curled and flowed over her shoulder; she wore a white dress with sneakers. She was laughing and grabbing her stomach.

"Very funny!" Everly rushed out. "I almost maced you."

Holland blinked a few times, cleared her throat, and looked up at Everly apologetically. "I'm sorry, but I couldn't resist. Let's go."

Holland was a nonstop chatterbox their whole way out. "Look what Kerrigan sent me!" Holland turned her phone to reveal a reel video of Kerrigan dancing around an all-white office with a big fluffy pink chair and matching laptop. "Isn't she so lucky!" Holland sighed. "To be her own boss!"

Everly had never met the elusive Kerrigan but had heard and seen plenty of stories about the perfect older sister.

They must have walked for nearly a half mile through back trails before the path sloped. Through the trees, they could see a roaring bonfire.

"All right!" Holland yelled as they exited the woods onto the private lakefront secluded from the rest of the world.

"Where are we?"

"It's an old boat launch."

"Isn't it trespassing?" Everly asked.

Holland shrugged. "Not really. Who's going to call the cops on us? There's no one here. Relax, Everly. Have fun. It's your welcome to Gravemark party!" She nodded with her chin toward a group of students lounging on stumps by the bonfire.

As soon as they arrived, they were almost immediately approached by a thin boy with a mole on his cheek. He had a long tube of sugar candy and tipped his head back to take a swig.

Everly hoped it was just sugar in the tube and not anything else.

"Hey, Holland, can we talk real quick?"

"Yeah, sure, Thomas. I'll be back, Everly." Holland excused herself, leaving Everly alone. She walked along the waterfront, staring at the water moving across the rocky shoreline, and spotted someone sitting on a beached log by themselves.

It was Kat focused on her phone. Everly was surprised she got any cell service out here. She moved to stand behind the log and watch the girl in fascination play a fighting game. Kat's character, just like her real personal life, had a cat tail, large metal claws, and ears. Whenever she would win a battle, the avatar in the game would lick her metal claws and then brush her ears.

"I can hear you breathing over my shoulder," Kat muttered angrily.

"Sorry." Everly leaned back to give the girl some space. "I'm just fascinated by your avatar."

Kat turned her face away from the game and looked at Everly. It was the first time the two had made eye contact, and her unusual eyes took in Everly. Heterochromia. Kat had one brown eye while the other was a green, and they almost glowed by the light from the bonfire.

"Your eyes." Everly's mouth dropped open, and Kat swung her head around and looked back at the game.

"It's called heterochromia. Hetero from the Latin word *different* and chroma from the word *color*."

"I know what it is," Everly said. "Well, no, I didn't know the Latin for it, but I'm sorry, I was just caught off guard by how beautiful your eyes are."

"Thanks, I guess," Kat muttered, dropping her head so her black hair covered her eyes. "Most people call me a freak."

"I definitely don't think so."

Kat nodded and leaned back so Everly could watch her

play over her shoulder. That's when Everly noticed that the feline avatar Kat played also had heterochromia eyes.

Since it didn't seem like Holland would return anytime soon, Everly moved around the log to sit by Kat and began watching people. The position of the downed tree trunk sat diagonal to the lake and was far enough from the bonfire. Everly took off her boots and buried her feet in the sand.

A large projectile hit the lake only feet from where Kat and Everly were sitting, sending a splash that hit her cheek.

"Hey!" Kat yelled up at the boys.

"Sorry, my bad!" The boy tested the weight of a second rock and threw it again, this time having more control and almost hitting the small swimming dock fifteen feet from where she was sitting.

"Did you see that?" Everly pointed toward the woods. She thought she saw eyes reflected at her.

"See what?" Kat asked, never even looking up from her phone.

"Never mind."

Kat shrugged. "Okay."

Everly stared at the woods behind the guy tossing rocks, swearing that she saw something move through the brush. Maybe it was just a reflection of the moonlight in the thicket playing a trick on her mind.

Everly was surprised to see Ian on the party's outskirts. He was leaning against a tree off by himself. Why was he here if he was going to be all antisocial? She wouldn't approach him, not after their awkward encounter this afternoon.

Then she watched as he slunk off into the woods alone. *Where was he going?*

"Want one?" A guy with acne scars and glazed eyes tried to hand Everly a beverage.

"Pass." Everly knew the danger that came from an unsupervised drink at a party. It wasn't worth the stomachache, hang-over, or threat of being roofied.

The red cup swung toward Kat's face, almost spilling on her phone. "If you dump that on me, you will lose an arm." The cup retracted as if on a zipline, and the guy moved on to the next girl. Everly recognized Maddie Eerie. Maddie was wearing a white romper dress similar to Holland's.

Kat glanced at Maddie from her phone and shook her head. "Stupid."

Holland and Everly hadn't arrived early and were probably the last to make it to the lake. Or so she thought until a familiar laugh had her cringing. She didn't want to look but couldn't help herself. Coming down the path was Hunter, looking bored, in a gray jacket, hand in hand with Aimee in a cute pink sundress.

Neither one noticed her, and Everly hoped to keep it that way; she didn't want to get into another confrontation with Hunter. Not tonight.

"I hate parties," Kat muttered.

"Then why did you come?" Everly asked.

"I'm here because I'm supposed to be here."

"What is that supposed to mean?"

"Someone needs to keep a level head when the grievers get wasted and start to do something stupid. That's our job. We're Batman's Alfred. The man in the van." Kat's eyes flickered to Maddie. She frowned. "Wait a minute." Kat paused her game, got up, and stormed over to Maddie. Kat swiped the cup from a surprised Maddie's hand and sniffed it. Her mouth snarled in disgust. She tossed the cup on the ground, and Maddie started to pout.

"I was drinking that." Maddie hiccupped and covered her mouth with a hand that held a sparkly pink cell phone.

Kat sighed. "Consider your BMI versus the amount of

alcohol you've consumed in the last thirty minutes, which is equivalent to two and a half beers. Based on my calculations, it puts your blood alcohol level at around .121 and your stupidity limit at about a thousand."

"What?" Maddie looked up at Kat, confused.

"Go home, Maddie. You're drunk."

"I'll take her." The boy from earlier popped up with another full red Solo cup.

Kat's eyes flashed angrily. "You're nothing but a low-life predator, trying to trick young girls into getting wasted. You don't even attend this school." She whipped out her phone, flicked her finger up the screen, and turned it to face the boy. "Eric Mulligan, age twenty-one, lives with his grandmother at 221 Ferris Lane and works at the local Kwik Mart."

"How did you find that?" Eric gasped. He slowly backed away toward the lake, but Kat was on his heels—an angry fuchsia-colored fireball.

"Oh, I know all about you and your addiction to *SpongeBob SquarePants* and a certain crush on a cartoon squirrel."

Eric had backed up to the waterline, and Kat only stood up to his chest, all five feet, two inches of her. But she was a fiery inferno of temper, and it was phenomenal to watch.

Kat shoved her purple-painted nail into Eric's chest, jabbing him, punctuating each word. "Leave! Take that barrel of poison with you. And if you ever show your face near any of us again, I will make your whole internet browsing history public."

"But I was paid to be here. I was—oof!" Eric slipped on the wet sand and fell backward into the water. His arms were pinwheeling as he tried to save himself but couldn't. With a loud splash, he ended up falling backward into the lake.

A loud group of laughter followed, and Eric dragged himself out of the water and ran up the path.

"The keg, stupid!" Kat yelled back.

Eric turned and grabbed the keg and the hose and frantically tried to roll it up the hill unsuccessfully. He lost his footing in the sand, and it slipped back down. The barrel was moving toward the water. But no one was going to help him.

Maddie walked away, talking on her cell phone, arguing for her friend to pick her up.

Kat moved to the bushes and pulled back the branches to reveal another keg. "There you are, sweetheart!" Kat crooned. "Here, I need help moving this. It's a two-person job."

"More beer?" Everly asked.

"This is my special recipe. It's better than beer. It has sarsaparilla root, ginger and bug root, dandelion root, birch bark, anise, and sugar." Kat tapped the keg, poured the brown liquid into a cup, and handed it to Everly, who gave it a cursory sniff and then laughed.

"It's root beer!"

"Exactly! I told you, better than beer. My secret ingredient makes it safe and turns a bright orange if any other chemical compound is added."

"Smart!"

"I know." Kat gestured to the group, who were now safely drinking out of blue Solo cups. "Grievers can't afford to let their guard down. If people really want to act stupid, they can do it without alcohol. Getting drunk is just the excuse people use to give permission for their bad behavior and claim ignorance for consequences of the night before."

Kat was vicious in her self-righteous anger about alcohol and drinking; her dark eyes flashed, and her hands shook.

"Something happened to you?" Everly asked.

Kat looked away, and her lip trembled for the barest moment. "No," she added defensively, but Everly could tell she was lying. She was starting to hate her gift.

She had seen a lifetime of victims and heard the stories from Nina and her father. She could see the signs in Kat's body language and her desire to protect others and hide in the online world. Everly didn't want to assume, but she felt something terrible must have happened to Kat in the past, and she was still a stranger.

"I'm here if you ever want to talk. I'm a great listener. I don't judge, and my lips are safer than Fort Knox," Everly said, referring to the US gold reserve bank, one of the safest places on earth.

Kat shook her head. "No good. I hacked the computer system and gained the access code for the vault when I was ten. The codes were encrypted and spread out among ten staff members, each knowing only a portion of the code. It took me two hours to break it. I even have an escape plan that has a roughly 86 percent success rate at the moment. Now, once I get my pilot's license, that plan moves up to the 90 percent success rate. So, I don't know if I trust your security clearance of secrets yet."

Everly thought Kat was joking, but the look of absolute certainty filling her face told her don't laugh at the girl.

Holland came walking over to them from the woods, her face flushed, mascara running as if she had been crying.

"Are you okay?" Everly stood up and looked around for the perpetrator.

"I'm fine," Holland said dismissively.

Kat jumped into the conversation, her eyes never leaving her phone as she started to rattle off information. "Statistics say that when a female says she's fine, it actually means she's *not* fine because of one of the following reasons: she's hungry, stressed, angry, on her period—"

"Kat!" Holland fumed, turning on the girl, her voice raising in fury. "I don't need to be psychoanalyzed right now by a—a psycho!"

Kat flinched at Holland's eruption. Holland's mouth dropped open, and she looked around at the scene she just caused. Kat was uncomfortable with the attention, and her eyes turned glassy with tears. She grabbed her phone and ran into the woods.

Everly jumped up to try and calm the situation down. "I don't think Kat was trying to be mean; I think she was just in her own way trying to say we could tell something was wrong and you were upset. If you need to talk, we're here."

Holland wiped her eyes and looked around at the stunned faces of the crowd she was drawing. "I can't take this emotional kumbaya right now. I'm out of here."

Everly stood stunned. Two girls had stormed off in the last few minutes, leaving her alone. Thomas walked past her.

"Hey, Thomas, what did you say to Holland?" Everly grabbed his sleeve.

"Nothing?" Thomas seemed to shrink under her glare.

"You called her over to talk." Everly wasn't about to let him get away with hurting her friend's feelings.

"I swear, I didn't do anything." He held up his hands and shook his head.

A chill ran over Everly, and not the kind from the cold.

Her father always said to trust her intuition. It was time for her to leave. She headed up toward the bonfire to warm her toes and put on her leather boots before making the trek to her car. She kneeled to retie her shoes. Directly across from her, on the other side of the bonfire through flickering flames, she saw Hunter. Aimee, oblivious, was shivering on a stump, her hands outstretched toward the fire.

Hunter and her eyes met, and her stomach dropped. Everly looked away. Her fingers fumbled with the laces on her boots in her attempt to quickly tie and move on, but it was as if her mind betrayed her because with Hunter staring at her, her fingers couldn't seem to tighten the laces on her boot right.

Finally, success that would make a kindergartner proud. She laced her boots and took off up the hill. She was hoping to find Holland before something terrible happened.

CHAPTER 14

Everly drove cautiously as the patchy fog rolled in, making the narrow roads more dangerous. Whenever she entered a fog patch and lost visibility, she clutched the steering wheel tightly until she emerged safely on the other side and could see again. The city's unique name, Misty Creek, resulted from the altitude and the earth's temperature creating these unnatural pockets of fog.

Everly slammed on the brakes as a girl all in white darted across the road in front of her.

Her heart was hammering in her chest as she looked in the rearview. It looked like a girl. It looked like—

"Holland?" Everly whispered under her breath. She put her car in Reverse and backed up until she saw the gravel turnoff that was almost hidden by the overgrowth of bushes.

She wasn't that far from the party location; Holland could have easily walked here on foot, especially if she was angry enough and wanted to prove a point.

Everly turned onto the gravel road, her speed slow as she looked ahead, searching for any clue about what she saw.

"Where are you?" Everly asked, squinting as she passed through another patch of fog, and then it cleared, and she could see that she had reached the lookout bluff. She pulled into the parking lot that was barely big enough for four cars, stared at the protective railing, and turned in her seat, scanning the woods for any sign of life.

Maybe it was just her imagination?

Everly pulled out her phone and decided to call Holland and test her theory. She would turn around and go home if she answered and was safe.

No bars. No cell service.

"Just great!" Everly closed her eyes and leaned her head against the headrest. Maybe she had just imagined it? But her gut told her she hadn't.

She was startled when she heard a slight knock on the window and realized someone had snuck up on her. Suddenly, a bright searchlight was pointed at her, making it even more challenging to see.

"Hey, you can't be here after dark!" a deep voice warned.

Everly squinted against the flashlight beam into the tan uniform. She saw the green-and-gold patch on his right shoulder, signifying a forest ranger. His name badge was starting to tarnish but was still legible. E. Danville. The park ranger seemed to be in his early forties with dark blond hair and dark eyes.

"Sorry, I pulled over to type in directions," Everly lied. "It's always better than texting and driving, but..." Everly held up her phone. "No signal."

"Do you have ID on you?" he asked.

"Am I under arrest?"

She pulled out her wallet and handed over her driver's license.

"No." The ranger stood up and flashed his light across the card. "You're Everick Hart's daughter?" he said in surprise.

"The same," she answered politely.

The sourness of the strict ranger disappeared as he started to reminisce. "Your dad helped with many of my rescue calls. He was well respected in our community."

"He was," Everly agreed but felt her smile crack as she saw movement by the bluff.

"It's a shame. Your father will be missed." He handed her back her license. "You didn't happen to see anything strange tonight?"

"Strange?" Everly felt her heart racing as her gaze flickered to the bluff's edge.

"I got a call about someone lost on these back trails. This whole area is closed off because there are dangerous predators around." He leaned down to rest his arm on her window ledge. He leaned through the door of her car, and Everly felt a moment of hesitation. "I hold myself responsible whenever I can't find someone. It's dangerous for them."

She saw the five o'clock shadow, the dark rings under his eyes, and the faint smell on his breath. Was it alcohol?

"Well, not anymore. I heard Ranger Raglan shot the cougar, correct? So everyone's safe now." Everly focused on his posture.

Ranger Danville stilled. "Yes, that's right. Raglan caught him." As he spoke, there was a slight raise in his left shoulder. A half shrug. He was lying or didn't believe the dangerous animal had been captured. Maybe the forest rangers hadn't caught the cougar and only released the statement to ease the city's fears.

Everly was feeling the urge that she was missing something significant. She needed to get to the bluff's edge to check out that clue, but she couldn't if Ranger Danville was still babysitting her.

A crack of lightning lit the sky, making them both jump; seconds later, rain followed, quickly drenching them.

"Okay, you need to be heading out now." He seemed reluctant to back away. "Are you sure you didn't see anything odd?"

Everly shook her head quickly. "Nope, I'll get going now." She rolled up her window and started her car.

Ranger Danville nodded and walked to a four-wheeler in the tree line. No wonder he was able to sneak up on her. That mode of transportation was the only way to get through some of the back trails.

Everly pulled out of the parking lot and turned onto the dark mountain road, and moments later, she saw the headlights of the four-wheeler head back into the woods. She drove a half mile, did a U-turn, and returned to the bluff.

This time a car from the other direction followed her to the lookout point and parked twenty feet away. Music blared from the speakers, and Everly groaned as the bass thrummed loud enough to shake her rearview mirror.

She knew what was about to happen. A hot and heavy make-out session, but she didn't want to be privy to seeing those windows steam up. She exited her car and stepped out in the rain, one foot in front of the other as she walked toward the cliff. The cold air was biting her skin, but she continued, propelled by the need to solve the puzzle.

"Everly?" Ian rolled down the window, and the music blared louder.

She ignored him and headed toward the bluff, using the light from her phone to guide her steps. The sound of his wipers made a rhythmic whoosh as he cursed under his breath and opened his door. A few seconds later, he was rushing up to her side.

"Hey, what are you doing?" Ian called out as he caught up to her, holding a large Maglite flashlight.

"I'm looking for something," she muttered against the rain. She tried to scan the rocks below, but it was too dark. "Can you point your flashlight down there?"

"What for?" he asked.

Everly pointed down the bluff. "There... right there!"

Pressured by adrenaline and her fear, Ian scanned the cliff-side with his flashlight to reveal rocks. Then a reflection shone back.

"There! Do you see it?" Everly called out excitedly.

"See what?'

"Hold the light right there. Don't move!" Everly ducked under the railing bar and slowly descended the more even incline.

"You should let me do this. I'm the rock climber," Ian called down.

"No time. I'm already halfway there."

With hand gestures and more directions, Ian kept her path lit and safe until Everly had crawled down the side, the water rushing quickly off the cliff, creating dangerous streams that could easily wash out the rocks she was balancing on.

"Over there!" Everly pointed again. She waved her hand for him to spread the light until she saw the reflection again, now dimmer because of the dirt and rain. Everly kneeled over the object, brushing away the debris, and held up a sparkly phone—Maddie's.

Immediately Everly started calling out her name, over and over again. The rain swallowed her cries. Everly tucked the phone in her pocket and tried to make her way back up the cliff. She took her time. One foot in front of the other.

She had almost reached the railing and the safety of the light from above when something snagged her boot. Everly looked down, expecting a tree root, but instead encountered a sickly pale hand with impossibly long fingers wrapped around her ankle. It tugged, and she started to slip, but she dug her fingers into the dirt and rock, trying to fight the creature holding her.

"Ian!" Everly cried.

A weird burble of hissing came behind her, and she felt another stronger tug. Everly lost her hold, and she slid down the side of the ravine. Then she was airborne, her hands reaching out for help.

CHAPTER 15

Everly woke up in the front seat of a car that smelled of leather and hydrogen peroxide. She wrinkled her nose as she tried to sit up, and Ian pushed her back onto the chair.

"Don't move. You're still recovering." He reached behind him, pulled something out of his duffel bag from the back, and leaned over her.

"What is that?" Her vision was still spinning.

"Don't worry. It's clean." He pressed a white piece of cloth to her head and had her hold it.

Ian opened his glove box and pulled out a first aid kit.

Everly pulled the white cloth away from her forehead and looked at it closer.

"It's a sock?" She gave Ian a look of disbelief.

He shrugged. "I told you it was clean." Ian reached into the opened first aid kit and pulled out a Band-Aid. "I think it stopped bleeding."

"You really are prepared for anything," Everly teased as Ian tore open a packet of ointment and spread it across the cut.

"Well, as a griever, I've learned a thing or two. Head cuts don't have to be deep to bleed a lot. But it stopped for now." He ripped open the wrapper of the Band-Aid and placed it on her forehead. His thumb pressed gently across the ends, smoothing them down. Ian tossed the Band-Aid wrapper in the cupholder.

"Why are you here?" Everly asked. "I saw you leave the party."

He shook his head. "I did. I was returning when I saw you take this service road. I wanted to make sure that you didn't do anything stupid. It turns out you did."

"What happened?" Everly asked, looking down at her wet and muddy clothes. "I thought I saw Holland and followed her here."

"You fell into a level three's trap," Ian answered. "Level threes are lures. They're dangerous. They trick you into following them to your demise. Luckily, I was there to chase it away and save the day."

"I fell victim to a level three?" She felt disappointment take over. "But I saw something. Really." Everly tried to convince Ian.

"No."

"Then how do you explain this?" Everly pulled out the glittery phone. "This is Maddie's cell." As Everly turned it, she saw the red spot on the edge, and her breath caught in her throat. "Ian, it's blood."

He carefully took the cell from her and flipped the overhead light on.

"Do you think the blood is hers?" she asked.

Ian inhaled, his eyes closing briefly. "Yes," Ian said.

"How can you tell?" Everly asked.

Ian made a face, pulled away, and swore under his breath. "I need to go."

"Go where?"

Ian exited his car and headed to the back, lifting the rear

door. Everly hopped out into the rain after him. He pulled out a black duffel and slung it over his shoulder.

"Stay here." He slammed the rear door.

"No," Everly said firmly, stepping before him, forgetting how tall Ian was. The rain was running down his face, making him seem solemn. "Rule number one. You never go after a grimm alone."

"Except when you have a newbie. You'd only slow me down or get in my way. I already had to rescue you once tonight. I don't plan on doing it again."

Everly's stomach dropped. "You wouldn't even be going after Maddie if it wasn't for me. I sensed something was wrong. You can't leave me behind." She was shouting into the rain.

Ian glared at her, shook his head, and headed toward the side of the bluff.

"I'm just going to follow you," she called out after him.

He froze, his shoulders stiffened, and she knew the minute he gave in. He reached into the bag and tossed her a weapon, a thin blade in a sheath. It was as long as her forearm and black. It didn't reflect in the moonlight.

She knew what it was. A never blade. A griever's primary survival tool.

"Ever handled a blade like this?"

She shook her head. "No, but I've read about them in the griever journal." Her voice took on a faraway tone. "Made of silver, forged under the moonlight, the bane of all grimm."

Ian rolled his eyes. "And don't forget blessed by virgins."

"That's not true—" Then she saw the teasing look in his eyes and knew she fell for it.

"Just don't stick me with that end." Ian pointed to the end of the blade. "It's poison for grimms but will make a human deathly ill. The tip of the blade is silver, and the edges are iron. We can stow most grimms with this."

"Except for level fours and fives," Everly answered.

"True, but Everly—" His eyes met hers in the darkness. He took a deep breath, reluctant to finish. "This may not be a rescue mission."

"What do you mean?"

"If Maddie was taken by a level three. There's a good chance this isn't a rescue but a recovery mission." Ian's blue eyes held hers, and an unasked question was behind them.

Could she handle whatever the outcome was?

Everly's eyes went cold at the prospect of failure. "Stop talking, more hunting."

CHAPTER 16

THE RAIN WASN'T LETTING UP. CORVIS WAS NOWHERE near. She kept mentally calling for him, and Ian explained ravens couldn't fly in heavy rain.

Everly followed behind Ian as they worked their way down the side of the bluff, following in his exact steps.

He held up his hand to signal a stop. "Make sure you *only* step where I step; it is imperative when hunting not to show how many grievers—" He turned around to correct her footing to find that she hadn't left a second set of tracks. "Never mind. Carry on."

Everly saw his nod of approval and knew she had done one thing right, but she couldn't let him or Maddie down. Ian picked up his pace, and Everly kept up with him. It was almost impossible to see where they were going or what exactly he was tracking.

He swore under his breath as he scanned the darkness.

"What now?" Everly came up beside him.

"I don't know. The trail ends here. It could be any level three. Water type would have dragged her into the river. If that's the case, there's no hope of finding her."

"What type of trail are you following?" she asked.

Ian refused to answer.

Ian kept scanning the riverbank. He walked up and down the embankments looking for clues, but she could feel his inner frustration. Just then, the rain began to let up, and Everly saw a dark shape fly to a nearby tree.

"Corvis," Everly called out. "Help!"

"Across the river to the south," he said. "Movement. Lots of breaking of branches and noise by the giant sycamore."

She searched until she saw the tree. "There." Everly pointed and immediately stepped into the river, trying to cross at the shallowest point.

Ian followed further upstream, and he joined her when she made it to the other bank. "Can your raven show the way?"

"He can."

Corvis flew low, tree to tree, leading them and stopping as they ran to catch up. Then they came to a small clearing of short grass and clover. The rain had died, and the clouds no longer hid the moon's soft glow.

"Watch your step," Ian warned, pointing to the ground and the small white mushrooms growing in a circle. "Never step in a fairy ring, or you can become trapped. This tells me we are dealing with a very clever little level one."

"I thought you said it was a level three?"

"It still could be."

Ian stepped into the clearing, carefully avoiding the circle of mushrooms. He held his knife in front of him and walked into the moonlight. Like a dancer, he stayed limber, his blade in front of his face, his left arm held out to block an attack. Everly held back, waited behind a tree, and watched in awe as Ian turned in a circle, keeping his eyes on the shadows.

Everly felt her breath catch in her throat. It was like reliving a page out of her father's journal. He was a true griever in action, and she felt excited.

"What do you see?" she asked.

"Trouble."

A childlike giggle echoed into the night, and there was a flutter of movement as a white light flew toward Ian. He ducked but not quickly enough as a bright red slash of blood now coated his cheek.

Everly gasped. That was so fast, she didn't even see it, and it was no bigger than a dragonfly. How did this thing manage to kidnap Maddie?

A flutter of bright light flickered in and out of the branches of the trees. And a tinkling giggle that would have sounded like a child playing now seemed sinister as the creature was toying with them.

A fairy.

Everly tried to rack her brain; what had she read about fairies? It was one of her talents not to forget anything she had read, but this wasn't like the stories.

The fairy zipped out of the tree line, screaming like a mini banshee.

Ian drew back his blade, swung, and the fairy twisted at the last second, dodging his attack but tearing a hole in his shirt.

"Stupid fairy!" he grumbled. "That was my favorite shirt."

The fairy zipped around and came back for another attack. Ian leaned down, keeping his weight on his back foot, and right when he swung out, a flash of light appeared, and the tiny fairy became full-size, slamming him into the ground.

The fairy's wiry hands wrapped around his neck, its mouth filled with razor-sharp teeth, and its long white hair, ratted and gnarled, covered it like a dress. Sexless, this thin creature squeezed, and Ian used his weapon he clubbed it in the side of the arm.

The fairy screamed and rolled away in a flash of light,

disappearing back into a killer dragonfly. Ian coughed and got to his feet, rubbing his neck, which was red and raw.

"Are you okay?" Everly asked, stepping from behind the tree.

"Stay back!" Ian commanded as the homicidal fairy swooped around again.

"That's a fairy?" Everly stated, watching the crying ball of light zip through the trees and head straight up into the night sky. "That's nothing like Tinker Bell."

"That's not Tinker Bell; that's *Tinker Hell.*"

"And it can change sizes?"

"Yep, nasty little buggers, but they don't necessarily attack humans; they tend to play with them until they get bored. Their favorite game is tricking humans into a fairy circle and watching them dance. They don't normally act like this. Something is up."

A shriek filled the sky again, and Everly didn't waste any time; she moved to the clearing, jumping over a second fairy ring this time, and stood out in the open.

"Let's do this," Everly said, feeling determined. She held the never blade by her thigh so it was out of sight.

"What are you doing? I can handle this." Ian waved her away.

"Are you sure? It seems like you're getting your butt kicked by a fairy."

"I'd like to see you do it."

"Then I can get all the glory for my first catch?" Everly asked.

"You couldn't catch a cold if it wasn't for me."

"Let's see who can nab her first," Everly challenged.

Ian's eyes lit up, and his grin grew wider. "Game on. What are the stakes?"

"I win, you can no longer call me grimm bait." Everly gripped the handle of her blade.

"And I win, you will always be grimm bait." He tossed her something out of the duffel that looked like a control pole dogcatchers use, except this one had a net on the end.

"Fine," Everly snapped and ducked as the maniacal fairy swooped in to take a slice at her face. She turned at the last second and felt a cut across her shoulder. The fire burned where it touched her.

"What in the?" She reached to touch her arm; it came away with a clear substance.

"Oh, didn't you know? Fairies have poison in their nails. Their cut causes an instant fiery burn." Ian ducked and swung out with the end of the weapon, missing the fairy again.

"That hurt!"

"The goal is not to get bitten or scratched. Maybe we should take off points for each wound." He pointed behind her as the fairy zipped past the ground, slashing at her ankle for a second slice.

Everly dropped to her knees and released a painful hiss from her clenched teeth. It was just a minor cut, but the wound caused the pain receptors in her brain to fire. It was a trick only. Even though it felt like her limb was burning off, she was still there.

Kneeling low, Everly kept her head down, trying to make herself seem small and helpless, while her hand gripped the pole.

It was just like playing lacrosse with Hunter. She just had to catch the ball, except this one was flying at speeds way faster than any throw she had received.

"Eee," the fairy screamed, zipping past, and Everly lifted the net; it would have been a perfect catch, except the fairy

changed size right before hitting the net and bowled Everly
over.

She gasped as the wind was knocked out of her lungs.
White hair hung in her face as the fairy screamed and clawed
at her cheeks. Everly lifted her forearms to protect her eyes as it
clawed at her jacket, ripping it to shreds. She was so unprepared for this creature that she had misjudged her skills and
dropped the blade. Everly did what any desperate female
would do. She grabbed a handful of the fairy's wild hair and
jerked it hard to the side. The fairy cried out, but Everly wasn't
going to let go. She used her moment of surprise and rolled over
to be on top of the fairy, pushing her face into the ground.

At full-size, the fairy was still only the size of an eight-year-
old child, but its strength was double hers. Using her other
hand, Everly wrapped up another pile of hair and ripped at it,
causing the fairy's head to lift.

Tears started to form in the fairy's beautiful black eyes, and
she cried out, whimpering. Her voice turned to that of a child
again. She could feel the fairy try to curl in a ball underneath
her, and Everly let her grip slacken. The fairy cried out,
shaking and terrified. Silvery pale wings with translucent veins
fluttered and curled around it, trying to protect the fairy like a
cocoon.

Guilt flooded her. She had hurt this childlike fairy. She
removed her hands from her hair but shifted her weight to press
down.

"No, don't let it go!" Ian warned too late.

"Whee!" With a burst of mighty wings, Everly was flung
backward, and the fairy was flying in a small burst of light.

"Stupid!" Ian yelled at her.

"Well, at least I caught it."

"And you let it get away. There's no point in almost
capture."

Everly felt anger rise within her. She had been tricked and fell for the big water-filled eyes of a fairy. *Newbie move.* She knew they were tricksters. Knew they did anything to survive.

"Got it!" Ian crowed, holding his never net high in the air, and she saw the fairy fighting against the glowing strings. It screamed, shaking and gnawing at the net. "Nasty little bugger," Ian leaned over to show her. His eyes were gloating, and she wanted to punch him.

"I think you forgot something," Everly said, looking at the tree behind him and seeing a second glowing light lifted from the branches.

"What?" Ian was full of himself.

"I don't think fairies are ever alone." Everly pointed at a second screaming ball of light flying straight for her head. Ian didn't have a second pole, and the fairy knocked Everly's out of reach.

But a darker shadow launched from the trees straight for Everly.

"EEK!" The screaming stopped as Corvis swallowed the fairy midair. The ball of light instantly dimmed.

Corvis landed on the ground. "Yuck," Corvis said, hopping from leg to leg, bobbing his head as if in pain. "Yuck. Yuck. Yuck."

"Did you just eat the fairy?" Everly asked.

"Yes." Corvis hopped again and let out a gross burp.

"Why didn't you do that in the beginning?" Ian countered.

"Because you two weren't in danger of dying, and I don't like eating fairies. They taste like crunchy jalapeños."

Everly snorted. Ian rolled his eyes, and the fairy inside the net became very still, watching Corvis in terror.

"Can't the fairy change shape again?" Everly asked.

Ian shook his head. "No, the net will get tighter and tighter if it does. It prevents any surprises like that."

"But where's Maddie?" Everly asked. "Why would the trail lead here?"

Ian scouted the area but was coming up empty. "It's like she's everywhere but nowhere."

Everly looked at the freshly churned earth. "Did they bury her?"

Ian's face paled, and the two dropped to their knees and quickly began digging at the dirt.

"Maddie," Everly cried out, scooping handfuls of dirt and tossing it to the side.

How long ago was she buried? When did they do this? Was she even alive?

She could feel her emotions begin to well up and hope slip away.

"Come on, faster," Ian commanded, his face covered in dirt and blood as he used his strength to lift an impossibly large rock out of the way. The more they dug, the more she figured they were recovering a body. But then they hit a root system, intertwined, creating a wall or a cocoon.

Everly dug at the root and tried to pull one up, but it was tightly interwoven. There were gaps, and she could see something white—Maddie's dress.

"It's her. I see her!"

Ian reached into his pocket and pulled out a pocketknife, which he used to slice each root until they had an opening large enough to put their hands in and pull them apart.

The hole expanded, and then Everly saw the shoe and the foot attached to the shoe, which was lying very still. They worked at the roots, opening them up to reveal more of Maddie, and she looked to be sleeping. A slight coating of dust covered her face.

But in the darkness and dirt covering her hair, she looked different, like a brunette.

"Kerri?" Ian's voice choked up, and he struggled to keep his composure.

"Is she dead?" Everly asked, afraid.

Ian reached out to touch her neck. "She still has a pulse."

Everly released the breath and tears she didn't know she was holding.

"I have to save her." Ian leaned down and pulled Maddie's arms up, wrapping one around his neck. He lifted her from the shallow grave. "I can't fail her."

He stood in the darkness, the moonlight illuminating his cut and injured face, as he held a beautiful girl in a white dress. His eyes took on a faraway look, and he didn't seem himself. *Were those tears in his eyes?*

Ian picked up Maddie and didn't speak to her but ran back the way they came.

Everly was left alone. She looked around the clearing and at the fairy circles. There wasn't just one; there was a whole field of them, and she could see flickering lights in the trees above. It would look like fireflies blinking at night to the average observer, but instead, she could see them for what they were.

Fairies mourning. It wasn't just one but hundreds.

She stared at the fairy in the trapped net and reached down to pull the net away. The fairy stared at her in surprise. It was only the size of a dragonfly with two sets of wings.

"I'm sorry about your friend," Everly said, "but we were trying to rescue ours. I hope you understand."

The fairy's pupils grew larger, and it nodded before flying off, not in a straight line, but in a zigzag. The fairy's wings were injured as it flew to join the others.

Everly watched the flickering of their lights. One at a time, they flashed until they joined together as one, then went dark.

Everly's stomach dropped, and unshed tears burned in her eyes, followed by a sour feeling that ran through her stomach.

"It's time to go," Everly said.

With Corvis's help, she found her way back up to the bluff, and when she came to her car, she saw Ian leaned over Maddie, buckling her into the front seat. He got into the driver's seat and turned on the vehicle. His eyes met hers across the parking lot, and he nodded.

She heard the gravel kick up as Ian exited the parking lot and raced to school. Everly waited a few minutes, letting her emotions calm down. She had fought in a battle against a fairy and won. But the cost was more than she wanted to bear. It didn't seem right. Why would the fairies kidnap a teen girl?

Everly turned the key in the ignition and heard the sputter as her car started, then quickly died.

"Come on," she pleaded as she tried again and felt relieved when the car engine roared to life.

Everly gave another shiver of cold as the chill of the rain soaked through her clothes. Her windshield started to fog up, so she hit the defrost button. As she did, the fog on the inside began to dissipate, and standing in front of her car illuminated by her headlights was a person wearing a dark rain jacket, their face covered.

Her breath caught in her lungs as the image shifted. Their fingers lengthened into dagger-like claws.

Grimm!

Everly threw her car into Reverse and hit the gas.

The tires spun on the gravel for a split second before finding purchase and launching her backward just as the grimm jumped on her hood. Still covered by the poncho, all she saw was the furry claw digging into metal, and the nails scraped across it, trying to find purchase as she whipped the car around and the grimm slid off into the tree line.

Everly was running out of road and was about to run into a line of trees. She hit the brake, turned the wheel, and did the fastest three-point turn in the world, making her driver's ed teacher, Mr. Gant, proud.

She looked in the rearview mirror and only saw the heavy fog roll across the road, obscuring her view of her pursuer. A sharp turn appeared out of nowhere, and she almost went off the road in her attempt to continue her speedy getaway.

She wasn't going crazy. She wasn't. That was a human-sized level-five grimm.

And the four claw marks in her hood proved it.

CHAPTER 17

EVERLY ROLLED BACK INTO GRAVEMARK CLOSE TO 1:00 a.m. Fearful of being out late or getting in trouble, she quietly returned to her room, making a quick stop at the bathroom to clean her wounds. As she collapsed on her bed, her phone started to buzz with incoming texts from Hunter.

> Everly?

> Where are you?

> Are you there?

Not wanting to deal with him, she powered down her phone and fell into an exhausted but nightmare-filled sleep.

Long-fingered claws kept reaching for her face, scratching her arms. Everly rolled every which way to try and escape its grasp. But she could never outrun it. Her legs became like molasses, and the ground seemed to swallow up her shoes, causing her to sink into the earth and become engulfed by roots like Maddie. Then she was underground and could hear her blood whooshing loudly in her eardrums as she pounded on the underside of the root-made coffin.

She could feel the air grow thin, her lungs struggling, the heat of her breath hot against her skin, and the pounding to escape continued as the earth was dumped on her; she could feel the sand and grit settle against her cheek. She was going to die.

Everly blinked against the sunlight pouring through her open window, enough light to know that she had probably slept through her first block of classes. Cursing herself for turning her phone off and, thus, her alarm, she groaned and laid one arm across her eyes, blocking the light.

Ms. March would be frustrated that she was already missing classes and would probably have much to say about her attendance record.

Everly looked at her phone and remembered to power it on as she headed to class. Once it powered on, she grimaced when she saw the twenty-four text messages from Hunter.

"Geez, now let's talk about a stalker," she mumbled under her breath. She deleted the message thread without reading them. But she needed to get moving, or she would be late for biology.

Mr. Wilcox was busy writing on the board the challenge for the day. Everly quickly looked for an empty lab table, and they were all full. There were only two spots open. One next to Hunter Abernathy, whose eyes met hers across the room, and he nodded with his chin for her to sit beside him. She quickly scanned the other open seats to see the lab station across the row from Hunter. One occupied by Ian Holmes.

Everly's ears were burning. She could sit next to Hunter and get lectured the whole hour on why she didn't return his texts or sit next to Ian, who took off and abandoned her the night before. She hated both choices.

She headed down the middle aisle, her feet sticking to the

tile like glue, walking as slowly as she could as she struggled to make up her mind.

Hunter leaned over to remove his notebooks from the seat next to him. Had he reserved it for her or blocked it so no one sat next to him?

She slowed when she came to his table. Hunter at least didn't seem angry; he seemed relieved to see her, but then he saw the cut on her cheek, and that relief turned to anger. His eyes darkened, and he clenched his jaw. She detoured and slid onto the stool next to Ian at the last minute.

He looked up in surprise as she sat next to him. His eyes were a bit unfocused. A white bandage covered the wound on his cheek, and he smelled of body wash and disinfectant. She noticed that his knuckles were bandaged, and the bites on his neck had a pink lotion covering them. Was it calamine? And where did Ian get it? Everly was ready to gnaw her arm off.

Everly subconsciously started to scratch at her cheek.

Ian frowned. "You didn't go to the medical wing and get those bites taken care of."

"I didn't know I was supposed to. It's not like I was given instructions after you left."

"Ouch, yeah." He rubbed the back of his neck and looked chastised. "That's my fault. After every reaping, we always check in with the medical. You should go right now."

"No," she said worriedly. "I think I can wait. I have already missed one class. I don't want to skip another. Unless you think I need to." She held out her arms, and he glanced at the red welts.

He looked over her wounds and sighed, obviously disagreeing with her choice. "You'll burn and itch like crazy, but you'll survive. Just don't scratch them."

Everly bit her lip when he said "scratch" because that was precisely what she wanted to do. She wanted to rub her backside all over the doorframe, and the cactus on the windowsill looked pretty good. She could imagine pulling it out and using it as a back scratcher. Oh geez, she was in trouble.

She wiggled in her chair to rub a bite on her back. "I take full responsibility for not forcing you to see a doctor last night. But last night was not like regular reaping. We were unprepared. Protocol wasn't followed."

"It's okay." She grunted, rubbing her arm against the edge of the table. "Ahh."

Ian held back a smile at her apparent attempt at not scratching. "By the way, I should warn you. I'm horrible at grimm biology, so no one wants to partner with me." He flashed a nervous smile.

Mr. Wilcox confirmed Ian's comment and discussed the upcoming lab assignments, including a group project. There was a groan from the class.

"Mr. Abernathy," Mr. Wilcox called out. "Since you don't have a partner, why don't you join one of the other groups? We will have one group of three."

The sound of a stool scraping across the tile made Everly's skin crawl, and she didn't need to look to know that Hunter had moved his chair to their lab table. She could feel the heat of his body as his arm was only inches from her. Everly was now pinned between Ian and Hunter. She sat up. Her back ramrod straight, so she wouldn't accidentally touch either of them.

This was not good. Not good at all.

How was she supposed to focus?

Hunter pulled out his phone, typed a message in his Notes app, and turned his phone so she could read the screen, not caring that the text was big enough that Ian could read it.

We need to talk.

Everly shook her head and mouthed, "Not now."

Hunter's jaw clenched. He typed a message below the table and turned the phone toward her again.

Why didn't you answer my texts last night?

Everly tried to stare straight ahead, but Ian read the text. Hunter nudged her arm for an answer, and she pinched her lips.

Ian pulled out his phone. He quickly typed his response. He placed his phone directly before Everly so both could read it.

SHE WAS WITH ME!

Everly's cheeks flamed red, her neck grew warm, and her back started to sweat.

But apparently, that was all the hint Hunter needed because he looked up at them in surprise and backed off—tucking his phone away like a good boy and pulling out his computer to open Google Classroom.

Ian opened up his laptop and the digital class file. He pushed his computer over toward Everly, and she felt relieved. It gave her an excuse to move her stool closer to Ian's and lean toward him to read along with the assignments.

In Grimm Biology, they were learning the aftereffects and poisons used by different grimms and their toxicity to humans.

Every single time they talked, Everly couldn't help but feel the burn in her arms, the scratches that were still needing treatment. She could see Hunter staring at the angry cut on her cheek, and she reached up and covered it with her hand.

The two-hour block was killing her, and by the time class was over, she had a stiff back from precariously leaning away from Hunter. How was she going to handle a few weeks of this?

CHAPTER 18

WHEN THE BELL RANG, SHE JUMPED OFF THE STOOL so fast it toppled over, but Everly didn't stop to pick it up. She sprinted out of class, pretending not to hear Hunter calling her name.

"Everly!"

She fled, something she never did, but it was either run or hash it out very loudly in front of a room full of strangers. She knew what it would entail. They were both passionate people, and it wasn't pretty when they disagreed. It was better to argue somewhere else... or not at all.

She made it to the hallway with windows overlooking the parking lot when Hunter caught up with her.

"Everly, what happened? I've been worried about you."

"Why?"

"Because someone died last night, not far from Hollow Lake, and you weren't answering my texts. I began to imagine the worst."

"Died? Wait, what? How?"

"It's on the news. They haven't released any information. There's too much police presence for us to go in and investigate. We have to wait until they release the crime scene now that your dad can't loop us in, but Gravemark's no longer buying the cougar story. They're sending Gemma and her team out as soon as possible."

"That's horrible," Everly said. "I wish I could have done something."

"We're on it. We should have been on it from the first attack, but Ms. March held us back. But Everly, where were you? Why didn't you answer my texts? You look like you got in a fight with a porcupine."

"Oh, sorry?" she said in confusion. "Didn't you hear? We rescued Maddie; fairies captured her."

"Who's we?"

"Ian and I."

"Is that how you got all these cuts? I can't believe Ian took you reaping on your second day." Hunter lifted her arm to inspect each of her wounds. "You weren't ready. This proves it."

"I didn't give him a choice," Everly countered. "I would have gone after the grimm alone if he hadn't shown up."

Hunter froze, his body tense. "You didn't just say that. You can't be that stupid."

Anger flooded her at being called stupid. He had no right. "I'm not stupid."

"That just proves that you don't belong here; you broke a cardinal rule."

"But I saved Maddie," she breathed out between clenched teeth.

"Don't you mean Ian did?"

"No, *we* did. I saw a girl... No, I guess it was a full-size fairy." Everly trailed off as she tried to figure out what she saw last night. Everly shook her head as if to clear the cobwebs of thoughts. "Either way, my hunch led to finding that Maddie had been kidnapped. I helped by saving her."

"Helped?" a deep voice cut in from behind. Ian stood there and shoved his hands into his pant pockets. "I don't know if what you did would be considered helpful. More like attempting not to screw up. By the way, where is the captured level-one fairy? It wasn't brought in for processing, nor is it in the oubliette. So I have to assume that you lost it?" Gone was the Ian from class who was asking forgiveness. Instead, he was acting like a team leader, harsh and critical. Or maybe it was because they were in front of Hunter.

Everly's cheeks burned; she would rather admit to losing it than letting it go on purpose.

Hunter stood before Everly to protect her from the big bad Ian. "Back off, Ian."

Ian stepped closer, going toe to toe with Hunter. "She's not your trainee, Hunter. She's mine."

Hunter flung out his hand and pointed at Everly's face. "Is this any way to treat your trainee?"

Ian followed Hunter's finger, and his face became stony.

"She survived." Ian shrugged.

"Just making sure history doesn't repeat itself." Hunter's voice dropped to a threatening tone. "You have a way of letting your team down."

Ian's eyes darkened. "That was a one-time event."

"That's why I won't let it happen again. I won't let you hurt someone I care about again." Hunter stepped forward, his hands curling into fists.

It seemed there was some unfinished business between the two grievers, which had nothing to do with her. She was just a catalyst that allowed them to get it out of their system. But she needed to distract them.

Everly stepped between the two of them.

"Maddie!" Everly shouted. "I'd like to see her."

Ian didn't look at her. His jaw clenched as he glared at Hunter. "She's in the hospital wing recovering."

"Which is where you should have taken Everly," Hunter responded.

"I was busy," Ian shot back.

Hunter bristled, grabbed Everly's arm, and pulled her into the hall after him, muttering about stupid, pigheaded trainers.

Everly stayed quiet, and let Hunter lead her back to the dorms. Once they passed into the living area, she pulled her arm out of Hunter's grasp. "I'm fine."

"No, you're not."

"Really, it's nothing that a hot shower and disinfectant can't fix."

"E—" His voice dropped low, and she could feel his emotion welling up. "I can't help this. I don't like seeing you here and injured, not to mention that you are lying to me."

"I'm not lying, I swear."

"Then tell me what happened for real?"

"We encountered a level-one fairy."

His eyes turned dark, the muscle in his jaw ticked, and he grabbed her wrist and pulled her over to the window that over-looked the parking lot. "Then what kind of fairy did that?" He pointed to the hood of her car, and she saw the three-foot-long deep scratches in the paint. In the morning light, it reflected at her.

"It was real." Everly rubbed her forehead. "I honestly thought I imagined it."

Hunter was still holding her other wrist, and his grip tightened.

Everly didn't pull away. She could feel his anger, but it wasn't toward her. It was toward himself, at his helplessness.

"I should have been there," he choked the words between gritted teeth.

"Why?" Everly asked, turning to look into his tanned face.

His eyes were glassy, and he realized how tightly he held her. He released his fingers one by one, and her wrist fell to her side. It seemed like he wanted to reach out again and grab her hand in his. His chest was heaving, the scar on his chin visible as it quivered.

"Because if something were to happen to you, I—"

"Stop," Everly commanded harshly. Hunter's head snapped up, and he looked at her in surprise. "I am not your responsibility. Ian's right. I need to take better care of myself. You go to class. Ian will see me to the infirmary."

"Are you sure you don't need—"

"Go!" Everly pointed her finger and watched as he struggled to leave her. Finally, he turned away, grabbed his bag, and headed to his next class. Ian passed him on his way into their shared dorm living area.

"Did your babysitter finally leave?" Ian teased. He took off his blazer and tossed it on the arm of the couch, and he dropped his bag by the entrance of the boy's dorms. All signs that he would take it back to his room later. Ian seemed very comfortable in Serenity Hall. How had she not known he lived in the same hall as her?

"He's just worried about me," she said, but she couldn't help but think, *Unlike you.*

"Yeah, I don't think it's just that. Hunter doesn't act that way when his girlfriend or sister go out on reapings."

"Act what way?"

He cocked his head and looked at her through half-closed eyes. "Possessive."

Everly shook her head. "He's just a friend."

"Does *he* know that?" Ian crossed his arms, watching her reaction closely. Under his scrutiny, she couldn't help but blush.

"Yeah, he's made that perfectly clear."

"And he has a *girlfriend*," Ian added.

"That too."

"That will soon change." Ian glanced out the window and saw the destroyed hood of her car. There was a slight change in his expression, the barest grimace on his lips. "When did *that* happen to your car?" Ian asked.

Everly sighed and tried to explain what happened after he left.

"That's my fault. I shouldn't have left you alone. I just needed to make sure that..." Ian paused . "Maddie was safe."

"Last night. When you saw her—your reaction. It changed. You called her by a different name."

His mouth tightened, and his face turned stony. "I don't know what you mean." Ian flicked his wrist for her to follow him and took off without even waiting for her.

Everly stood there, her lip curling in disgust and her eyes narrowing in frustration. He was treating her like a dog. All she needed to do was say woof. But if he was her mentor, who was she to make things even more complicated? Her feet felt like lead weights as she trudged after him.

As she turned the corner into the main hall, she stopped short, almost running into his chest as he turned to wait for her. "You did..." He struggled as if trying to find the right words. "Good."

Everly felt her mood brighten for a bit. It was the first compliment that anyone had given her. "Thank y—"

"Don't let it go to your head," Ian quickly interjected. "You still sucked, for example, losing the fairy, but you didn't suck as bad as you could have. Still have a lot to learn."

Everly tried to hide her smile as she walked behind Ian. It was a compliment, smothered in sarcasm and criticism, but if it was the best Ian could do. She would take it.

When they entered the infirmary, Everly remembered her first trip here after getting her omen. She had forgotten how big the room was. Large windows lined the hall, with rows of beds with pressed mint green sheets. Privacy curtains were set up between each bed, and a doctor on staff was ready to greet them.

He was tall, with soft brown skin and dark eyes filled with kindness, and he wore blue scrubs with a white jacket.

"You must be Everly." The doctor came around the check-in desk and shook her hand. "I'm Dr. Madsen."

"I know. We met briefly when you treated my head bump."

"Oh, that's right." Dr. Madsen reached for a dish of suckers and handed her one. Everly took the green one, and Dr. Madsen put three in his pocket before walking her back to the medical wing.

She took the first exam bed, and Dr. Madsen closed the curtain, giving them privacy.

"So I heard you had your first encounter with a fairy? Didn't expect them to bite like that, did you?"

Everly let out a relaxed chuckle and lifted her sleeve to expose her shoulder. "I didn't. It's nothing like what the movies make it out to be."

"They never get it right." Dr. Madsen began to clean the wound and applied a cream that instantly began to numb the fiery pain. "And your omen? He's fine after eating a fairy? No adverse side effects?" He pressed a little too hard, and Everly winced.

"Corvis seems fine."

Dr. Madsen nodded. "Many of the grimms have different antibodies, and their bites, scratches, or even weapons can have a negative effect on your nervous system. Like had it been a redcap. They would have laced their weapons with a hallucinogenic. One cut and an hour later, you would be in wonderland."

"That's good to know."

"I'll be right back." Dr. Madsen stepped out, went to his desk, and grabbed another handful of suckers. Everly stood and went to see if Maddie was recovering. She wasn't in any of the beds.

"Where's Maddie?" Everly asked Ian, who was sitting in a waiting room chair.

Ian looked up from his phone and scanned the room. He pointed to the second bed on the right. "She was right there just an hour ago."

When Dr. Madsen returned, they directed the question to him.

"Oh, she's been transferred to one of our sister clinics up north."

"Why?" Everly asked.

"That falls under patient confidentiality." Dr. Madsen wouldn't even look her in the eyes, telling her there was more going on than he wanted to say.

"I wanted to talk to her."

"I'm sorry, but that's impossible." He fidgeted with his charts.

"Did anyone interview her before she was transferred about what happened? How did she get kidnapped?" Everly pressed.

Dr. Madsen again grew silent.

Ian picked up on Everly's line of questioning. "We usually have to report to our advisor after every hunt. Did Mr. Halsey question her?"

"I'm sorry, he signed off on her transfer." Dr. Madsen retreated. "If you'll excuse me, I have some paperwork and phone calls that need to be conducted." He went into his office and closed the door.

"What just happened?" Everly asked.

"I don't know, but she was transferred fast. That is unusual." Ian turned and headed back down the hall.

"Where are you going?" Everly called out.

"To class," Ian answered.

"Are you not at all worried about interviewing her?"

"Look, Everly, I'm a griever. I hunt, train, and reap grimms. That's all I do, and that's where my job ends."

"But there's so much more information that needs to be explored. I mean, my dad would have—"

"You are not your dad," Ian cut in. "You don't have jurisdiction. You don't have the power, money, or resources to track her down and play detective. If you are so worried about her, you should talk to her griever team lead and pressure them to follow up on her well-being."

"Maybe I will." She crossed her arms in defiance and then uncrossed them. "Who was her team lead?"

Ian grinned, taking pleasure in this moment. "It's your *not boyfriend.*"

Everly was confused. "Hunter?"

Ian's eyebrow rose in affirmation.

"Then how come Hunter wasn't as worried about her when—"

"Exactly." Ian's eyebrow rose even further. "That's what I want to know. Tries to rake me across the coals when we've got bigger things—" He froze when a notice appeared on his phone.

Ian lifted his screen and read the text. His eyes turned dark; his knuckles gripped his phone until they were white. "I've been benched."

"What?"

"A team of grievers is going out tonight to investigate this latest attack. I want to go, but the Grimm Society is putting me under house arrest."

"Why?"

"Look, you've probably noticed I'm unlike other grievers. People don't like me, and because of that, speculation begins and fingers start to point."

Everly's phone beeped as well. She lifted hers to read the text and was surprised when it was from Ms. Bellcamp. "It says I need to report for my GCS appointment. What is GCS? It sounds like some disease."

Ian barked out a laugh, and then his grin turned mischievous. "This might make up for my house arrest. Lacie Duvall heads up that department. Good luck with that." He gave her a two-fingered salute, and she stood there.

"But what is GCS?" she called out to his retreating form. All she got back was another laugh.

CHAPTER 19

"SMILE!"

A flash of a camera blinded Everly as she held the coffee cup up to her lips, being very careful not to mess up the latte art as she set it back on the table.

"One more!" Lacie commanded, and Everly lifted the cup back up for another shot. She was sitting at a generic cafe table before a green screen. On the metal chair beside her were four shopping bags from department stores Everly had never heard of nor could afford without selling an arm and a leg.

"You look stiff and uncomfortable." Lacie leaned out from behind the camera light ring and frowned.

"I *am* stiff and uncomfortable," Everly said through a fake smile.

"Loosen up," Lacie said and did a little shake to demonstrate.

Everly mimicked Lacie but forgot to put the cup down and shook the cup. The latte art of a beautiful heart with an arrow now bled into the edges of the cup and resembled a decomposing organ.

"Sorry," Everly said when she looked at the pitiful cup.

"It's fine," Lacie said. She handed the destroyed coffee

drink to Kat, who already had one cappuccino on her desk and was working on the desktop computer in Photoshop.

"She always turns into a statue whenever there's a camera pointed her way," Holland said, bouncing into the studio with a designer bag overflowing with items. "It's like she has a sick sense."

"Don't you mean sixth sense?" Lacie corrected.

"No, I mean sick. Just look at your images." Holland went over to the closet and looked through the hangers' items.

"She's right," Kat said from behind her monitor screen. "She looks half dead or on the verge of puking her guts out in all these."

Lacie wrinkled her nose and went to stare at the desktop with Kat. "You're right. We can't use any of these. Can you Photoshop them?"

"Hey, I'm good with computers, but I don't know if I can fix this," Kat said, bored. "Unless I like superimposed someone else's face."

Everly grimaced and tried to tame the flyaway pink fur vest that kept blowing into her face from one of the many fans that simulated wind.

Now, she knew why Ian had told her good luck and abandoned her.

GCS stood for Griever Cover Stories and was in a separate classroom that doubled as a photo studio. Lacie Duvall practically tackled Everly as soon as she came in and took her to the dressing room. There were racks of clothes, swimsuits, winter gear, and items for every sport and hobby imaginable. There were also rooms full of various props to set up scenes for cafes, bookstores, and even restaurants.

"But you've got her esthetic all wrong." Holland put her hands on her hips. "No one would believe Everly would be wearing that." Holland pointed to the black-and-white-striped bags. "And she doesn't care about shopping or anything designer. If it's dusty, old, and someone probably died in it, she'd wear it."

"That's not true, I—"

Holland gave Everly a look. "What was that thing that you wore last Halloween?"

"You mean my great-aunt's wedding dress—"

"And where is she now?" Holland tapped her foot.

"Dead. Okay, I get it." Everly cupped her hands over her face in embarrassment.

"Well, she can't just wear her old clothes," Lacie said. "Now that she's at Gravemark, people have to believe she is one of us."

"We have to post some updates," Kat added.

"Wait, I don't have social media accounts," Everly corrected.

"Oh, you do now," Kat answered, pointing at her screen. "I made them for you. See?"

Everly came around the computer and stared at the images of her on campus, talking to Hunter in the parking lot on her first day of class and eating at lunch.

"Where did you get these?"

"I accessed the campus security feed. You are quite photogenic when you don't think people are watching." Kat hit a button, and the back of Everly's head came into view. Kat had accessed the school live feed.

Everly stiffened, and she looked around the room awkwardly, searching for the cameras. She saw the blinking light in the corner and turned to face the screen. Everly tried to smile and look natural, but her body position was stiff again.

"Great, Kat, now that she knows they're there, we will never get a good shot again." Lacie sighed.

"Go change!" Holland shoved the bag at Everly, and she went into the changing room.

Everly opened the bag and saw a pair of ripped jeans, sneakers, and her favorite blue peacoat.

When she came out, Lacie nodded. "Okay, I see it—vintage chic."

The stage in front of the green screen was replaced with an oversized chair. Holland patted the cushion and held out a book.

Everly's eyes went wide when she saw the latest crime novel. "But it hasn't even been published yet? How?"

"My dad knows the publisher. It was your birthday present from me, but it didn't arrive in time. I tried." Holland handed her *Fashion Crime Spree.*

Everly opened the book to see it was autographed. "I love it." She hugged the book to her chest.

"I know." Holland grinned and pointed to the chair. "Now sit."

Everly hopped into the chair, folded her legs under her, and immediately began reading, ignoring the sounds of the camera or the movement of the lights as they adjusted the setting around her.

The world faded into background noises as she found herself in the inner city, in an alley, being chased by thugs. The popping of the camera in her mind attuned to the shots of a gun being fired.

Everly barely even noticed as a beverage was placed in her hand, and she took a sip. Or when Holland guided her to a picnic blanket. She continued to read, taking a bite of a sandwich handed to her. She was a puppet and didn't care as she followed the opening chapters and the victim was revealed.

"Gruesome!" Everly said as she turned the page, but the book was pulled out of her hands. "Wait, I wasn't done."

"You are for now!" Lacie took the book and pointed to the computer screen, filled with images of Everly engrossed in the book. Her face had softened as she read the intro, stretched into a grin as she laughed at something funny, and then furrowed when the crime had been revealed. The book had been cropped out of most of the photos, and they looked almost like candid shots, except she knew better.

"We've got loads, and I think we should hold onto this and let you read each time we need an update."

"But—" Everly reached for the book.

"Not bad, grimm bait. They even got the fairy bites all but covered up."

Everly's head snapped up, and she zeroed in on Ian standing over Kat's shoulder, her book forgotten.

"What are you doing here?" Everly could feel a panic rise within her. She didn't want him to see photos of her.

"I got a text to come here." He shrugged.

"I didn't text you," Everly said.

"I did," Lacie added. "You need some shots with a cover man, and since Ian's your mentor, I told him he had to fill in."

"Cover man?"

"Holland said you don't have a boyfriend," Lacie said. "So we assign you one for candids."

"Holland," Everly growled out. "That's no one's business."

Holland smiled sheepishly. "Hey, my cover boo is Terrell."

Everly let out a breath. Yes, Holland usually had a new crush every week, but the guy that she had seen the most in her photos was Terrell.

Lacie dragged Ian away into the closet, and he came out moments later in a black denim jacket, white shirt, dark jeans, and boots. She had run gel into his hair to give it more waves.

Ian walked up to the green screen and stood there waiting.

"I can't do this," Everly said under her breath, turning to

Holland in a panic. "If you think I have a sick sense, wait until you pose me with a boy. You know my mouth doesn't shut up, and I get stupid."

"C'mon, grimm bait. I don't bite," Ian taunted; he had already run his fingers through Lacie's work and messed up his hair.

"This isn't going to work in the studio," Holland told Lacie. "If you don't want her to toss her cookies on your props, your best bet is to catch some candids with her. She'll never pose with a hot guy."

"Fine, let's take it on the road." Lacie grabbed her camera, tripod, and ring light. Holland followed with a bag of props, and Kat stayed put, waiting for the images to return to her screen.

They headed down the hall, and Everly fell into step beside Ian. "Why are you doing this?" she asked him.

"Because I'm in charge of you. Your cover, training, it's all my responsibility, and I knew that you'd probably screw it up if I didn't come. It looks like I was right."

They passed through the doors into the outer yard. He walked toward the stream and turned to wait for her. He gave a wave for her to hurry. She picked up her pace to catch up. He slowed when he came to the wooden bridge over the stream and stopped at the top.

He turned to look over the bridge, pressing his forearms onto the wooden railing. Everly stopped and turned to watch what he was staring at. It was a leaf on the water's edge, swirling around, caught in the wind. Her eyes followed his gaze, and she stared mesmerized at the moving water. A few tadpoles were darting around the speckle of the river stone underneath the surface. She noticed it all with her sight.

"Having a boyfriend won't be believable to anyone who

knows me. If I suddenly appear with a strange guy in photos, I think people will be even more suspicious."

He turned and tilted his head to look at her. "That's why we do this. You and I already went out on an unsanctioned reaping. We are going to go on more assignments, although sanctioned this time."

She chuckled. "I'll try not to track any without you."

"That's a good girl."

He turned and leaned against the bridge, lifting his head and looking up at the sky, closing his eyes and letting the sun hit his face at the right angle.

Everly froze, her heart hammering in her chest as she stared at his strong jawline, tan skin, and a faint scar that crossed his throat. Where did he get that? It looked old and healed. She wanted to reach up and touch it. Find the story behind that battle scar.

"Are you ready for the next assignment?"

He looked down, took a step toward her, and she backed up until she hit the edge of the railing. Ian put his arms on either side of her; he still never made eye contact but looked intently beyond her left ear. And she was glad for that. If she looked into those eyes, she would feel like prey trapped by a predator.

"Am I ready?" she questioned.

Ian smirked, leaned forward, his lips coming right to her ear. She could feel his breath on her cheek. "Not in the least."

She raised her hand to push him away. Instead, he grabbed her wrist and gave a harsh command. "Don't move. There's a bee!"

Everly froze. Her anger dissipated into fear. Ian's other hand grabbed the back of her head, and she felt him pull her into his chest.

"Don't!" he warned as she stiffened and tried to pull away.

"Stay still. I'm about to flick it away. The bee is caught in your hair."

Everly obeyed, her face pressed into the denim jacket. She felt his warm hands on her neck and could smell his aftershave. She could hear his heartbeat in his chest. While hers raced, his was steady.

"Is it gone?" she asked, feeling her legs tremble. Ian gently touched her chin with his fingers and turned her head to meet his gaze. His eyes darkened, his lips parted, and he leaned forward as if to kiss her, but she felt the lightest flick on her hair.

Then he stepped back, shoved his hands in his pockets, and looked to Lacie, who gave him a thumbs-up.

Her knees barely held her up as Ian strode across the bridge and looked at the digital display of Lacie's camera. Everly's heart was racing, and she blinked in surprise. *What just happened?*

"Did you get the bee?' she asked Ian.

"Uh, yeah," he said uncomfortably.

"That's it. You're done." Lacie grinned.

"Wow! These are good!" Holland cheered. "Come see, Everly."

Everly felt her stomach roll. She didn't even notice that they were shooting. She wasn't prepared to see the awkward photos on the digital screen.

Lacie clicked on the first picture in the library, and the photo took her breath away. Ian was handsome, a model in every shot, but what surprised her more was how natural and beautiful she looked next to him. There was a shot of him smiling and waving to her and her running to catch up.

Then one of them both looking over the edge of the bridge at the water. Another of Ian looking up, and Everly seeming to be fascinated by him. He looked like Adonis, and she looked in love. Then, when he pinned her against the railing, the camera hadn't caught her face or reaction. Instead, it looked like they were about to kiss. Then, it looked like they were kissing. He was blocking the view with his shoulder as he was supposed to get a bee out of her hair.

Holland whistled and fanned herself. "These are hot! Yikes, I would think you two are madly in love if I wasn't here to see it in person."

Lacie nodded. "It's like a whole love story played out in pictures."

Everly felt duped. She didn't even notice when Ian started manipulating her into poses. He was back to being a stone gargoyle, his arms crossed across his chest as he stared at nothing.

The whole thing was beautiful but fake. Everyone was going nuts over the photos, but Everly felt hollow, like Ian had stolen something precious from her.

She walked over to him, and he looked at her. "There wasn't a bee, was there?" she asked, trying to keep her anger under control.

"No." His eyes met hers. "Lacie texted me the problem. Said you were beyond hopeless with staged photos. That I needed to work my magic to get them from you."

"Did you know I am deathly allergic to bees?" she said.

"I read your file."

"I have a file?"

"All new grievers do. You weren't given to Hunter as a trainee because you knew him from before. It's best always to know everything about the people you work with. Especially when lives are at stake."

"You used my greatest fear against me," Everly said. "You manipulated me."

Ian's head tilted, and his eyes narrowed. "As you did me the other day. When you profiled me. I think, then—we're even."

She couldn't help the angry tears from burning in her eyes. She didn't want to stay and look at the photos but had to.

"Can I see the camera, Lacie?"

"Sure." She handed the camera to Everly and started to talk to Holland excitedly.

Everly quickly selected all the photos taken and deleted them from the camera, then took the memory card out and slipped it into her pocket.

"There must be something wrong," Everly said innocently. "I can't find the images."

"What?" Lacie grabbed the camera back. "Oh, no! There must have been a glitch. Ian, Everly. We are going to have to retake them." She started to wave Ian over.

"Not on your life," Everly said, glaring at Ian. "I'm done. I don't need a manipulator or a liar as my mentor slash fake boyfriend."

"You can't just dump me like that," Ian said.

"Watch me!" Everly snapped and stormed off, heading back into the building and toward Ms. March's office.

CHAPTER 20

"I'm sorry, I cannot grant your request," Ms. March said from behind her desk.

"Why not?" Everly asked.

The headmistress's office was right out of a Mother Goose story. Hand made doilies under every plant, and even the chairs had knitted covers to protect their armrests. Birdie would be green with envy at the number of doilies.

The office was pristine, not a speck of dust, filled with bookshelves and books, with a lovely view overlooking the school's inner courtyard.

"Because your reasons for wanting a change in mentor are invalid. Ian took on the mentorship, stepped in, and helped you take photos for the GCS department; he didn't report you for the unsanctioned reaping. In fact, he was the one that took the demerit on his record. He said it was his idea. Are you saying that I punished the wrong person?" Ms. March sighed, putting her glasses on the table and leaning back in her chair to stare at her.

Everly shrank in her chair.

"He has a drinking problem. I've seen it. It's in a little flask he carries around." She felt terrible trying to throw him under the bus.

Ms. March's eyes focused on Everly. "We are aware of Mr. Holmes's current afflictions."

"But it's not safe—"

"Agreed. In some circumstances, he may be considered not safe. But after he saved you from the ogre, I thought you would be more inclined to overlook his peculiarities."

Everly fell silent.

"Then it's settled. You are still under Mr. Holmes's purview. If you have any issues, you can take it up with your resident advisor. That is all."

Ms. March dismissed her.

Everly left Ms. March's office feeling dejected; her shoulders slumped, and her feet dragged back to Serenity Hall. Ian waited for her in the living area as she passed through the double doors. He was sitting on the couch, playing the Xbox.

"You couldn't get rid of me, could you?" Ian said, not even looking at her but somehow sensing when she entered the room.

"No," Everly growled out in displeasure. She stormed over to the fridge and opened it to pull out a bottle of water. "Why are you always around?" she snapped.

Ian paused his game, got up, and moved to the fridge near her. "It's because I live here too. Get used to it." He pulled a silver flask from his back pocket and took a long drink before replying. "Just to let you know, I tried earlier too."

"*You* tried to get rid of me?" Everly scoffed.

"Yep, after that first training session," he answered. "I knew we weren't a great fit together."

"The feeling's mutual," she said, raising her glass to his in salute.

"It is," he closed the fridge door and jumped up to sit on the granite island. "We seem to rub each other wrong, and you have too much emotional baggage."

"What?" Everly snapped. "You didn't just say that I have—"

"Sorry, I call it as I see it. As a new griever, you let your feelings cloud your judgment. You don't listen; let's not forget you let a grimm get away. All the makings of a terrible griever."

"I hate you!" Everly seethed quietly.

"Good." Ian's voice rose. "Then use that hate and prove me wrong."

"I will!" she yelled.

"Okay, then." His eyes were fire. He slid off the counter and strolled back toward the boys' hall, leaving his video game unfinished. Did he play that so he could be in the living room when she returned to the hall?

Everly stood there shaking in frustration.

What just transpired?

What was worse was that they had an audience. Maddox stood by the boys' hall. When he saw her, he retreated backward into the shadows.

Everly sighed and stormed into her room. Something was nagging her about the hiker case, and knowing Ian was on house arrest meant she wasn't going anywhere near the sites or solving it unless she got someone else to mentor her temporarily.

The first thing Everly did was open up her laptop and start catching up on all the online reports of the attacks. It would help more if she had her father's case files instead of the media. But she wasn't going to nitpick.

The victims had nothing in common. The first victim was Shelly Miller, a dental hygienist. The second was Rocky Cordon, a lawyer in his thirties. The latest was unidentified. But all of them were dead.

By the way her father reacted after the attack—the woman who had been lost hiking—it was a grimm. He'd said as much. There was no doubt in her mind that they were not hunting just a cougar, and from what she saw that night on the bluffs, it was probably...

"A level five." Everly opened up her text to read everything she could about the werewolf. Shift any time with or without moonlight, but their minds are less human under a full moon. They tend to go crazy. Those who are bitten can keep the were-wolf curse at bay as long as they never take a life. The curse will take hold permanently once they have their first taste of blood.

Everly moved back to her dad's journals; maybe there was more in there.

March 7, 2002

I was wrong; Eugene isn't recovering from the werewolf attack. He was bitten. He tried to hide the fact from Dr. Madsen, but it was apparent. Every full moon, he has become unstable. We have to lock him up in a cage made of silver because he loses himself to an uncontrollable rage.

This is no way to live.

April 1, 2002

Redcaps are murderous little goblins that soak their hats in blood and favor iron weapons and boots. I accidentally discov-ered they hate the sound of praying. Note to self, memorize the Lord's Prayer.

May 10, 2002

I had my first experience with a fairy kidnapping at a public park near college. I'll never understand fairies' obsession with swapping out changelings for human babies. I found the closest fairy circles and luckily stole the baby back before he had eaten fairy food. But having to explain to the parents why I had picked up their swaddled infant in a public park without permission and ran into the woods, to return ten minutes later, was another thing. I almost got charged with kidnapping myself. Thankfully, Officer Mitchell was there and saved the day.

May 16, 2002

I can't stop thinking about that baby I rescued. It made me start thinking of the future and what it means to be a griever and have kids. I pray that I survive until graduation and am lucky enough to get married. I'll do everything I can to prepare my kids, so they don't have to deal with the stress of being a legacy. Or better yet. Pray they don't ever come to Gravemark.

June 3, 2002

I did it! I survived graduation from Gravemark. My griever abilities are still going strong, so I'm one of the few that can still go on reaping assignments while at college. There are a few other Gravemark students that are attending the local college with me. I refused to date, until graduation. I dare not let anyone distract while on assignment. Maybe, now I can lower that guard around my heart.

October 19, 2002

Eugene and Carol got engaged and are to be married next October. It's a reason to celebrate. Their griever marks are fading, which means their gifts will disappear too, and they can retire. I'm still worried for Eugene. I think it's too soon to get married with the werewolf curse, but Carol says it doesn't matter. She loves him.

I'm a terrible friend because I don't trust him. I live in constant fear with a silver bullet always loaded and ready.

Everly closed the journal and pondered the sacrifices her dad and his friends made when they were just teenagers. Chasing down monsters, almost dying. They had so much riding on their shoulders. But if it were a werewolf, it would most certainly make it hard for the police to track it down. It would need someone to find their human counterpart, their motivation. Find the grimm behind the human mask.

Everly's neck was getting stiff. She sat back up and began to write down how to find the creature that could pose as a human. If only someone had seen the grimm or werewolf. Everly's pen fell from her fingers to clatter against the notepad; it rolled off the pad and onto the floor. She grabbed her phone and dialed Hunter.

It went to voicemail. Everly waited a few minutes and tried again. Hunter denied her calls. Was his silence his payback for her turning her phone off? It wasn't funny.

She stormed out of the hall.

Maddox was in the living room, playing Ian's game he had abandoned.

"What hall and room number is Hunter Abernathy?" Everly asked.

"Why?" Maddox jumped back as he tried to dodge an attack from the screen.

Everly moved toward the Xbox, her finger hovering over the logo. "Don't make me hit the power button."

"Okay, it's right there!" He gestured with his elbow to the boys' hall and the first door on the left.

"Really?" Was she really that much of an introvert that she didn't know who lived in the guys' hall?

"Why would I lie? Although, he's hardly ever there." Everly immediately began to picture him with Aimee. "He's usually training or hanging out in Liberty Hall with Aimee and Terrell," Maddox answered.

Everly relaxed and went down the boys' hall. Knocking on his door, she got no answer. "Hunter!" Everly yelled through the door. "Stop ignoring my calls."

Hunter came down the hall, having changed out of school clothes into comfier gray sweatpants and an NYU sweatshirt. He was talking on the phone and held up a finger for her to pause. "Uh-huh. Love you too, Aimee." He moved past her into his room.

Everly waited at the entryway for him to finish his conversation. When he put the phone away, she descended on him with anger.

"You're not just Maddie's team lead. You're her mentor," she rushed out.

His eyebrows rose in disbelief. "Yeah, I know."

Everly had never been inside Hunter's room at his home and had only seen it when she passed the open door on her way to Holland's room. Like Holland's, his room looked like it was hardly lived in. There weren't even shoes on the floor. All the books were lined up on the shelves, spines out and alphabetized. Everything in his room was stacked in very neat piles. His computer chair and desk were the one slightly messy area with a state-of-the-art gaming system and high-end flat-screen monitors.

She released the information like a volcano ready to explode as soon as he closed the door. "Maddie was transferred out of Gravemark."

"So," Hunter said, not seeming to catch Everly's clues. "It happens. When a griever is wounded, they are sent to another facility for healing."

"But when she wasn't interviewed by her advisor?"

"Maybe they didn't think it was necessary." He went and sat down at his desk chair.

"Or maybe she knew something. It was an encounter with a level-one fairy. What is the worst that can happen? Nasty bites, scratches. Why would they transfer her out? What if she saw something? What don't they want us to know?"

He shook his head. "That's a lot of questions."

"Exactly, no one knows what happened. No one questioned her. Can we go to this facility and ask her ourselves?"

Hunter was still. Too still. He knew something and wasn't saying anything. He wouldn't make eye contact, just stared at the floor, his shoulders drooped, and he looked lost, which meant deception.

Everly marched forward, put her hands on the armrests of his chair, and leaned forward within a few inches of Hunter's face in full intimidation mode. Something her father had done when trying to gauge the truth from someone.

"Hunter, look at me," she demanded. "I can tell you're hiding something from me. I can read it in your body language. What is it that you're not telling me?"

Hunter looked up, his green eyes meeting hers before quickly lowering to her lips. She heard the intake of his breath, or was that her own? The tension between them was electric. It almost broke her. She wanted to lean in and close the distance, pressing her lips to his. Then she felt the barest touch of his thumb on the underside of her wrist, sensual.

She gasped. Hunter leaned forward, his hand reaching for hers, his fingers brushing across her palm as she escaped.

Moving across the room to stand by the door, she wrapped her arms around herself as if to comfort or protect her heart. She wasn't sure. She was trying to play him, force his hand, but somehow, she was the one who retreated.

"Everly," he breathed out her name, half desire, half pain. Before dropping forward, he buried his face in his hands. "You make me walk a fine line between honor and temptation. And I fear I will be left burning in the end."

She backed away, her hand on her heart as she tried to calm the frantic beating. Had she read the situation right, or was it her overactive imagination?

"Tell me about Maddie," she pressed, ignoring the truth that they both were dancing around. "I need questions answered, and you're the only one who can help me get them. Where is she?"

"She's been transferred to one of the Grimm Society hospitals up north. Once someone goes up there, they don't usually come back."

"What's that mean? Was she that badly injured?"

He grew quiet and refused to speak. He knew more than he was saying.

"I'm tired of the lies; I just want to know the truth."

"And what if the truth changes how you see us... or me?" Hunter stood up, the chair rolling away from him.

"The truth won't change how I feel about you," Everly said. This time it was her turn to look away and avoid eye contact.

He came and stood by her, keeping two feet between them, but it felt like mere inches. Her heart was beating out of control; she was struggling to take a deep breath.

"And how... do *you* feel about me... Everly?" He took another step, closing the gap even further.

"You're my best friend's brother." Everly reached behind

her for the door handle, feeling the cold metal in her hand. "That's all there is to it. I care about Holland."

"That's it?" He reached out and brushed a stray strand of her strawberry blonde hair that had stuck to her lip in her hasty escape to his dorm door. She was trapped against the closed door. He leaned forward. It was a slow move, one meant to test boundaries, to watch her reaction the same way she had done to him.

"That's it."

Everly closed her eyes and inhaled as his lips brushed her jaw as he whispered, "Some secrets, Everly, should stay buried. Trust me." Her eyes flew open as he pulled the door open, it hit her back and thrust her into his chest, but he moved away and left her standing in the open doorway. "But if you want answers, I'll take you there. But they may not be the answers you seek."

"Thank you, Hunter. Thank you. I'm—"

He cut her off with a wave of his hand. His eyes were blazing with anger. "Stop. You've proven your point. You're willing to do anything, even tempt your best friend's brother, to get what you want. You are more like Holland than I thought."

"That's not what I—" Everly started to argue but realized he was right. She pressed and only thought of herself and not the consequences of hurting others. "I'm sorry. I just really want to find out what happened."

Hunter nodded. "Okay. I will see what I can do."

"When?"

"I'll let you know when I'm ready to go. There are a few things I have to do first. You know the way out."

The dismissal was abrupt. She was pushed out of his room, and the door slammed closed in her face. Everly was left standing in the middle of his hall, confused and with her cheeks burning in embarrassment.

CHAPTER 21

ONE OF THE GREAT THINGS ABOUT GRAVEMARK WAS THAT most classes were held Monday through Wednesday, and the rest of the week consisted of private tutoring and online courses, which slowed down and gave them time to study. It gave the grievers flexibility to go out on reaping assignments from the society. Friday morning, Everly sat at the kitchen island with her notebook and pen, writing her thoughts about the attacks, and watched as the students headed out of the hall to run errands or go into town.

As she sat drinking a can of seltzer, she saw Lacie had already changed out of her school uniform into fancy heels, skintight jeans, and expensive sunglasses. She was storming out to her car and yelling into her phone.

"Of course, yes. I'm coming home for the weekend. No. I will not be stopping to pick up your dairy-free frappe. Get your other favorite child to do it. You know I hate coffee."

Everly smirked. Even the rich and powerful had weird family dynamics.

She listed all the types of grimms that could be responsible for the attacks that looked like cougars: vampires, bugbears, chupacabras, lycanthropes, therians, werewolves. She understood the dilemma now. There were quite a few that could mimic one another. She closed her eyes and then started to eliminate them all again, coming down to circle the last one, werewolf. She tapped her pen on the word while bouncing her leg on the footrest.

She really would feel better if she knew what happened the night that Maddie was kidnapped.

"Hey, can you talk?" Ian came into the kitchen and leaned across the counter.

"Did the other grievers come back with anything?" Everly asked.

Ian frowned. "No, the police still have the site closed off. All they could do was try and track the surrounding area, but Sergeant Mitchell saw the griever and escorted them out. Ms. March isn't thrilled, but what can you expect? They can't exactly track as well as I can."

Ian's eyes drifted to her notepad and list. He frowned and swallowed nervously. "Hey, Everly. Have you heard any rumors about me?"

"You mean other than you're a jerk, ice prince, or—my favorite—Mad Max."

"Who calls me Mad Max?"

"Oh, wait." Everly teasedly punched him in the shoulder. "Those are the names I call you."

Ian dropped his head, and his cheeks showed a hint of color. She embarrassed him.

He licked his lips, reached for his flask, and took another sip, causing his face to sour in disgust.

Everly felt her stomach drop, and her opinion of him also did. "Do you need to do that?" she chastised.

His eyes widened, and he got defensive. "Yeah, I do. You don't understand."

"Yeah, I do. You have a problem. An addiction."

"No, there are some things I think you should know. I'd rather have you hear it from me than someone else."

A shadow fell across the counter, and Everly knew when Hunter had arrived without looking. She could feel his presence, the power that radiated off him from being an Abernathy.

"You ready?" Hunter dropped a duffel on the counter. He had changed into jeans and a green V-neck shirt.

"For what?" Everly turned on her stool, grateful to be saved from this awkward encounter.

Hunter leaned onto the island. "You wanted to interview Maddie. I'll take you to her."

"Right now?" Everly asked in surprise.

"Yeah." He grinned. "Unless you have other plans." Hunter swept his open hand toward Ian.

"No, I'm good." Everly scooted off the stool, eager to escape. Hunter headed out, and Everly entered her room to get her crossbody bag and change out of her uniform into jean shorts, a band shirt, and light blue flannel.

"Everly," Ian called her name as she passed him. It sounded sad, so she slowed. "I just want you to know I will be unavailable for a day or two."

"Okay." Everly was confused as to why he was telling her.

"So, don't do anything"—he shoved his hands in his pockets and raised his eyebrow at her—"that would require me needing to save you."

"I won't," she added and turned to catch up with Hunter.

She hurried out to Hunter's Jeep Rubicon. She tossed her crossbody bag onto the seat and grabbed the door grips to pull herself into the car. Hunter's movements were methodical, turning the car on and looking in his rearview mirror to check before backing out of the parking spot. Ian was standing behind his Jeep.

Hunter honked his horn, and Ian moved out of the way, but he only shifted over a few car spaces before stopping to watch them pull out.

Aimee came down the front steps, confused at seeing Everly in Hunter's passenger seat. She brushed her hair behind her ear and mouthed his name, but Hunter didn't even seem to see her.

Everly kept quiet. A few seconds later, Hunter's phone rang, and the Bluetooth screen kicked on, showing the caller's ID as Aimee Stillwell. He hit Ignore, and Everly got a sour feeling in the pit of her stomach. Something was wrong. She sat upright in her seat, her seatbelt buckled but her hand on the door handle for safety.

Hunter drove down the winding stretch of mountain road that led to their school. Five minutes later, he pulled onto the interstate and headed north. Only when they were on the freeway did she see his shoulders relax, and twenty minutes later, he put on the radio, and the sweet tones of Brendon Urie and Panic! At the Disco came over the speakers.

Everly released her grip on the handle and looked around Hunter's car. Like his room, it was impeccable—clean interior with a hint of new-leather smell. Not a speck of dust anywhere. She could see a duffel with his lacrosse stick over the rear seat headrest in the back trunk space.

"Sorry to ruin your date with Ian Holmes," Hunter said, breaking the silence.

"It's okay."

"Really?"

"Because it wasn't a date. We were just talking," Everly said. She traced her finger along the glass windowpane. "He's my mentor. Plus, Ian is the last person I would want to take me on a date."

"You're kidding? I wouldn't know from the pictures on your Instagram."

"What?" Everly pulled out her phone, opened the app, and groaned when it showed a photo of her running up to Ian. "I thought I deleted those."

Hunter started to laugh.

"Why is that funny?" She made a face. "I don't want people to think I'm dating anyone."

"It's just not what I would have expected. I would have thought there would be people lining up to date you."

Everly sighed. "Not so much when your father was a detective and ran background checks on every suitable guy in the vicinity. Anyone near me was put under a microscope, analyzed, and fingerprinted. It tended to send most people running."

He studied her face, the tense lines of her mouth. "You're not kidding?" he scoffed.

"I wish I were, but my family was a bit paranoid. Whenever someone did express interest in dating me, it wasn't for very long."

Hunter's brows furrowed. "Why is that?"

Everly gave Hunter a pleading look, not wanting to state the reason was his sister. "They would just lose interest," she muttered.

He made a noise in his throat and shook his head like he didn't believe her. "Is that the lie you are telling yourself?"

"It's not a lie," Everly stated. "Any time I showed interest in a guy, or vice versa, they would find someone more interesting than me."

She knew the moment Hunter put two and two together. "You mean Holland would swoop in and steal—"

"Not steal," Everly interrupted. "Can't steal what isn't

yours to begin with." She crossed her arms over her chest, wishing the questioning would end. She looked around the clean car and wondered at the lack of dirt.

The only signs of uncleanliness came from the Starbucks receipt between the center seats.

"Caramel Frappuccino." Everly read the receipt out loud. "This isn't your receipt. You don't buy Frappuccinos. I've never seen you drink anything except for iced americanos," Everly accused, changing the subject.

"You know my coffee order." He bit his lip to hide his smirk and shook his head in disbelief.

"Why is that surprising?" She crossed her arms and leaned back in the chair.

"I mean, it shouldn't be knowing you, but Aimee doesn't even know my coffee order, and we get coffee every week together."

"That's because Aimee is a self-cent—" Everly stopped. "No, I'm better than that. I won't insult your girlfriend out loud or in front of you."

"No, but you'll *think* it."

"Of course," Everly admitted. "There's no hiding that I *think* you two are wrong for each other, but I won't *say* it out loud to your face."

"You just did." He grinned.

"Yeah, I know. I'm in a *mood*." She tried to keep a straight face.

"I can tell." Hunter chuckled.

She turned on him, her eyes blazing. "Don't you act all high and mighty. It is because of you that I'm this way."

Hunter dared to laugh. "You are going to blame me for your snippiness?"

"No, for your coldness."

The smile died on his lips. "Well, I haven't been in the best of moods myself lately. I'm surprised you haven't given me the first degree on the facility we are going to. You always have a million questions rattling around in that brain of yours."

"I figured you'd tell me eventually. We're stuck in a car. It's not like you're going anywhere. I have all the time to interrogate you."

Hunter relaxed. "Interrogate away, but I may not answer all your questions."

"How long is it going to be?" Everly asked.

"It's a five-hour drive up north."

"What?" Everly sat forward in her seat. "I wasn't expecting it to be so far. I thought..." She leaned back in her chair. "I don't know what I thought." Everly zipped her lips, afraid to ask the questions that would solidify her conclusions. Saying it out loud didn't make her feel any better.

A light rain started, and the sound of the Jeep's wipers calmed her nerves. They stopped an hour later to fill up and get food.

Everly stretched her arms and legs and walked around to the side of the car as he filled up the tank. They were at a small derelict gas station with only two pumps. The inside store barely held room for the attendant and a few drink coolers. She stepped inside to ask for the restroom key and took the giant license plate with the key attached to the back outside.

Headlights illuminated her as another call pulled into the station, and she inserted the key and stepped into the restroom. Inside was a map on the wall, a toiletry dispenser, and soap. There wasn't much to say about where they were except that she suspected they had crossed over into another state while she was sleeping. That and the giant license plate keyring told her.

Everly brought the key back inside to the attendant in the

booth, and Hunter was inside paying for his gas. He was buying burritos, chips, and bottled water.

Through the rain, Everly could make out a black sedan but not the actual make or model of the other car. The driver never exited the vehicle to get gas or snacks.

"Ready?" Hunter had his hand on the door, and when she nodded, he opened it, and they ran back out to the waiting car.

Once inside, she shivered from the chill in the air. He took the snacks and handed Everly a burrito. Which was already steaming up the window. Hunter leaned over and adjusted the heater and then the vents, so they blew on her lap.

"Th-thanks," Everly said as the heat warmed her up. Something didn't feel right about the other car, so she kept watching the driver out of her side-view mirror.

"Yeah, I have done this trip before. There isn't much out here for the next two hours. The snacks will get us through." He buckled his seat belt, tossed a bag of chips into her lap, and handed her the bottled water.

"Got it. Eat junk food and be prepared to sing bad karaoke," Everly teased.

"No karaoke, I beg of you," Hunter said, popping a chip in his mouth.

They ate their food in the car and tossed the wrappers into the garbage can by the pump before pulling out of the gas station. Everly watched the other car suspiciously until she was sure the sedan didn't follow. She sighed in relief and took another sip of her water. *Why was she so paranoid?*

The next hour passed quietly. Everly didn't sing karaoke, but she couldn't help but hum along to some of the songs on the radio while Hunter drummed along on the steering wheel. The tension from the first hour of their trip had dissipated with the rain as the clouds parted, and they could see the sun.

After another hour, Hunter was trying to stretch out his neck while still driving.

"Do you want me to drive?" Everly asked.

Hunter looked at her, his eyebrows raised in surprise.

"No. I can do it."

"I can," Everly offered. "You don't have to be all macho and do the driving yourself."

He laughed. "Believe me. There's nothing macho about driving long hours. It's just that I care about my car." He rubbed the dashboard. "But I do appreciate the offer. Aimee never offers to drive—"

As if speaking her name summoned her, the phone rang again through the speakers. Aimee Stillwell's name popped up.

"You should really take the call," Everly said.

"I'm sure it won't be a pleasant call. I didn't bring my headphones and don't want you to have to hear us argue."

"It's fine. All couples argue."

"Do they?" he asked, looking to her for reassurance.

"I don't know." Everly shrugged. "I've never had a boyfriend. I'm just basing it off what I see on TV."

The phone stopped ringing. Everly thought that would end it, but it started again.

"Oh, please, just pull over and answer the phone already. I will get out of the car and go for a walk." She pointed to a trail, and Hunter took her advice and pulled into the gravel drive. Everly opened the car door before Hunter shifted into Park and headed toward the wooden sign that marked the park trails.

As soon as the door closed, she heard Hunter say, "Hello," but not get another word out before a high-pitched yell came across. Everly needed more distance.

Everly walked a few feet down the trail and found a bench to sit on. It was still wet, but she didn't care. She tried to collect her thoughts. When she said she didn't know if couples fought, that was not true.

When she was seven, she remembered her parents fighting, the arguments, and the doors slamming. She never knew why they fought, only that it happened frequently. Then the fighting stopped, and her mom was gone.

When she asked about her mom, Everick had said, "She left us."

Not, she left *me*. She just left us. *Plural*. It left Everly with a feeling of not being good enough or valuable enough since she didn't take Everly with her.

Was she such a burden that she didn't want her daughter?

It was those feelings of neglect that made her so self-sufficient. She didn't ever want to be a burden on anyone else again. And it was her fault; her mom was gone. Her dad was gone.

None of them stayed.

Everly didn't know when the tears started.

She heard the car door slam and tried to wipe away the signs of her weakness, but they wouldn't stop. Even when he came up behind her on the path, she stood and tried to turn away.

Strong arms pulled her into an embrace, and she turned, burying her face into his shoulder. She cried, letting her heart mourn for her father. Hunter only held her, wrapping his arms around her back, rocking her softly. His cheek rested against her head. He smelled like his car, the burrito, and his aftershave. When her crying stopped, she pulled away, but he was reluctant to release her. Finally, he let go, and she felt cold once more. Alone.

"Thanks," she whispered, unable to look him in the eye. "You give good hugs," she said, trying to make light of the situation.

"Do you want to talk about it?" he asked.

She sniffed and shook her head. "No. If I do, I'll cry again. I want to get going. The sooner I learn the truth about Maddie, the better." Everly marched past Hunter, leaving him on the path and heading back up to the Jeep, but not before she heard his parting remark.

"I don't know if knowing will make it better."

CHAPTER 22

"How was the call?" Everly asked as they pulled back onto the road, referring to the call with Aimee. "As expected," he said.

"That bad?"

"Worse. She doesn't understand why you are with me. Nor why I won't be able to see her tonight, especially when we had plans to take her father's boat out one last time before the weather changes."

"Yikes," Everly said, twisting the ends of her flannel into a knot.

"It is tough because I won't tell her where I'm going."

"Why not?"

"Because this is something that I can't tell Aimee... ever."

"But you can tell me?" Everly dropped her flannel and looked up at Hunter.

Hunter glanced at her before returning his gaze to the road. "Yes, because you're different. You're like family."

Family? Family wasn't the word she wanted to use, not when she had a crush on him and had been hiding it for the whole time they'd known each other. But it was a good word to help her remember where the lines were drawn. And she had to step way back over to the safe side and stop blurring them.

Holland was like a sister to her; besides her dad and Birdie, she was the most important person in her life.

Everly yawned, leaned her head against the window, and watched the headlights of the oncoming cars; with each passing moment, they got brighter until her eyes were closed.

———

"Caramel Frappuccino and an iced americano, please," Hunter spoke into the intercom.

Everly woke up as they pulled into a drive-through.

"Have a nice nap?" Hunter smiled at seeing her sleepy face. Her heart fluttered at seeing those dimples.

"Can we also get two grilled paninis and an iced cold brew with cream?" he asked the barista.

Everly stared at Hunter like he had two heads. He knew her coffee order.

A few minutes later, the barista handed three coffees through the window, and Everly juggled them. She put Hunter's and the second drink in the center console while holding hers.

"Where are we?" she asked, putting the straw in his americano without him asking. Things she automatically did for her father whenever she was with him. She was taking care of the driver. Everly also unwrapped the sandwiches, turned the wrappers into holders, and passed one to Hunter.

She took a bite of her panini, the cheese burning her mouth. "Hot!"

He gave her an amused look as he took the sandwich. "Almost there."

They left the little suburb area fifteen minutes later,

heading up a mountain path with cabins on every side. They passed a no-trespassing sign and then another.

"Okay, if this ride ends in a *Cabin in the Woods* type horror movie, you will end up dead, and you won't be killed by the main antagonist but by the quirky side character."

Hunter snorted. "You consider yourself the quirky side character?"

"Of course." She took a sip of her drink. "They're the ones that usually survive."

"You like horror movies."

"No. Never horror; too much unnecessary gore and blood, which they never get right, according to my grandma. But I do love a good thriller or mystery."

"Good to know." Hunter pulled the car into another driveway, and the land leveled out, and the gravel turned into pavement. They passed a sign for the Dorian Institute.

Hunter got out and waited for Everly, who took longer to get out.

When she stepped out of the car, she could feel the tightness at the thought of being in another hospital. The building was ancient, with high walls, and surrounded by gardens and hospital attendants. Her feet froze, her hand still stuck to the door as if glued. It reminded her of Mayfair Hospital.

"She's here?" Everly asked.

Hunter came around the car and could see her hesitation. "She's here."

"I hoped...." Everly trailed off. "As long as she's okay."

Hunter waved her forward, and she moved, each foot like a lead weight as they headed into the facility. Seeing her struggle, Hunter tucked his arm through Everly's for support.

They entered through one of the big double doors.

An Asian woman stepped forward to greet them. "Mr. Abernathy, you're back again. Would you like to visit you—"

"Yes, Ms. Kim," Hunter rushed out. She bowed, giving a small smile, and then waved her hand. "Right this way, sir, but I'm under orders that only family may visit." She cast a questioning glance at Everly.

"It's fine." Everly tried to untangle her arm from Hunter's.

"No. It's not. We didn't come all this way for you not to see her." He released his hand and walked over to lean down and speak to Ms. Kim. This time her expression did change; it wavered to worry, and then she nodded and brightened again. "All right. Come this way."

Hunter grabbed Everly's hand, threading his fingers through hers.

"What did you say?" Everly whispered in distress. Ms. Kim used a key card on a door and a buzz sounded followed by an unlocking noise.

"I said that you are family. We just recently got engaged but don't want the media or distant family to know yet." His lips pulled into a half smile, taunting her.

Everly tried to untangle her hand from Hunter's, but now that he had her hand in his, he wasn't letting go. He winked and swung their hands a bit.

"Don't worry, it's just a facade," he said softly.

"But you're not related to Maddie Eerie, are you?"

"Shh." He squeezed her hand, and her cheeks warmed. "Details."

Ms. Kim gestured to the elevator. "Floor three."

They stepped into the elevator, and with fingers interlocked locked together, he used the knuckle of the hand holding the coffee to hit the button. When she tried to pull her hand away, he tightened his grip.

The doors to the elevator opened, and they stepped into the foyer. There was a mirror directly across from them, with a small table and potted plants. Down the hall was another locked door and monitored check-in desk.

They moved toward the door. Once they reached it, they had to wait to be buzzed in. Everly gave up on separating her hand from Hunter's because now she clung to him for support.

"Hunter." She licked her lips as she struggled to breathe. "What is this place?" She could tell it wasn't just a hospital. It had way more security than usual.

"It's where injured grievers come to live out their lives. Ones that can't go back to society just yet."

"What do you mean, 'can't go back to society'?"

"Sometimes our job leaves grievers scarred. Mentally and physically, the time it takes to recover can be weeks, months, or years."

There were multiple sitting areas. A few patients and nurses were working on a puzzle. A gentleman with dark hair was rocking back and forth and staring at a mirror. His eyes were wide with terror, and he focused solely on the mirror.

Hunter gestured with his chin. "That's Delaney Byrne. He survived a gorgon raid fifteen years ago but now can't stop staring into mirrors. He screams if he's moved away from his reflection."

"That's horrible."

"The Grimm Society doesn't advertise this place. I only know because there's someone here that I... " He trailed off when they came upon the person they were looking for.

Maddie was curled up in a chair, a bathrobe wrapped around her, and pink fuzzy slippers on her feet. Her blonde hair was pulled into a messy bun on her head that was falling to the side as if the bun itself was exhausted from trying to stay perky. Her face was slack, her eyes vacant as she stared at the sun.

Hunter released Everly's hand and moved to sit in the chair

before Maddie.

"Hey, Maddie. How are you doing?"

As Everly drew closer, she saw that Maddie's right foot was in a cast as well as her left arm.

Her beautiful hazel eyes widened when she saw Everly. She licked her lips, and those sad, hollow eyes filled with tears. "You were there. You saved me."

"I had help," Everly replied. "Ian was there as well, but Maddie, we came to find out what happened that night."

"I already told him." She pushed the coffee away and buried her head into the tops of her knees. "It was awful; I don't want to discuss it."

"Told who?"

"Dr. Madsen. I told him, and he said it would be better if I didn't tell anyone what happened."

Everly cast a wary look toward Hunter. "Why would he not want you to talk about it? You should have reported it to your advisor."

"Advisor. I'm so embarrassed." Maddie started to cry soft sobs. "I don't even know what to tell my parents. They don't know what Gravemark is. They still think I'm attending a normal prep school. But I can't. Not after the mistakes I made."

Everly held out her arm and pulled up the sleeve of her shirt to reveal a bandage, which she peeled back to display the soft scratch that had faded from a bright red to almost pink. "I made the same mistakes. I thought fairies were soft and pretty and granted wishes. Wrong. Did you know they bite, and if they scratch you, it burns like fire? Oh, and if you eat one, they taste like crunchy jalapeños. So don't recommend that."

Maddie snorted, her lips hinting at a smile. "Did you...?

"No, that was Corvis, my omen."

Maddie slumped her shoulder. "I'm not even good enough to get an omen."

"Hey, my sister didn't get an omen until after six months at Gravemark." Hunter tried to cheer her up.

Everly frowned but didn't correct Hunter, knowing that Holland didn't have an omen.

Maddie continued to cry.

Hunter looked at Everly helplessly. "Don't look at me; tears are my kryptonite. I feel utterly helpless."

Everly dropped to her knees in front of Maddie. "Listen, what happened to you was horrible, but you survived. Someone else that night did not. And whatever you tell us can help us get a better picture. That night on the bluff, I saw something horrible too, but I need your help to put the pieces together. That's what we do. We're grievers. We save people by putting the bad grimms away." Everly took a deep breath.

"I don't remember much," Maddie started to speak. "I was upset; Kat told me to go home. I remember not feeling okay, so I called Terrell to drive me. I was supposed to meet him by his car, except—" She pressed her fingers to her temples. "I got lost on the way back to the road. I took the wrong trail, and then—I saw something."

"What did you see?" Everly asked.

Maddie stared into the distance, trying to recall what she had seen. "It was a flashlight. I thought someone had gotten lost. So, I followed the light and overheard two people on the trail. They spoke in low voices about the attacks and said the illegal big game poaching story held off the suspicion, but they needed to come up with something else."

Everly's fingernails dug into her palms. *This was it. This was the evidence she needed.*

"Who? Did you get a good look?"

"I tried to sneak up on them to get the license plate of the black car, but I tripped and crashed into the trunk. My cover was blown." Maddie's hands clenched into fists.

"It's okay."

"They gave chase. I collided with two guys, knocking them down. Despite hearing a scream, I kept running and didn't even stop to help them. I tried to return to the lake but got lost and ended up on the bluffs. But then he showed up offering to protect me, but it was a trap." Maddie covered her face. "It was so awful; I don't remember what happened, except everything went black. I told Dr. Madsen about the person I met on the bluffs. He said no one would believe me. I needed to keep quiet."

"I don't understand why he would say that?" Hunter said. "We should question him."

"No." Maddie got angry. "No. Don't."

"Why, Maddie?" Everly asked, watching her body language. Her face paled, and her hands were trembling. She was scared of someone.

"Why would the doctor tell you to keep what you saw secret unless...?" Everly closed her eyes and tried to play through the different scenarios. He could be right in trying to protect the Grimm Society. But the other reason seemed more plausible.

"You think the person you saw on the bluffs was the killer," Everly said.

Maddie's mouth dropped open, her eyes widened, and she inhaled.

A confirmation.

"And you recognized them," Everly added.

Maddie's eyes filled with tears, and she nodded.

"Why would you agree to come here then?" Everly asked.

Maddie's bloodshot eyes found Everly's, and her voice became a hoarse whisper. "He said I wouldn't be safe at school, that they would get me there. The only way to protect a secret... was to come here or take it to the grave."

CHAPTER 23

"Oh, Maddie." Everly's heart broke for the girl.

But no matter what, they tried. Maddie refused to say more or even name the person she saw on the bluff. They were trying to press Maddie for more information when they were interrupted by a beautiful girl in a painting smock.

"Hunter James Abernathy," the female called out in excitement.

Hunter grimaced but turned around and gave a big smile. "Hey, Kerrigan."

Kerrigan? Everly snapped up to look at the long-lost sister, the one who had gone overseas to work as a CEO of a fashion startup. Kerrigan Abernathy. She was just as tall as Hunter with similar green eyes. She wore an oversized white shirt dress with a tan belt and slip-on shoes. A matching headband pulled her slightly curly locks out of her face, and she wore a canvas smock with red and green paint on it, and there was a splash of green color on her nose.

"What are you doing here?" Kerrigan asked.

"Came to visit my favorite sister," Hunter teased, putting on the charm. He stood up and moved a few steps away from

221

Maddie. Everly followed, still holding the caramel Frappuccino.

"Don't let Holland hear you say that." Kerrigan waved her hand and then gave a curious look to Everly. "Who's this? You don't normally bring people to see me."

"This is Everly." Hunter stepped back and swept his hand to her.

"*The* Everly?" Kerrigan raised a blonde eyebrow. "The one you don't stop ta—"

Hunter made a play to tackle his sister, and she yelped and backed away. "Stop, truce." When she regained her composure, she wiped a hand on her apron and smeared more red paint on her fingers. "Oh, I got paint—"

She raised her hand to her face, and she began to tremble. Her face slackened, and she fell to her knees, reaching out for the floor, her hands searching for something or someone that was no longer there. "There's so much blood. I can't. I can't feel a pulse. Help!" Kerrigan started to scream.

Hunter reached for her. Grabbed her arms and pulled her back, wrapping her in an embrace.

"No, Kerrigan. It's okay. You're safe."

"No. No, no." Kerrigan shook her head. Reliving a nightmare that replayed in her mind alone. "Not Dean."

Kerrigan collapsed on the floor, sobbing. The orderly came over to help, but Kerrigan became violent, swinging at him with her fists. "Don't touch me. Please leave me alone. Who are you? Where's Kit? I need Kit!" She swung her hand and knocked the Frappuccino up into Everly's face. Caramel and whipped cream hit her head, slowly dripping down her T-shirt and flannel.

More orderlies came running, and Ms. Kim approached Hunter. The welcoming smile was gone. Her eyes narrowed in barely contained fury. "I think it's time you two leave now," she said.

"Okay." Hunter tapped Everly, who stood frozen with iced coffee running down her face, hair, and shirt.

The tap was all she needed to snap out of her shock. During the chaos of Kerrigan being sedated, they were escorted to the parking lot, and the doors were shut in their face. They went to the Jeep to get cleaned up.

"I don't understand," Everly said as she dug for more paper napkins from the glove compartment to wipe off the stain from her shirt. "Why is Kerrigan here?"

"I told you; this is where they put broken grievers."

"But Kerrigan, I never knew she was a griever. I've seen your family pictures of her and heard you and Holland talk on the phone with her. How long has she been here?"

"Going on almost two years," Hunter said. "And Holland doesn't know."

"What?"

"Promise me, Everly, that you won't tell Holland."

"What happened?"

"She was the first in our family to show signs of being a griever. She lost her omen in a reaping and has mentally deteriorated ever since."

"Is that who she was calling out to?"

"Yeah, Kit was a fox. He sacrificed himself for her. She tried to come home, but she wasn't quite the same. Muttering to herself, talking, seeing things that weren't there."

"The other name, Dean?"

Hunter pressed his hands to his mouth and sighed. "That was the day we all became grievers. Kerrigan was driving the car when she lost control, and we went off the bridge. Her boyfriend, Dean, was in the front seat and was killed. Holland and I were in the back. Holland doesn't remember the crash, so her griever abilities haven't kicked in. But one day, it will come flooding back, and she'll remember. Kerrigan was doing great at Gravemark. She was blossoming and even getting over Dean's death. Being bonded with an omen helped. Then her omen was killed, and the bond breaking triggered her. The Grimm Society stepped in and sent her here.

"My parents are among the few families that know of our school. My father wasn't pleased about sending her here, but he understands."

"Hunter, I'm so sorry."

"This is what happens to grievers. They don't put this in the manual." He pointed angrily at the Dorian Institute. He unscrewed an unopened water bottle out of the trunk, handing it to Everly so she could wipe off her sticky hands.

"I had no idea." Everly poured some of the water on a napkin and tried to wipe the stickiness from her hands but was only partially successful.

"Now you know everything. Why I didn't want you to come here. I wanted to protect you."

Everly nodded. "But you can't protect me. No one can."

"I know." Hunter took back the water bottle.

Everly bit her lip and looked back at the Dorian Institute. She needed to get that name from Maddie.

Hunter's phone rang, and he didn't look happy when he looked at the caller's ID.

"Aimee, again?" Everly asked.

"I wish." He hit the Answer button and put the phone up to his ear. "Yeah, I'm here visiting Kerrigan. They called you. I figured they would. No. I won't. Oh, really?"

The conversation had to have been between Hunter and his father, and it didn't sound good.

"Fine!" He hung up and, in frustration, kicked the rubber of his tire. "The facility called my father. He has banned all visitors. Even me. That's it. I'm sorry we didn't get the answers you were looking for."

Everly reached out, placing a hand on his shoulder to comfort him. "If it weren't for you, I wouldn't have even known where Maddie was—much less get in to see her. Thank you for your help. I'm just sorry you won't be able to come and visit Kerrigan anymore."

Hunter turned to face her, his eyes meeting hers with such intensity, that it took her breath away. Studying her, his face softened, and he opened his mouth to speak. "Everl—"

A notification on her phone interrupted him. She turned the screen over and gasped.

"Hunter," she breathed out his name and turned the phone for him to see the photo of them embracing on the mountain-side. "It's us."

CHAPTER 24

"How is this possible?" Everly breathed out, her hands trembling in fear.

Hunter took the phone from her with shaking hands. "I don't know."

It was a digital photo of the two of them, but someone scratched out Everly's face in red.

"Who would do this?" Everly spoke aloud again. "Who followed us? What do they want?"

"Can I buy a vowel?" Hunter asked in frustration.

She didn't say the other part that scared her. It meant someone had followed them and taken a photo while Everly had a breakdown on the mountain trail. From the photo's angle, it looked like they were in a lover's embrace, and she could see how it would give anyone the wrong idea.

"Maybe it was a prank?" Hunter said, watching the surrounding woods warily as he slammed the trunk.

"Could be, it was a text from a blocked number."

Maybe power it down to be safe," he said. Hunter held the button, swiped it, and handed it back to her.

"Is this photo... a warning—" Everly started.

"Relax, you're safe," Hunter said. "Nothing's going to

happen to you while I'm here." He reached out, touched her shoulder, and gently squeezed it. "I promise."

"Is this what being a part of the Grimm Society is like?" Everly asked, feeling the paranoia set in. "Stalkers, monsters, and secrets? And if you're ashamed of one, you lock it away and throw away the key."

"We do it to protect those we love," Hunter reminded her. Everyone has a secret. I bet you have a secret you haven't told anyone because it would hurt someone you care about." His voice dropped low, and he leaned against the back of his Jeep, observing her.

She looked into his green eyes and could almost see her feelings reflected there. But it was her imagination. Her eyes flickered to his lips, and then she glanced away, breaking the tension between them.

"Yes," she breathed out.

"Then you're just like the rest of us," Hunter said, and he stepped away.

When he did, she could feel the distance rip them apart. As two halves of Velcro ripped apart—it hurt. He opened the passenger door for her, and she got in and slammed the door harder than she meant to. *Why did first love hurt this much?*

He put the Jeep into Reverse, pulled out of the parking spot, and drove down the mountain pass. Despite Hunter's reassurance, an uneasy feeling settled in, and her worried thoughts filled the cabin. The silence of unsaid words between them became overpowering.

As the trees zoomed by, it almost made her fall into a hypnotic state.

Hunter pulled over at a truck stop. "Maybe you should go get changed." He gestured to her flannel and T-shirt with a brown coffee stain on the front. "This one has a bathroom." He got out of the Jeep, went to the trunk, unzipped his duffel, and pulled out an oversized Gravemark lacrosse shirt. "Here. It's better than nothing."

"Thanks." Everly gingerly took the shirt and headed inside the truck stop.

When the door opened, there was a jingle, and she immediately looked up at the security mirrors to see who else was in the building. Three others were perusing the food and snack aisles. One was in the walk-in cooler, and a woman and child were putting toppings on a hot dog. She made a beeline for the hall with the showers and restrooms.

Everly changed and tried to wipe the whipped cream residue out of her hair with wet paper towels. Everly stared at her face in the mirror. There were slight circles under her eyes; her face seemed pale, probably from stress over the last few weeks. She pinched her cheeks, and blood rushed to them, giving them a faint pink color. She flipped her head down and dried her strawberry blonde locks the best she could with the hand dryer.

Her coffee-stained shirt was put in a plastic bag she got from the truck station, and Hunter's shirt, which had his faint scent, fell past her hips. It was a weird feeling to wear his shirt, which should have been reserved for his girlfriend. Everly stopped on the way out and bought food for the trip back: turkey sandwiches, two glasses of water, chips, and pink frosted donuts for dessert.

As she headed out to the car and opened the door, she was surprised to see that Hunter had reclined his driver's seat and was fast asleep.

She closed the door softly and watched him. The sun brushed against his tan cheeks, making them appear even more golden. His lashes were dark and long, and his lips—

Everly turned away, unable to control the beating in her heart. She wouldn't betray Holland. She couldn't become that girl. She closed her eyes and swallowed, imagining the confrontation of Holland yelling at her. "You traitor, you were only friends with me because of my brother! I hate you!"

It was a good hour before Hunter woke up. Everly didn't have the heart to wake him knowing that he had driven the whole trip.

"Sorry," he said sleepily. He looked at his watch. "We can make it back before dark if we get going."

"All right," Everly said softly. She handed him a turkey sandwich.

"You're quiet," Hunter said.

"Contemplative," Everly sighed, leaning her chin against her fist as she watched the trees pass by.

"About what?" He dug into his bag of chips and popped them in his mouth.

"Your sister, school, this grimm that keeps eluding the grievers. I think..." Everly sighed and thumped her head against the seat headrest. "I don't know what I think."

"Let it out," Hunter encouraged. "You always need to talk things through. I'll be your sounding board."

"What did you find when investigating the hikers' murders?" she asked. "Walk me through the griever side of the case."

"I don't know much; it wasn't my team that was assigned it. Victims were torn apart, hard to recognize the species of animal that did it," he repeated. "But we never get the first shot at the evidence. No one lets teens around the crime scene. But your dad would loop us in, even though it could have cost him his job. He sent us evidence files and photos. Except since he passed, we're in the dark."

She never knew how much her dad did and tried to help the grievers even though he was technically blind.

"The police ruled the first attack as death by wild animals, so we didn't investigate. That's the one your dad was in charge of... when he...." Hunter swallowed and moved on. "The second one, Rocky Cordon, alerted us to a serial and came across as a possible grimm. But we have nothing to go on. No crime scene photos. All we can do is try to hunt a far enough distance away to not interfere with the investigation or become a nuisance."

Everly nodded. She could only imagine what the Misty Creek PD would think if every time there was a dead body, many students in Gravemark uniforms kept showing up to stalk the scene. When she had attended Misty Creek High, she had heard the creepy rumors about Gravemark. One student swore they heard howling coming from the grounds every full moon. Another said they looked into the eyes of a teacher and felt like they were bewitched.

She rubbed her eyes. "My dad was working on the case... right before he went into the hospital. He said, 'It's grimm.' At first, I thought he meant it was horrible. But if he found some-thing... a clue that it's not a human. I think we have to follow that lead."

"Now, remember, your dad was working blind. He didn't have his sight."

"Yeah, I know, but he was still a griever, and you don't lose your instincts. I was raised to trust my gut, and I feel the Misty Creek PD got it wrong."

"Based on..."

"Based on what I saw that night."

"But we've investigated each location where the attacks happened and got nothing. The rain keeps washing away all the physical evidence, even the tracks. It's like the attacker only strikes if there is guaranteed rain."

His phone rang again, and it was Aimee. This time, he answered. Everly tried to ignore the conversation between them. Lots of reassuring promises, like: "*Miss you. I can't wait to see you. Be back soon.*" The sweet nothings hit Everly hard. Everly bumped her head against the window and sighed. She let the puff of air heat the window and let it steam up on the inside of the glass.

A few minutes later, they pulled into the school parking lot. It was late evening again, and she was getting hungry. She wasn't just hungry, though; she was confused.

Hunter had barely parked when Everly was out of the car, looking up at the school.

"I know that look. What's wrong?" he asked.

"We missed something."

"What do you mean?" His brows furrowed in question as he came around the Jeep to meet her.

"I think I need to speak with Nina and see if I can get a hold of the case files."

"What now?" Hunter moved to get in the car again, but Everly shook her head. "No, it's too late. Tomorrow after school."

"What time? I'll come with—" The phone went off again. He answered it, and Everly rolled her eyes when she heard Aimee's voice over the line.

"Where are you?" Aimee demanded loudly from the phone.

"I'm here, but—"

Everly started her car and drove away, leaving Hunter to deal with his girl problems. She had a much bigger grimm to catch.

CHAPTER 25

"You know this is a highly unusual request?" Nina said, sitting behind the receptionist's desk in the Misty Creek PD. She leaned forward and whispered, "I just can't let anyone see active case files."

Everly was wearing her school uniform and sunglasses, having come here after her last Friday study block, and Ian was not answering her texts or phone calls. She didn't think going to talk to the police would be considered doing anything stupid.

"Just the photos," Everly said. "You don't have to show me anything gory or bloody. I want to take a look at the crime scene photos."

"What do you hope to see?" she asked.

"I don't know. Something that would put my mind at ease. This was the last case my dad was working on when he passed. And I need closure."

"I could lose my job for this," Nina whispered.

"You won't because I'm not going to say anything, and you're not going to say anything. Like the fact that I was within a quarter mile of that last attack, and I may have seen something that will help the police out."

"Everly." Nina's voice squeaked. "You didn't?"

"Something attacked my car." She pointed out the front of the station through the glass toward her hood.

Nina stood up and gasped when she saw the scratches. "Maybe it will help find this cougar. So are you going to help me or not?"

"This is so going to get me fired," Nina said.

"Not if we play this the way I say."

"Fine." She stood up and straightened the papers on her desk. "Give me a few moments. Who do you want?"

Everly thought for a few moments. "Give me Stevens."

Everly went into interrogation room one. She had been in here enough with her dad as a kid. It wasn't at all scary like on some of the TV shows. There was a metal table and two wooden chairs, and the walls were a boring beige, but there was a water cooler in the corner of the room with disposable cone cups.

Everly purposely took the chair closest to the door, with her back facing the only entrance. The seat the interrogator usually took. She would use every tactic she had to get the upper hand.

Stevens entered the room, and Everly stood up, clutching her keys.

"I'm so glad it's you." She played the part of a damsel in distress.

She had chosen Officer Stevens because he was the youngest on the force. He wasn't half bad to look at with sandy hair and those golden eyes that could melt a girl. He also idolized her father, so she thought he would be the easiest to manipulate, and it didn't hurt to flirt with him.

Stevens blushed slightly, pulled out his notepad, and clicked his pen to take notes. She saw that he had the case files under his pad, which she told Nina to hand him right before he came for the interview. She bet he didn't even know what files they were.

Everly set her keys on the table, and his eyes automatically went to the pink pepper spray container and the Gravemark key chain. The corner of his mouth lifted into a knowing smirk.

"Always have to be prepared." Everly shrugged. "Dad taught me that."

Stevens nodded. "Nina says you came to report vandalism on your car while at the bluffs a few nights ago?"

"Yes."

"Why didn't you come to report it earlier?"

Drat! It was time to turn on the waterworks.

First, she tried to think of her father but was mentally exhausted, and her tears dried up. She switched to an old technique that worked on her old school nurse. Everly stared unblinking at the sunlight streaming through the window over Stevens's right shoulder until her eyes burned and glazed over with tears of pain. She dipped her head, letting the carefully built-up crocodile tears fall, before blinking rapidly and looking up pitifully into Stevens's face. She let her bottom lip quiver ever so slightly.

"Because I was scared that Birdie would get mad at me for being at a party on a school night. She's terrifying, and then look at the damage to my car."

Everly wiped her eyes for effect. She knew she would most certainly get caught. Only an idiot would believe the lies she was spewing forth like confetti at a baby gender reveal party, but sometimes you have to gamble with everything you got, especially when the stakes were this high.

"What party? Who organized it?" Stevens leaned forward, his golden eyes widening. Everly reached forward and pulled a tissue from a box on the table.

She covered her mouth as she mumbled and shook her head, "I *can't* say."

Cast the line, Everly thought.

Stevens blinked in confusion, sitting back in her chair, stunned. "What do you mean, 'you can't say'?"

In Everly's mind, she could see the imaginary red-and-white fishing bobber floating along the still waters, and Stevens, the wide-mouthed catfish, rising from the murky bottom to inspect the disturbance of his mundane police ticket life.

"I don't want to get them in trouble. It's a pretty influential family."

He frowned and clicked his pen again. "Did you see what animal damaged your car?"

Everly's mind flashed back to the grimm, the rain jacket, the long-clawed fingers. She shivered.

"I didn't see an animal exactly." She decided to go with a half-truth.

"Was there anyone else on the bluffs with you that night?"

Now, I was going to have to lie to protect a griever. Oh, she was going to H-E-double-hockey-sticks.

"No."

There was a knock on the door, and Stevens looked up as Nina peeked in. "Stevens, there's a call for you on line one."

"I'm busy, Nina." Stevens wrote in his notebook. "What time were you there?"

"It's your mother."

Stevens's face paled, and he practically jumped up from the table. "Excuse me, Everly," he said, rushing for the door.

Nina held it open and gave her a wink. "You have two minutes." She closed the door.

Everly moved the notepad, opened the files, and looked at the photos, trying to let her eyes see the clues. If Hunter was right and none of the grievers could access the evidence, they were hunting blind. She flipped the first file open.

There was a close-up of an arm with long, deep scratches across the wrist. From teeth? Claws? She moved the photo to the back and took in the crime scene markers. A yellow tent card was placed near the first tracks beside the body. A picture next to an evidence ruler of a footprint marked a size ten woman's hiking boot print—nothing else surrounded her body.

That didn't mean anything; the victim was a hiker, which could be her print. There wasn't anything else that stood out. Except the file felt very light. A medical report said she died of blood loss due to a severed carotid artery.

Everly had to take a few deep breaths; this was more detailed than she expected. She used her phone to snap pictures of each evidence file before opening up the second file and the next victim. Overall, the photos were of the scene; not much was left as it was dark and raining again. This was Rocky Cordon, murdered similarly, but he died wearing a suit and tie —not clothes one would wear to hike.

There wasn't anything that was jumping out at her. No glimmer of a grimm, no major clue was shifting or revealing itself to her in the photos. Maybe this wasn't a grimm at all, but a real cougar.

She opened the latest file. The unidentified victim was found about six hundred yards from the lake. Male. John Doe. Heavy lacerations to the face. Unrecognizable.

She lifted the paper to look at the photo underneath and gasped. It was only a photo of the victim's chest, but it was enough. She recognized that Hawaiian shirt and the red Solo cup photographed in the next crime scene photo.

Her mouth went dry, and she quickly closed all the files and tried to stack them as they were. The pen rolled off to the side, and she moved it back to its original position as Stevens entered the interrogation room.

"So sorry, Everly." Stevens didn't seem happy. He sat back down, ran his hands through his hair, and reached for his pen. "We were talking about the damage to your car?"

"The last victim." Everly struggled to get the words out.

"What about him?"

"He hasn't been identified yet... correct?"

Stevens's brows furrowed. "That's correct."

"I know..." She took another deep breath. "I know who it is." She touched the bottom file folder gingerly, her hand trembling slightly.

"You looked in my files?" He pulled them toward him.

"Yes, I'm sorry, but... I thought you should know. In case, his family. I mean, his grandmother..." She couldn't breathe. She needed to get out of there. Everly pushed the chair back, and it scraped across the floor.

"Everly?" Stevens stood up.

"I'm sorry, I can't do this." She brushed her hand across her forehead; she was overheating. "The victim's name is Eric Mulligan, twenty-one, works at the local Kwik Mart."

"How do you know?"

"I recognize this Hawaiian shirt." She backed away and went for the door. "Please, excuse me. I need some air." Everly left the police station in a hurry.

CHAPTER 26

EVERLY DIDN'T GO BACK TO GRAVEMARK; SHE WALKED around downtown. She now understood why Holland and Hunter retreated home whenever they could. It was an escape from the reality of what they faced. And Holland's friendship with her didn't depend on hunting grimms. It was just movies, gossip, boys—things every teenage girl wanted to discuss.

She needed someone like that to help her when she was overwhelmed.

Everly wished she could go back, rewind time before she knew about the Grimm Society, and forget all the death. Everly walked into the Kwik Mart on autopilot, putting odd items in her basket. Chewy candy, Ho Hos, chocolate. Yes. Lots of chocolate. She had intended to go home, slip into a sugar coma, and watch a mystery. No, something silly. Maybe a rom-com. Anything to distract her.

As she walked the aisle, she couldn't help but picture the crime scene photos. What was wrong with her? Yes, she needed some air after discovering the identity of the last victim, but once that shock wore off, there was a pressing need to solve his murder. Because now it was personal.

What was the missing link? When she went to the

checkout to pay, her mind couldn't help but wander. Is this why she found herself shopping here? Did she subconsciously come here to see the common thread?

What did Shelly Miller, Rocky Cordon, and Eric Mulligan have in common?

"That will be fifteen twenty-three," the cashier said, a young man with too much aftershave and a name badge that read Roy. He looked to be the same age as Eric, and she even noticed that he had a red store cap on.

Everly handed him cash but continued to stare at Roy. Maddie said that she ran into two boys. One had a red cap. Everly was good at gambling.

"Here's your change," Roy said in a monotone voice.

"Do you know Eric Mulligan?" Everly flashed him a sweet smile.

Roy looked up from his register in surprise, and that's when she saw his unibrow that desperately needed plucking.

"Yeah, we hang out sometimes."

"Where?" Everly dropped a quarter on the counter and took one of the quarter suckers out of the plastic tub by the register. Peeling off the wrapper, she put it into her mouth and leaned on the counter as if interested in him. She was making sure to curl her hair around a finger.

Roy's mouth dropped open before he answered. "Places."

"Anywhere cool? Or is it a secret?"

"We had a place where we liked to go." Roy nodded, brushing his polo to try and straighten it. "To hang and do stuff."

"What kind of stuff?" Everly toyed with the lollipop.

"Party. Drink beer. We make our own."

"Cool, I like partying and stuff." Everly tried to keep her face to one of interest, but she secretly wanted to barf at her attempt at flirting. "You should take me sometime."

His face paled, and he backed up, bumping into the register. "No, we don't go there anymore. It's... I can't...." Roy was terrified. "We don't go there anymore," he stated firmly.

"Where was it?"

Roy shook his head. Everly had enough of being the nice girl. She slammed her palms on the counter, and the bowl of lollipops shook. "Look, Roy. I know that you and Eric tapped your beer, took it to a party at the lake, and gave it to minors." She was lying; she didn't know Roy was involved. But she knew there was no way Eric made his way to the party alone with a keg. Just like Kat admitted to having Terrell carry it for her, it was a two-person job.

"How did you know—"

Everly took her wallet out, quickly flashed her student ID card, and tucked it away. "I'm investigating what happened that night. You know as well as I do. What really happened to Eric?"

Roy immediately started to bawl. He keeled over and wept like a baby. "I'm so sorry. I don't know what happened. We brought the keg to some old cabin we used to brew booze. Some terrified girl bowled us over, and then I heard some animals busting through the woods. I was out of there like I rolled a plus twenty for dexterity. I thought Eric was right behind me, but then he wasn't, and I was too scared to go back."

Roy reached for Everly's sleeve. "His screams. I can still hear them."

"Why didn't you notify the police?"

"Are you crazy? You said it yourself; we were serving illegal booze to minors and trespassing. I just thought Eric got lost and would eventually show up for work in a few days."

Everly reached for the Misty Creek map in the acrylic display. She dropped it before Roy and took a pen from the plastic register cup.

"Circle it, Roy. Where is this cabin?"

His hands shook as he gripped the pen, opened the map, and circled a spot near the bluffs. It was within a mile of the lakefront. Everly took a different color pen and put an X where each of the other victims were found.

There was a pattern.

"Thank you for your cooperation, Roy." Everly dropped the sucker in the garbage can on her way out the door.

All the attacks happened near Hollow Lake or the bluff.

She reached into her jacket and pulled out her cell phone to call reinforcements.

———

"Here." Everly put the map on the table and stabbed her finger at the circle. "This is the cabin where Eric and Roy used to sneak in and party."

She convinced everyone to come and meet at her house on Saturday since Summer usually went shopping at all the farmers' markets. It was more people than she'd ever had at her home. The first person she had called was Holland, who brought Kat along. Then because he was her mentor, the last person she called was Ian. He wouldn't return her calls and didn't even pick up till this morning. He sounded like he had spent the previous two nights at a rave. His voice was gravelly, and even this morning, his eyes were bloodshot with dark rings under them.

Thankfully, Summer was out of the house, and Birdie didn't mind the swarm of students. She was having fun, making tea and serving biscuits, and eavesdropping.

"Are you sure we can talk around her?" Kat asked suspiciously.

"Yeah, she's one of us," Everly answered.

Kat looked skeptically at Birdie as if she didn't believe that the woman with the silk shawl could ever have been a griever. But she took the offered tea and began to load it with sugar cubes, even popping one in her mouth to suck on gleefully.

"It's so nice to be solving crimes again," Birdie sighed, pushing the sugar bowl out of Kat's reach.

Ian stood by the fridge, leaning against the counter, looking out of sorts in the homey kitchen, sipping his flask, and staying quite far from them. His eyes kept glancing over to Birdie's solarium and her exotic plants.

Everly moved to stand by him.

"Great griever team you put together," he whispered. "It's like the island of misfit toys. A squint, sib, newbie, and granny into deadly plants." He pointed with his chin to the plant with purple berries. "Is that nightshade I see over there?" His eyebrows rose in surprise. "And wolfsbane?"

"That's why you're here." Everly tapped him in the chest.

"What, to take the fall when you screw up? I already told you what I thought about cleaning up your messes." Ian sighed and crossed his feet.

"No, to ensure I do it right," Everly said. "Thanks for coming. It must have been some rager you went to. You look"—she wrinkled her lips—"like death."

"This wasn't a party for the faint-hearted. You'd blush at all the language and music we listen to. Trust me." Ian took another sip. "Why'd you assemble this team anyway?" He looked around her kitchen and reached over to pick up a cookie.

Great. Ian seemed hungover, and he had the munchies.

"I interviewed Maddie Eerie. She said she overheard someone discussing the attacks. I think Eric was just in the wrong place at the wrong time. So I want us to investigate if there is any connection between the victims."

"Wouldn't the police have already done that?" Holland asked.

"Not if they're convinced it's a wild animal. They would have no reason to look for a motive," Everly said, pushing her laptop in front of Kat. "So that's where Kat comes in."

"Oh, uh." Kat seemed nervous opening the laptop case. Reaching for the mouse, she pushed it around the table and struggled to get it to the search bar. She squinted and began to finger-type one by one. "How do you spell the victim's names?"

Holland seemed completely aghast as Kat painstakingly typed out each name on the keyboard. She leaned over to whisper to Everly, "Maybe she's one of those people who only knows how to text on a cell phone." Holland danced her thumbs midair, pretending to text.

"I didn't think of that."

Holland pulled the laptop away from Kat. "I got it. At least I'm good at something." Holland searched for the names Shelly Miller and Rocky Cordon and got no combined hits. "Oh, Rocky Cordon, Esq. He's a fancy lawyer for—the same firm my dad works for, H. C. Andersons. I wonder if this has anything to do with the court case against the city?"

"What court case?" Everly asked.

Holland opened the state's circuit court access portal and typed in Shelly Miller and the county. A whole list of court cases popped up.

"Whoa! Look at this. Shelly was suing the City of Misty Creek for a pretty hefty sum regarding an aggravated assault with a city employee, and Rocky Cordon is her lawyer."

"So they are connected," Ian said. "I can't believe that you know how to access this."

"I was begging my dad for more allowance a few weeks ago and saw him access this website when looking up court cases.

It's a public portal." She shrugged. "No big deal if you know where to go."

"Does it say anything else?"

"When does it go to trial?" Everly asked.

"Next week. That's when each side will present their witnesses on the day of testimony. We don't even have access to that."

"What about Eric Mulligan?" Ian asked.

"Just wrong place, wrong time. We need to focus on our strongest connections. Shelly and Rocky. But it's a weak link. A lot of people in our town know one another. We need to gather evidence that they were specifically targeted."

"How?" Ian asked.

"I think we need to go here." Everly pointed to the map and the area that Roy had circled. "We know how the victims are connected, but now we must figure out who is behind them. We need to go to the cabin."

"I need to change my shoes!" Holland grinned, getting up and stretching. "I can't ruin my Gucci sneakers!" She grabbed her keys and headed out the kitchen door.

Kat continued to steal sugar cubes.

Ian had left the kitchen and walked down the hall, staring at the family portraits. His hands were shoved in his pockets, and he seemed solemn. That's when she remembered Ian didn't have a family. He was a griever orphan—a foundling.

Ian seemed fixated on a particular photo. It was one of her dad's earlier photos of him and his buddies fishing. She didn't know it then, but they were probably other grievers. Everyone was a lot younger, more clean-cut, and had big grins. Ian was focused on someone in the group.

"Who is it?" she asked.

Ian pointed to the photo and tapped the young man beside

her dad. He was the second tallest in the group, with a serious face that seemed familiar.

"It's my dad." He struggled to get the word "dad" out.

"I didn't know our parents knew each other."

"I didn't know either. I didn't have many photos of him. This is one of the first ones I've seen." His voice got slightly choked up, but he cleared his throat and moved away. He refused to look at any more photos. He marched back to the kitchen and took his place by the fridge as he eyed the solarium.

Holland returned from her car, having ditched her designer sneakers for designer boots.

"Hey, Alfred," Everly addressed Kat. "Do you want to navigate us there with your phone?"

Kat looked at her blankly, not catching the joke. "I forgot my phone. But I can get you there."

They piled into Ian's Bronco. Holland and Everly were in the back while Kat got in the front. The mood shifted, and everyone became silent and contemplative as they headed into the national park.

"Turn left in three hundred feet. There's a park access road up ahead," Kat directed without looking at any maps.

"There's not a road here," Ian argued.

"There is. Trust me," Kat said.

Ian almost missed the turnoff; it was overgrown, but he followed the trail.

Holland leaned over the front bench seat and looked over at Ian. "So, um. Is anyone else worried that we'll find a big, bad scary thing at the end of this scavenger hunt?"

His cold eyes met hers, and she retreated into the back.

Then, under her breath, she muttered, "No, just me? Okay. Cool."

Ian slowed, and the car came to a stop when the road dead-ended. "Looks like we will go on foot from here."

They piled out of the Bronco and headed to the back, where he dropped the tailgate and revealed the collection of weapons.

"Choose your weapon," Ian said proudly. He handed Kat the never blade, and she avoided it, grabbing instead for a solid wood baseball bat. Holland reached for a sword, but Ian blocked it with his hand, giving her a raised eyebrow in question.

Holland's mask of sweetness disappeared. She grabbed the sword from the truck bed, unsheathed it, swinging it in the air with ease.

"Whoa," Everly gasped, seeing the talent with which she brandished the weapon.

"I'm an Abernathy, first in my class at the all-girls fencing championship. Despite what people say, I do have some skills." She made a face at Ian.

Everly looked over the weapons—swords, knives, and clubs—and hesitated.

"Here." Ian handed her a staff. "You seemed to handle yourself well with martial arts weapons."

Everly thanked him.

"Let's move out." Ian led the way, and they spread out, taking the woods.

Everly and her team searched as they walked. She was looking through the brush, checking for broken branches and bent blades of grass or plants. Anything to show something having passed this way. The ground opened up before her, and a path became visible. Everly followed the path, her eyes searching.

"Hey," Kat whispered, pointing toward a dense area of trees. Standing just outside the trees was a cabin.

"It's an old ranger station," Holland said. Her boots made

little noise as she walked across the deck and looked in through the window. She waved to everyone. "It's empty."

Ian hung back as Holland tried the handle. "It's locked."

"Not for long." Everly dropped to her knees and pulled her lockpick kit out of her crossbody. She eyed the keyhole and grabbed the appropriate tension wrench and a pick.

"I guess we should thank your dad for all those training games." Holland kneeled and watched wide-eyed as Everly inserted the wrench and focused on getting the pick to the last pin. It only took her about thirty seconds before they heard a click as she unlocked the door.

"They don't seem so stupid now, do they?" Everly teased as she pushed the door open. It swung inward to reveal a dark one-room cabin. There was a cot on the far wall, with a sleeping bag and the remains of empty cans of food and a portable stove, a boiling pot, and siphon tubes—everything for a home distillery.

"Someone was living here." Holland moved to pick up the can and give it a cursory sniff.

"Maybe it was a homeless person," Ian said from the doorway. He kept his eyes focused on the surrounding area.

"Or troubled teens," Holland said. When they explored the cabin, they came up empty. "Let's check around back."

Holland led the way as they walked around the back side of the cabin and came to an underground cellar. She ground to a halt and didn't budge. "Nope, not going anywhere near that. Last time I went into a cellar, a boggart tossed his head at me."

"Baby." Kat reached the door first and pulled the right side open; the door fell backward and hit the ground with a thud.

Holland moved toward the opening to peer in. Kat moved to her side, grabbed her arm, and yelled, "Boo!" making Holland scream.

"Not funny, Kat." Holland clutched her heart. A musty

scent came from below, and she pulled out a mini flashlight and illuminated the stairs. "Shall we play rock paper scissors?"

"Make the guy go into the deep dark pit." Kat pointed toward Ian, the farthest from the cellar opening.

Ian's face had lost all its coloring. He seemed pale, scared. "It smells wrong. Can you smell it?"

"I don't smell anything," Holland added. "Maybe it's the alcohol."

Everly noticed the change in him, so she decided to take the lead. "I'll go." She grabbed the flashlight from Holland and went down the stairs first. The halo of light guided her down each rickety step. When she got to the bottom, the floor was dirt, and the room was barely half the size of the cabin above.

When it seemed like Everly wasn't immediately eaten by a boggart, Kat came down second.

"Whoa!" she breathed as Everly's flashlight flickered across something metal. "What was kept in that?"

It was a giant animal cage with heavy-duty bars and a mega door. There were paw prints along the dirt floor leading to the cell. The only area in the basement with a cement floor was where the cage was bolted.

"Whatever it was, it was big," Everly said.

"Mountain lion?" Kat asked, pointing to the prints.

Everly leaned down and looked at the tracks. "No, big cats have retractable claws, so there would be no claw marks around the pads. See this"—Everly pointed to the apparent claw marks —"means canine, probably wolf."

"So someone kept a wolf here?" Kat lifted her hand to her chin and began to process everything. "What would the motive be? Poachers? Or something else."

"And where is this big, bad wolf now?" Holland asked from the stairs, unwilling to come into the earthy basement. "Did it go to Grandma's house? Where's the owner? I don't want to stick around much longer in case either one comes back."

Everly was not eager to leave. She felt like she was close. "Any tire tracks?" she asked. "Check for recent treads."

"I'll check, but we've had many rain showers lately. But Everly, nothing here is saying grimm. Yes, wild animal poaching, but I don't know about grimm." Holland bounded back up the stairs.

Kat started to go up the stairs, but Everly stayed where she was, her gut telling her something wasn't right.

Everly touched the bars and the scratches along the surface.

"I wonder." Everly reached into her purse and pulled out her wallet. She opened the magnetic closure and let it brush against the metal. It slid right past. She tried a few more times, and it wouldn't magnetize.

"What are you doing?" Kat asked.

"Iron and steel have magnetic properties," Everly said. "This doesn't. There are only a few types of metal that aren't magnetic." She began to list them off. "Copper, gold, lead, titanium—"

"Silver," Kat answered.

"Silver," Everly repeated. "But do you know how much making a cage this big out of silver would cost?"

"A lot?" Kat answered.

"More than a mere poacher could afford." Everly leaned down and scraped some of the silver off the pole. "I'll test it back at school."

Kat stood there awkwardly for a few minutes. She didn't seem as obsessed with her phone as usual. "Where's your phone?" Everly asked.

"I left it at school." Kat bounced on her heels.

Everly's eyes narrowed suspiciously. There was something

not quite right about Kat, and not just Kat. Other people had been acting out of sorts lately.

"Can you go get Ian?" Everly suggested.

"Oh, yeah. I'll do that." Kat turned and headed back up the stairs.

Everly waited, and when she was alone, she stepped inside the cage and leaned down to brush dirt to the side. She uncovered a piece of torn green fabric. She turned it over and saw the edge of a green-and-gold emblem patch and another dark blot on it. Blood maybe? The Gravemark school crest. Her blood went ice-cold.

"What is this doing here?" she whispered under her breath.

She pulled out her phone and started taking pictures.

"Did you find something?" Ian asked from the bottom of the stairs.

Everly carefully tucked the cloth into her bag as she pulled out a random business card. "Just wanting to get a picture of these prints and need a reference." She placed a business card next to the print, lifted her phone, and took a few shots.

"You really are the daughter of a detective." Ian seemed impressed.

"Yeah, well, I'm not an expert, but these look bigger than a normal wolf print." She picked up the business card. "And this cage. I'm pretty sure it's made of silver." Everly watched Ian, but he didn't seem surprised at her announcement of a silver cage. He just seemed nauseous. "Are you okay? You seem a little out of it. You're pale, and you're sweating."

Ian ran his hand over the back of his neck. "I don't like to talk about it, but I have an irrational fear of small spaces, and this cabin only has one exit, and this basement is terrifying to me. It smells wrong... I don't know." He gave an unconscious shudder. "Can we go upstairs, please?"

"Sure," Everly said, slipping her wallet into her crossbody bag. As she came up the stairs, she had to wait for her eyes to adjust to the light.

"Well, that was an absolute waste." Holland stretched and raised her arms above her head. "Who's hungry?"

Kat raised her hand. "I want ice cream."

Everly grew quiet. Crawling into the back seat of the Bronco, she tossed her bag to the side. She worried at her thumbnail. What did a secret cabin, silver cage, wolf prints, and Gravemark uniform mean? Nothing good. Not only that, but it meant the Grimm Society could be behind the attacks, and they were covering it up.

"Can I borrow your hand sanitizer?" Holland reached into Everly's crossbody bag before Everly could stop her. Her eyes went wide as she pulled out a scrap of fabric. "Ew, what is this?"

"It's nothing." Everly snatched it back before she saw the gold emblem, tucking it into her bag.

"Was that blood?" Holland's voice got higher pitched. "That looked like blood. Did you find that in the cabin?"

"Holland," Everly hissed and waved her hands at Holland to be quiet. "Hush."

"Oh!" Her eyes widened, and then she caught Everly's hints. "Never mind."

The damage had been done. Everly looked up and saw Ian's cold blue eyes watching her.

CHAPTER 27

Sunday morning rolled around, and the sky was clear, unlike Everly's clouded mind. After church, Birdie, Everly, and Summer headed to the local diner Bake n Eggs, which had more pages on its menu than their church hymnal. Summer was ranting about that morning's service and how they wouldn't allow her to bring in and play her tambourine.

"It's because you were throwing off the rhythm," Birdie chastised her daughter, who lounged across from her in the red diner booth. "It was four, four times, and you played a three-count waltz."

Summer's mouth opened to argue, and Birdie reached over and shoved a dinner roll between her lips, silencing her for a few seconds.

Everly tried to hide her smirk behind the menu.

Summer bit off the end of the roll and chewed. Then proceeded to grumble about the menu. "I don't know what to order."

"Just get eggs," Birdie muttered. "Plus, you always order eggs."

"But not today. Today may be a French toast day." Summer waved her hand, the bangles jangling together on her wrist.

"It's not." Birdie looked at Everly and mouthed, "She's going to order eggs."

"What is shakshouka?" Summer asked, trying to pronounce the Mediterranean dish.

"Tomatoes and... *eggs*," Birdie answered.

Everly sipped her water and looked out the window next to their booth. It was on the corner of the main street in downtown Misty Creek and had a good view of the town square, which included a bookstore, internet cafe, pharmacy, general store, antique store, and numerous other gift shops.

After a few more indifferent arguments, Summer ordered eggs and bacon, much to Everly's amusement. Everly had just started eating when she saw a familiar person walk past the window just outside and head through the diner's front doors.

Ian Holmes.

He was seated a few booths down from Everly and her family. When he got a menu, he pulled out his phone and looked down, not noticing Everly.

Lacie Duvall entered the diner a few moments later, her head craning as if looking for someone. This seemed like somewhere other than the place an upscale rich girl would ever visit. When Lacie spotted Ian, her mouth tensed, and she moved to slide into the bench seat across from him. Her back faced Everly. Everly's fork hung in the air, her eggs getting cold as she became enthralled by their body language. Lacie was upset, her hands flying to punctuate each word. Ian crossed his arms and leaned forward. His mouth moved, and Lacie seemed to calm down, looking around her in alarm as if forgetting their very public setting.

"Do you need ketchup?" her aunt asked, setting a bottle in front of Everly.

"Shh!" She waved at her as she stared at the drama unfolding. Lacie and Ian were arguing, and she pulled out her phone.

He shook his head, leaning away from her. Whatever they were discussing, it didn't seem like they were on a date or very happy.

Summer brought out the dreaded pocket-size tambourine to prove that she could indeed keep a beat and, in doing so, knocked her water glass all over Everly.

A loud clatter followed as the glass hit the table. Everly gasped as the ice water hit her lap, followed by the ignorant remarks that flew out of Birdie's mouth. "Put that tambourine away, or I will burn it."

Everly lost all anonymity as every head turned to watch the drama unfold and Summer and Everly had to file out of the red leather booth. A server came and brought a towel to clean up the seat. Birdie dove into Everly's plate to save the bacon as her eggs became a floating island among water. But "saving" meant putting the bacon into her own mouth.

Everly stood in the aisle in the middle of the diner, her shirt and pants soaked clean through, looking like she had an accident. She glanced down the row, and sure enough, Ian and Lacie had seen her with wet pants. Everly shook her head and rushed down the hall toward the kitchen entrance and into the women's bathroom, where she pulled paper towel after paper towel out of the dispenser to wipe her pants.

"So embarrassing," she muttered. "Stupid." Could she hide in the bathroom eternally? Or maybe stay here until Ian and Lacie left. An older woman entered the bathroom and gave Everly a disgruntled stare, forcing her to vacate from the only sink as there was hardly room for two.

Everly exited the bathroom doors and ran into Ian, standing in the hall.

"Ian," she said nervously. "What are you doing here?"

"I came to grab a bite to eat. You?"

Everly looked into the diner and saw Lacie was gone from their booth.

"Sunday tradition." Everly cast her thumb toward the booth where Birdie and Summer were still arguing and cleaning up. "I'm sorry, but I never apologized for leaving to go off with Hunter and dragging you from your friend's party to help me investigate that cabin. That was rude of me." Everly dropped her head. "Thank you."

"You could apologize by telling me what you found in the cabin?" His voice was low. Ian suddenly grabbed her elbow and applied pressure. She started to yelp, but Ian quickly pulled her out of the way of a server coming out of the kitchen with a loaded food tray. "Watch out!"

When she was safe, he still didn't release her arm but moved her out of harm's way and back in front of the bathrooms.

Everly felt her pulse race as she struggled to read his body language. Was he threatening her or protecting her?

"I don't know what you mean?" Everly lied, making sure to keep eye contact.

"I heard Holland. She's not the most subtle. You found something in that cellar, and you're not sharing it with anyone. It's highly suspicious."

"Hmmph." An angry sound came from behind her. Everly moved out of the bathroom doorway as the same elderly lady from before wanted to get through.

"What if I said I'm still investigating it?"

"I don't like it when I can't trust people..."

"I don't like it when I'm being lied to." Everly clenched her teeth. "You're a griever. Not a sib. You knew full well that there was a werewolf in that cellar, and I have proof that someone from Gravemark was involved."

Ian grew silent. Not confirming or denying.

"You weren't even surprised. It's like you knew and weren't even curious about investigating. I don't buy your claustrophobia excuse for a second. You were trying to draw suspicion away."

Ian shoved his hands in his back pockets and leaned back as a server passed them with a tray of dirty dishes to head to the kitchen.

"Everly, I can explain. Just not here, not now."

"We're paid up and ready to go," Summer called out as she headed toward the door.

"Coming," Everly called over her shoulder before returning to Ian. "Sorry, I have to go, and you should get back to your date with Lacie."

"Oh, that." He seemed uncomfortable, shuffling his feet. "We were just meeting about a school assignment." His shoulder rose. He was lying. Everly was tired of his lies.

Everly tilted her head. "On a Sunday?"

"Yeah. When someone blackmails you, you answer," he snarled.

"What is that supposed to mean?" Everly asked.

"Nothing. It means nothing." He sighed. "I guess both of us need to work on trust."

"Maybe," she said cryptically.

Ian left first and headed out the diner doors. Everly stayed back and watched, as Lacie was outside waiting for him. He spoke to her, and she looked in Everly's direction and shook her head.

Lacie turned and leaned close to Ian, and Everly watched his body tense, his hands ball into fists, and then he stormed off down the street. Lacie watched him go, with a slow smile on her face, as she nibbled on a cake pop, before sauntering off in a different direction, like a cat that just caught a mouse.

A crack of lightning hit the sky, and seconds later, a roll of thunder followed. Everly sighed as the rain began to pelt her skin.

CHAPTER 28

SUMMER AND BIRDIE DECIDED TO HIT A MATINEE MOVIE across the street, and Everly declined, wishing to get home and study. And by study, she meant to go over her case notes. Everly was just as bad as her dad, unable to let things go until they were solved. Since Summer ruined her lunch, Everly raided the snacks left from the Kwik Mart she'd left in her car. A warm, slightly melted Ho Ho hit the spot. The storm came in quickly, making one o'clock in the afternoon feel like late evening. Auto sensors on the streetlights kicked on, and it was an ominous feeling driving home. As she pulled up the driveway, her headlights lit on the old medical building.

She grabbed her purse and the day-old snack sack and returned to the kitchen.

When she went inside, she flipped the light switch. No lights went on. The circuit breaker had probably tripped during the storm. Flipping the breaker wasn't a big deal in their house; they had to do it at least once a week. Everly grabbed the flashlight from the kitchen junk drawer and headed to the basement. Her feet slowed as she hit the last step. For some reason, it was much scarier to be free-standing in an old, creaky house in the dark with no one home than tied up and handcuffed when it was full of people.

It was because of the dead rat, Everly told herself. It was still down here.

Everly raced across the basement to behind the water heater, opened the electrical box, and flipped the switch. A hum filled the house as the fridge kicked back on and so did the air conditioner unit, but Everly was still basked in darkness, the bulb light not having been yanked on.

Above her, a crash came from the living room. Everly jumped. Her flashlight arced to the ceiling to where the sound came from. She tried to picture the floor above her on that side of the basement. It would be the sitting room, roll-up desk, end table, and lamp. Did Birdie and Summer cancel and make it home before her?

"Hello?" Everly called up the stairs. Her flashlight aimed at the top step. "Birdie?"

Just then, loud footsteps started running across the floor, and Everly knew it was not a cat. Instinct kicked in, and she raced up the stairs just as someone in black raced out the back kitchen door.

"Hey!" she screamed after the intruder as they fled on foot, their form disappearing into the darkness.

What had she just done? She ran toward an intruder. Some people, they have a fight-or-flight response. Everly's reaction was to fight.

Everly tried Birdie's cell, but it went right to voicemail. She had it silenced while they were at the movies.

She didn't dial nine-one-one but the direct line to Nina Hastings.

"Hello?" Nina picked up.

"Hey, Nina," Everly rushed out breathlessly. "Who's at the station tonight?"

"Officer Stevens and Mitchell? Why? What's wrong?"

"Can you send over someone? I interrupted a B and E; the intruder headed out the back door toward the maple and vine. They were about six feet tall, in all dark clothes and a black hood."

"What?" Nina exclaimed. "Everly, are you all right?"

"I'm fine, but send over someone as soon as possible."

"I will."

Not even ten minutes later, Everly heard the screech of tires before Officer Stevens came bursting through the door, his hand on his gun holster at his hip.

"Everly, are you all right?"

Everly was sitting in the front room. "It's good I unlocked the door, or you might have kicked it down."

Stevens looked around, motioned for her to stay there, and he thoroughly checked the house. She grabbed a book, settled into their overstuffed chair and waited. She could hear his footsteps as he went from room to room, checking out her dad's, her grandma's, and even her own.

The second police officer that entered was Sergeant Mitchell, one of her father's oldest friends, who was built like a bulldog, a thick-chested bruiser with a short temper regarding poker.

"Hello, Everly." Mitchell dipped his head in greeting. "Looks like the point of entry was the front door. They broke the sidelight."

Stevens descended the stairs and came back to the front room. "The house is clear."

"I know," Everly said. "I already checked."

Stevens's brows furrowed. "What do you mean you already checked? If an intruder is in the house, you shouldn't wander about aimlessly. It could be dangerous. You should wait for backup." He pointed toward himself.

Everly shrugged.

Mitchell shook his head and hid his laugh. "All right, give us a statement."

"When I came home, the power was out. I flipped the breaker and heard him run down the hall. I caught him just as he was racing out of the house," she said.

"Description?" Stevens pulled his notebook out of his uniform pocket.

"Yeah, I already told Nina Hastings. Tall, six foot, dark clothes."

"Is anything missing?"

"Not that I can tell," she said.

Everly pointed to the foyer and the broken glass. Stevens went to the front entrance and looked at the heavy wooden door. "What is this?" Stevens leaned down to examine the frame and the broken sidelight glass. He looked up at Everly in surprise. "Is this fingerprint powder?"

"Yeah," Everly said nonchalantly. "I was getting bored. I didn't lift any because there weren't any prints. They must have worn gloves."

"Everly!" Sergeant Mitchell's voice held a hint of awe. "I'm going to check the outside." Mitchell went out the front door and walked around the perimeter.

"Anything else you can tell us?" Stevens asked.

Everly closed her eyes, trying to replay everything she heard in the basement, the sound of the first crash, which turned out to be a footstool in the study. When she turned the lights on, it must have startled the intruder, and he knocked it over.

Listen, Everly told herself. *What did she hear?*

She had called upstairs and heard running. But there was something about the way they ran.

"I think they injured themself when they tripped over the

stool. They were limping as they ran out. The sound was as if they were favoring one foot over the other. Check the stool for blood."

Stevens used his pocket flashlight to look at the overturned cloth footstool with wooden legs.

"Surprised you didn't dust that for fingerprints," Stevens said sarcastically.

"Of course not," Everly said dryly. "You can't dust fabric for fingerprints." She kneeled next to the stool and saw the smear of blood on the wooden leg at the same time he did.

"What next, Ms. Hart?" Stevens asked, testing Everly.

"Elemental traces can be run through a mass spectrometer, but if it is biological, it goes to DNA."

"Impressive, I'll get this to our lab," Stevens said.

"Will you update me on the results?" Everly asked.

Stevens cleared his throat. "Not likely. You don't have a relative on the force anymore, Everly."

Mitchell reentered and cleared his throat to announce himself again.

"Uh, Everly, what happened to your car?"

Everly's face turned bright red, and before she could answer, Stevens did.

"She was up at the bluff on Wednesday night. I think that cougar did it."

"That's right where that kid was murdered." Mitchell was shocked.

"Oh, didn't I tell you?" Stevens said. "It was Everly that identified the Mulligan kid."

"Everly." Mitchell's voice dropped to one of warning. "What were you thinking? You shouldn't have been up there."

"It was just a gathering with some friends." Everly decided to stick as close to the truth as possible. "I parked my car and noticed the scratches when I left."

Mitchell rubbed his forehead and looked to heaven. "Your dad would have killed me if you got hurt. No, Nina Hastings will have my hide and use it for a rug. She's scarier than your dad ever was."

Everly laughed. It was good to laugh with her father's friends.

"Just promise me that you'll keep yourself safe. Stay out of the police's investigations. I know how curious you are."

She nodded.

"Everly! I got your text," Holland called as she rushed into the house, pushing Stevens aside. Her face was flushed, her chest heaving hard, eyes squinting as she scanned the surroundings. Her pink rain jacket skimmed rainwater off onto the carpet in puddles. Hunter stood on the porch in shock.

"What happened?" Holland's voice was high-pitched. "I'm never leaving you alone again. That's it. I'm moving in here." Holland looked around the dark halls with the creepy black-and-white photos. "No wait. It would be best if you moved in with me."

"Well, that seems to be everything we need," Stevens interrupted. "I can station someone outside for the night if you want."

"I'll be fine. Birdie should be home any minute," Everly said, looking at the clock in the hall.

"Are you sure? I don't mind being the one to stay." Stevens blushed and scratched the back of his head.

"Thanks, but I wouldn't want to inconvenience you. Especially since nothing was taken."

"Come on, Stevens." Mitchell grabbed the younger officer by the shoulder and pulled him out the door. "You're not wanted."

"Hey!" Stevens yelped as he felt the full grip of the bulldog, and they headed out to their unmarked black police cruiser.

Holland took a long breath when they left and started to fan herself. "Okay, he is hot."

"I don't know, I thought he kind of looked like a bulldog," Hunter added.

"Stop it." Holland smacked her brother before turning to Everly. "I could almost feel the tension between you and the younger one." Holland winked.

"No, there wasn't," Hunter argued.

"Did you not see the way he looked at her?" Holland added. They bickered for a few minutes and then came around. "I'm just glad you called us this time."

"I tried Birdie and Summer, but their phones are on silent."

"But it worries me that they didn't take anything. You said they were in this room." Holland looked at Everly, who stilled.

Everly jumped up, went to her dad's locked roller desk, and pulled it away from the wall to reveal the air vent along the floor. It wasn't screwed into the wall but had a tight enough seal that Everly had to tug before it popped it off. She reached inside.

"It's gone," she said in disbelief.

"What's gone?" Hunter asked.

"When we went to the ranger cabin yesterday—"

"What cabin?" Hunter interrupted. He didn't seem to enjoy this news.

"Oh, Everly interviewed Roy at the Kwik Mart. He was there the night that Eric was killed. They went to this cabin and were chased away by someone and Eric... Well, we know what happened to Eric."

Hunter stilled. His eyes raked over Everly's face, silently pleading with her that she hadn't gone and done something so stupid. "You didn't."

"I did, and in the cabin's cellar, I found a cage... made of silver."

"Werewolf," Hunter immediately added.

"But not only that." Everly pulled out her phone and showed the image. "A piece of a Gravemark uniform. The physical evidence may be gone, but I got a picture."

"Let me see that," Holland asked. Everly handed the photo to her best friend, who examined it closely. "You know, I don't think this is from our school uniform. The colors aren't the same. It's more hunter green than Castleton green, and this bit of thread here. It's fraying. This means it's not the polyester twill of our blazers but has a wool mixture in it. And while the patch color is similar, this one is older than ours. Much older." She scrunched up her nose in thought. "What school has colors similar to ours?"

Everly looked over at the photo in the hall of her dad in his police uniform, then back down to the enlarged picture. "You're right. It's not a Gravemark school uniform. Holland, you're a genius!" Everly gasped.

"Really?" Holland said excitedly and turned to her brother. "Did you hear that? I'm a genius. G-e-n-u-s."

Hunter glanced at Everly when Holland misspelled the word and chuckled. "Yep, verifiable. How about you spell that one?"

"Stop it," Everly warned and punched Hunter in the arm.

"What?" Holland pouted. "What is going on?" She didn't like getting left out of the joke.

"Nothing; I know what this is, and it points to someone outside our school. I don't understand why someone would break in and steal the incriminating evidence."

"Um." Holland raised her hand. "Not to be the one to point out the obvious, but the only people who were with us were..." Holland's hand rushed to cover her mouth when she realized it.

"Ian and Kat." Everly sighed.

"And Kat barely clears five feet. How tall is Ian Holmes?" Holland asked.

"Close to my height. Six feet," Hunter answered.

Holland gasped. "And you know he wouldn't go down into that cellar. It's like he knew what we would find because he is an accomplice. He knows who the killer is and is covering up for them." Holland was getting excited, her hands flailing in the air. "Geez, is this what it's like, Everly? The feeling of putting the puzzle pieces together."

Everly chuckled. "Yeah."

Holland put her hands on her hips in a superpower pose. "I like it. It's addicting."

A silent worried look passed between the three of them. "Now what?"

"We have to corner him, get him to admit that he broke in here, and confess to who he is covering up for."

A back screen door slam followed as Summer came in, shaking off her wet coat. "Was that a police car that just drove off? Why was there a police car here?" Her voice was getting filled with worry.

Birdie's quick gaze snapped right to Everly, who mouthed, "There was an intruder."

Birdie reached into her satchel and pulled out a silver revolver, her eyes going hard.

Holland gasped. Hunter made a move, but Everly stepped in front of him and waved, gesturing for the seventy-year-old woman to put the gun away.

Birdie wasn't going to be deterred. Silently, she stepped into the hall, the gun at the ready.

"No one harms my bug!" Birdie whispered. "Where is he?"

"Gone," Everly hissed. "We're fine. Put that thing away before Summer sees you and freaks out."

"Mom?" Summer stood in the hall, her face pale as she saw the gun. "What are you doing?"

Too late.

Everly bit her lip and looked between mother and daughter. How was her grandma going to explain the large revolver? Nothing would make sense for her to pull it out.

Birdie didn't even flinch. "Don't move. I saw a cockroach."

Summer jumped on the nearest kitchen chair. "Oh, for the love of God! Where?"

"In the front foyer," Birdie said. "So you stay there."

"Shoot it!" Summer shrieked dramatically. "Shoot it!"

Holland sputtered and covered her mouth to keep her laughter silenced.

Hunter glanced at Everly as he struggled to hold back his smile. Everly just shrugged. It was a typical day in the Hart household.

Birdie came over to Everly, her voice dropping low. "Are we good? Is there a grimm here?"

"We're fine. Officer Stevens already came and went. Just a break-in."

"So not a grimm?"

"No," Everly reiterated. "We think it was someone from school."

Hearing that it wasn't a grimm relaxed Birdie, and she put the gun into her impossibly small handbag. It was funny how a human break-in was far less disturbing than the other option. It made her wonder what kinds of creatures her grandmother had encountered when she carried a giant revolver. She puttered back to the kitchen and calmed a shrieking Summer. Minutes later, they heard Summer head upstairs and to the shower.

"Don't just stand out in the hall. Come into the kitchen and have some tea," Birdie called out.

Everly turned to give an apologetic look to Hunter and Holland.

Holland was still silently dying of laughter and had buried her face into a pillow. Hunter looked terrified of the former griever.

Everly took a seat, and Holland and Hunter followed suit. Birdie set a teacup in front of each of them. "Holland, good to see you again, dear. Hunter, it took you long enough to come over here finally."

Hunter cleared his throat. "Uh, well, I wasn't sure I was welcome." He gave Everly a shy glance.

"You're a Gravemark student. All are welcome. I'm going to make you a nice herbal tea." Birdie went into her solarium off the kitchen. "You sure it wasn't a grimm?" Birdie called from the sunroom.

"Yeah, positive," Everly said.

"I would rethink that assessment."

They entered the solarium and saw cracked pots and dirt everywhere.

"What happened?" Everly gasped. Most of the other plants were undisturbed except for the ones in the pink pots.

Hunter tensed. Everly tried to remember what was in the pink pots. Birdie tended to label most things even if she didn't know their medicinal uses. Everly knew where everything was.

"It's gone," Everly said, looking up at Birdie for confirmation, a worry line crossing the woman's face.

"What is?" Holland asked.

"The wolfsbane," Everly answered.

Birdie was solemn.

"But who would take it?" Holland asked.

"That is an excellent question." Birdie moved some of the plants around and held up an empty pot. "They took the vervain too."

"What does that mean?"

Birdie went to the kitchen and climbed a stool to reach a red-and-white plaid cookbook from a cupboard above the fridge. She dropped it on the kitchen table and flipped open the pages to reveal it was a false cover. Inside was an herbal book full of various concoctions and ingredients she couldn't pronounce. Birdie used the index and started to scan recipes that used wolfsbane and vervain.

"This one!" Birdie pointed to the page and read the inscription. "It's been many years since I had to brew this, so I wanted to be certain. Combined with wolfsbane and brewed for three days, it stops the heart of—" She looked up at the three of them. "Is someone planning to kill a werewolf?"

Everly looked between Hunter, whose face was watching her in complete trust, and Holland, who seemed confused.

"Do you think Ian would attempt to go after the grimm without us?"

Hunter raised his eyebrows. "Oh, yeah, he's cocky enough to try it."

Birdie nodded. "Then you have two days to stop him."

Monday morning, Everly returned to the Gravemark campus, pausing to speak her father's name to the gargoyle. This time when she pulled into the parking spot, Hunter was already waiting for her, leaning on the bumper of his Jeep.

"Ready?" he asked her, standing up when she pulled into the empty spot next to him.

"No," she said truthfully. "What if we're wrong?"

"Do you really believe that?" Hunter asked.

"I don't know. I know Ian is hiding something from us. He shouldn't be protecting the killer. We should go right to the headmistress."

"He won't go hunting for another day at least. And we don't have proof that he knows who the werewolf is. So act normal. Get through the day and remember." He placed his hand on her shoulder. "I'm here for you."

Everly bobbed her head and headed to her first class.

Listening to the lecture by Professor Stubbs was hard because she was hyper-aware of Ian sitting in the row behind her. Everything the professor said went in one ear and out the other. She sat there, drawing circles on her paper, trying to focus because something was still nagging at her. She couldn't quite get the whole picture.

Why would Ian steal from her?

Then her eyes fluttered to a foundling in the front row with a bag of gummy bears. They were noisily ravaging through the sack like they were starving.

After class, she went to the library for private tutoring with Mr. Halsey. She wasn't surprised that more griever journals were stacked on the table as she entered.

Everly took a seat, picked up a different griever's journal, and skimmed, only looking for every entry that mentioned werewolves. But none were as detailed as the journal she had back in her room from her father.

Everly thumbed through the pages, for once not interested in the past when she was overwhelmed with the present. "Mr. Halsey?"

Mr. Halsey looked up from his book. "Yes, Ms. Hart?"

"Has there ever been a grimm at Gravemark?"

"Do you mean besides the grimms that are on staff?

"Grimms as in plural?"

"Why? I heard that you saw Professor Stubbs's true form your first class. Did you not realize that a society that spans hundreds of years would need pax or, as we say, peaceful grimms to help facilitate the organization? It can't all be done by you children and blind adults. The Grimm Society needs us, and we need the Grimm Society. We balance one another."

Everly swallowed, feeling nervous. There was a certain way that Mr. Halsey was leaning over the books, the way his fingers dug into them like claws. She could see a glimmer in his eye, a hunger, but she had pushed it aside because he was so focused on his reading. She should have seen it sooner.

"Have you not figured out what I am yet?" His eyes darkened, and he stretched his neck and closed his eyes. "Maybe we should play a game, and you guess?" He rubbed his hands down his mustache, and Everly heard a deep rumble in his voice. She had yet to figure out how to make her sight work on command.

"It's not working. I can't see you." Everly felt defeated. "Why can't I see you?

"I'm old; the older the grimm, the better they hide their aura. Any guesses?" he asked.

Everly shook her head.

"Well, we will leave the surprise for another day." Mr. Halsey pushed his glasses up his nose and folded his hands. "Now, where were we... ah yes. You were asking about grimms in the school. Any captured and in for processing will most likely be in the oubliette."

Her eyes went wide. "I saw it open during my testing. An ogre came out of it. What is it exactly?"

"It is a place of forgetting. A place that is beyond time or reasoning. A well, dug out of the mountain by dwarves and enchanted by a pax witch, that has been turned into a prison for the reaped grimms. What did you think happened with the grimms you brought to school?"

"I wasn't sure."

Mr. Halsey snorted, his voice deep and resonating in his chest.

"But there wouldn't be any unsanctioned grimms in the school, right? I mean, you all can sense one another. It would be stupid for a grimm to try and sneak in here with all the grievers... right?"

"Is it? Sometimes the best place to hide is right out in the open. Even the weakest of grimms can hide if no one is actively looking for them. Why are you so inquisitive today?"

"No reason." Everly shook her head. "I'm just curious, is all."

"You know what I say about curiosity?"

"It killed the cat?" Everly said tentatively.

Mr. Halsey grinned and licked his lips. "Oh, yum, cats. Tasty little morsels."

Everly took a deep breath and shuddered. "Okay, then I have a question. Why did you send Maddie to Dorian Institute after the incident with the fairies?"

Mr. Halsey's brows furrowed. "The Dorian Institute? I was informed she was released from griever duty and sent home."

"No. Dr. Madsen said *you* signed off on her being transferred to Dorian."

Mr. Halsey took a few more puffs of his pipe, sending a furious circle of smoke around his head. "That is incorrect. I never leave my library."

"I went to the institute, and Maddie recognized her attacker. Someone from Gravemark terrified the girl so much that she would rather live in isolation. She is terrified of coming back to school."

"I didn't know." His deep voice softened, filled with guilt.

"You're her advisor. You should have known."

Mr. Halsey dropped his head in defeat. "I do admit that sometimes my obsession with knowledge makes me blind to other areas of concern. I feel awful that I didn't follow up on the poor girl. But Dr. Madsen said the girl had requested to be sent home. I didn't know about anything else. I swear."

Mr. Halsey looked utterly defeated as he took to smoking his pipe again. "This news is alarming indeed. I will speak with Dr. Madsen to ensure this never happens again."

"Okay," Everly said, flipping through the other journals and feeling bored.

"By the way, Everly, have you found any help in the family journal I gave you?"

"Yes. It's been an immense help in my transition here. It makes me feel closer to him."

"Him? Don't you mean her?" Mr. Halsey asked.

"You said it was my dad's griever's journal."

"No, I thought you knew," Mr. Halsey said softly. "That was your mother's. I thought you would like to read her entries when she was a griever here at Gravemark."

Everly's world dropped out from under her. All the tips and tricks she got had been from her mother. Not her father. Her mother was a griever too. She didn't believe it.

"She is not my parent; she gave up that right ten years ago. There's nothing I can learn from someone who abandons their family," Everly retorted with tears in her eyes.

———

Everly stormed back to the Serenity Hall, half blinded by tears. She was annoyed that all the help she had been receiving came from someone she didn't want to accept help from. She felt like Mr. Halsey had duped her into relating to her mother.

Everly pushed open the door to her room and froze—she stared in horror at what lay within.

Everything was destroyed. Someone had come in and tore her room apart. Her bedspread was shredded as if by a knife. All the pages had been pulled from her books and even her mother's journals. The wardrobe was emptied, and all the clothes had been ripped apart. Even the wooden hangers needed to be fixed. On the mirror in red marker were the words:

Leave Gravemark, grimm bait

Those words again.

Everly stood there shaking. Was this Ian?

There was a stirring behind her, and Everly heard someone gasp. She glanced over her shoulder to see Lacie in her school uniform. Her hair had a slight wave to it, and her makeup, as always, was perfect.

"Everly, what happened?" Lacie said, her voice full of concern.

"Oh, I just felt it was time to redecorate," Everly answered, refusing to show how much the attack on her room bothered her. She went to the dresser and picked up the photo frame of her dad. The broken glass slid off the desk as she did, but she salvaged the photo from inside.

"Who would do something like this?" Lacie stepped over many destroyed books and came further into the room.

"Someone that wanted to make a point," Everly answered, thumbing and caressing the photo.

Lacie noticed the mirror, and she inhaled. "Is that a threat?"

"It's sure not an invitation to a party." Everly turned to address Lacie. "By the way, you never came."

"What do you mean?" Lacie started picking up the torn journal pages and stacking them on the dresser.

"You were adamant about throwing me a party at the lake, but you never came."

"What party?" Lacie said. "I think I would have known if I threw a party. Are you feeling okay?"

Everly watched Lacie's face for a tell but only saw the truth.

"What about meeting with Ian yesterday?" Everly asked again.

"Are you feeling okay?" Lacie said, her pretty brows furrowing.

"No, I don't know. I think I need to be alone for a while." Everly escorted Lacie out and into the hall.

"Here." Lacie handed her the torn journal pages from her mother's book.

"Thanks." Everly closed the door. She leaned against it and looked at her destroyed room. She glanced down at the journal entries that Lacie handed her, and she couldn't help but read the first entry.

August 30, 2004

Carol's pregnant. It's only been ten months since they got married. She'll love him until the end. My fear now is that even though Eugene has suppressed his wolf, what does it mean for their kid? Will the curse pass on to the child? Will the child be forced to drink the bane of wolf poison like the father to keep the curse at bay? What are the ethics of having a child, knowing it will be cursed?

I've written to the Grimm Society and asked them to intervene. I feel guilty. I'm a terrible friend.

June 8, 2005

My fears are unfounded. Carol and Eugene are the proud parents of a healthy baby boy, and I've been named his godparent.

Ian Holmes Danville

Everly froze as she read the name one more time. Ian Holmes... Danville.

"Werewolf cursed from birth," Everly muttered, sliding to

the floor, her back pressing against the wood door. She was horrible. Treating Ian like a drunk when he was afflicted with a disease he fought daily.

The flask he was drinking that she accused him of sneaking alcohol in. It was wolfsbane. No wonder he was looking sickly. He kept poisoning himself to keep the werewolf curse under control.

That would explain his superhuman strength, hypersensitivity to smell, and why he could jump the oubliette to save her. There was no doubt in her mind that he was the one to rescue her from the ogre. And she had treated him like an addict.

Everly dropped her head to her knees in shame.

Her phone rang, and she answered it.

"Hello?"

"Hey, Everly, it's Officer Stevens. I did a precipitin test on the blood in your house. Well, it came back not human. Do you perhaps own a pet? The lab did a further test, and you won't believe what came back."

Everly leaned forward.

"Let me guess. Wolf."

———

Learning that Ian was wolf-cursed only shed light on one of the problems plaguing her mind. She went down the hall to knock on Kat's door. The door swung open, and Everly entered the dark room with computer screens. The curtains were closed, and Everly could hear the soft sound of video game music from the headphones on the table.

She went to the keyboard, moved the mouse, and lit the four screens. Each one showed the lock screen.

"You didn't think I would be that stupid to leave my baby unlocked," Kat said.

Everly turned in her chair, and Kat didn't seem bothered by Everly's intrusion. She had crossed her arms and was grinning.

"It's a complex password that changes by the minute." Kat seemed smug. Too smug.

Everly thought about it. She thought about Kat and her overcomplicated genius. Then remembered that Mr. Halsey said that sometimes the answers are in plain sight. Everly glanced at the clock on the upper hand of the computer screen and typed in the exact time without the colon. 1004

She hit Enter, and the screen unlocked.

"How did you...?" Kat's hands unfolded in disbelief. "No one has ever... I mean..."

"I want to access the school security feed," Everly demanded.

Kat nodded; she came to Everly's side and made a motion. "Shoo, no one can touch my baby but me."

Everly focused on Kat, studying her mannerisms, and then nodded, going with her gut to trust her.

Everly got up, and Kat slid into the gaming chair, her fingers flying across the keys as she pulled up the screen and over forty different folders pulled up.

"You got better at typing?" Everly decided to point it out.

Kat never even heard her as her hands danced across the keys.

"What camera?" Kat asked, grabbing the mouse and moving it to a specific location.

"Serenity Hall." Everly pointed to the folder with their halls.

Kat clicked on the folder, and the different camera views pulled up. Everly touched the one that showed their rooms. "Our hall."

A double click brought the screen to a bigger size. Currently, it was empty. Kat's door was slightly ajar, but there wasn't anyone in sight. Everly's room was the farthest from the camera, and her door was right where the camera almost cut off.

"Go back this weekend and see if you can find who entered my room."

Kat bobbed her head. "Gotcha." A few keystrokes later, the video was being played in reverse, and multiple times, they saw Lacie and Kat come and go, but no one went near Everly's door.

"What, what was that?" Everly said, gripping the desk. "Go back. There was a flash of light."

Kat slowed the video down, and sure enough, there was a slight change of light as the stairwell door opened, and the outside stairwell red emergency light briefly came into view. Then there was a shadow by her door.

"I think someone just went in." A few seconds later, in fast-forward, the person left.

"Can you zoom in?" Everly asked.

Kat clicked on the screen and brought up the image. She clicked again to make it larger, then dragged it into a different program to smooth out the pixels. The same thing she did with her photos for the photo shoots. A few seconds later, the image cleared, revealing a face.

"I don't understand." Kat's mouth dropped open in surprise as she saw the image. "It's Aimee. Why would she go into your room?"

"Has this footage been altered in any way?" Everly asked, focusing on exactly where Aimee put her hand. Her left hand touched the door, and her right hand turned the handle.

"No, I would be able to tell."

Everly chewed on her lip in thought. "Check a few more dates and times for me, will you?"

With each date and time that Kat double-checked, the

more certain Everly became that they were dealing with someone very cunning.

"Can you make me a copy of this?"

"Sure." Kat cut the clip, dragged it onto a USB drive, and handed it to Everly.

"Can you keep this between us for now?" She pocketed the USB drive.

"No problem, I'll be your Alfred anytime." Kat did a little salute, but Everly had already headed back out into the hall.

She went to the kitchen, grabbed a mortar and pestle, then searched her bedroom and began digging around the trashed room until she found her retractable pencil. Pulling off the eraser, she dumped the lead into the mortar and ground it to dust. She opened her pencil bag, grabbed a makeup brush she had never used, and went to the door.

With her makeshift fingerprint powder, Everly dusted the wood door for prints. And came away with an unmistakable, distinct set, which wasn't what she expected. She moved inside, looked around her bedroom, and returned to the photo of her and her dad. A picture that Lacie Duvall picked up the first time she came into her room.

Everly pulled out the powder, dusted it, and returned with nothing but round flat indents instead of prints.

"Very clever," Everly breathed out as she formed the picture of what was happening at Gravemark. "But not clever enough."

———

Everly was pacing her room, waiting nervously. Her plan was falling into place. She hoped.

A rap at her window told her Corvis had returned from his

errand. She opened the window, and he flew in before landing safely on the wardrobe.

"What the grimm?" Corvis used the grievers' favorite cuss word. "What happened?"

"Nothing but a bit of jealous girlfriend revenge." Everly stepped over a pile of ruined clothes.

She had gotten her room back into some semblance of order —a pile of salvageable clothes, books, and personal items. The garbage can was overflowing with broken glass and ripped bedding and clothes. She had done her best to sweep up the glass but didn't have time to put her whole room back in order. Not when she had other business to get to.

"Corvis, I know you know your way around this campus. You figured out how to get into the inner sanctum. What else do you know about Gravemark?"

"Quite a lot. I've lived here many years."

"I need to know if you've seen this wax seal stamp anywhere?" Everly held up her letter from the Grimm Society and pointed to the seal.

"Yes, one is in a golden box in the headmistress's office."

"I need you to steal it."

"I don't know what you mean; I never steal anything." He shook out his feathers. But Everly pointed to the one area she discovered while cleaning above the wardrobe. It was undisturbed by Aimee's rampage and had a whole collection of rings, jewelry, and even a familiar raven's eye brooch. Seeing that brooch set her on her current course of action.

"I don't know how that stuff got there." He pretended ignorance.

"Can you get the seal or not?" Everly asked firmly. "I don't have much time."

"I can get it."

Corvis flew away and was back within a quarter hour.

During that same time, Everly prepared paper, envelopes, and a deep red crayon. It wasn't the same wax the society used, but she didn't think it would matter.

Then it came to forging. It took her multiple tries to get the curvature of the G and slant just right, but it would do. Thankful that the Grimm Society's messages were always short and to the point, she melted the crayon using a spoon and lighter and then sealed them with the official seal.

When they were finished, she sighed in relief. Now she just needed a raven to deliver the messages. Because the Grimm Society only used ravens.

"What about other ravens? Do you know where they are?"

"In the northern aerie," he replied.

"Can you get these to them so they can deliver them to the Grimm Society members?"

"Yes, they listen to me."

Everly laid out her plan, organized the letters, and handed them to him. "All right, Corvis. You know what to do. Can you handle this one?" She held up a separate letter. "It's going to take the longest. How fast can you fly?"

"Faster than a normal raven."

"Then I leave it to you."

Corvis flapped his wings excitedly, picked up the stack of letters, and took off to deliver her messages.

Now came the final chapter, and she hoped she was right in her assessment.

CHAPTER 30

THE CLOCK STRUCK MIDNIGHT, AND EVERLY WAITED IN A pilfered green hood on the upper balcony. They weren't hard to find since all she had to do was sneak into Maddie's old room and take hers hanging in the closet. Getting into the chamber was easy enough as she had memorized the combination on the grandfather clock.

She waited next to the other grievers, all hand selected.

Hunter moved next to Everly; he touched her elbow. She jumped slightly, then relaxed. He leaned in to whisper. "I don't understand why you're doing this charade. We should arrest him now for being an accomplice and turn him over to the Grimm Society."

"Can you trust me, Hunter?" she asked. "I already put the wheels in motion and plan on solving two cases tonight."

Hunter nodded and moved toward the side stairs where she had stationed him. Everly moved to another griever. "Are you ready?"

Silence followed.

"Please, trust me."

The griever turned away.

Everly watched and waited for all the players to file in.

The handful of grievers she selected were in the student box totaling five. And she tried counting all the others in the Grimm Society member box. Six came. Five in silver masks, one in gold.

"What is the meaning of this assembly in our inner sanctum?" The speaker in the gold mask of the Grimm Society stood at the podium. "I did not sanction this meeting. Who would dare to impersonate one of us?"

Everly took a deep breath and lifted her hood. "I am that person."

There was a whispering among the society. Everly focused on the person in the gold raven mask wearing the collar.

"I have called this meeting for many reasons. One is to report an unsanctioned grimm that has been roaming the halls of our schools," Everly spoke calmly.

"Who is this?" a male voice behind a silver raven mask asked.

"Wait, and you will see; they will arrive any minute."

As Ian walked down the stone steps, his footsteps echoed loudly. Upon entering the chamber, he stood in the middle of the room. Suddenly, the heavy door behind him slammed shut with a loud thud, locking him inside.

The griever next to her tensed, ready to attack.

"Wait for it," Everly breathed out. She nodded toward the master of ceremonies with the raven's brooch, stood up, and moved to the podium.

They tapped it dramatically with a wooden mallet, cleared their throat, and announced, "Ian Holmes, you're here because you have been reported as an unregistered grimm."

Ian was blindsided. "Grimm?" His face paled, and he began to tremble. "I'm not a grimm. I swear. I'm human."

The master of ceremonies raised their voice. "As an unregistered grimm, I hereby sentence you to the oubliette." The dramatic speaker waved their arms, and two grievers came out of the shadows and took Ian by the arms.

"What is the meaning of this?" the leader in the gold raven mask shouted. "You cannot order a student to the oubliette."

"I can't?" The MC seemed surprised. "Oh. Okay, then."

Everly bit her lip to suppress her grin. She stepped up to the podium and glared at the person in the gold raven mask. "I present to you the rogue grimm that has been living unsanctioned in our school."

There was a loud snicker and hissing as members of the society started to laugh at her expense.

"We are well aware of this particular human's curse. He presents unique griever abilities, and he is well under the purview of Ms. Bellcamp. Isn't that correct, Ms. Bellcamp?"

Ms. Bellcamp stepped forward, lifting her silver mask. "I have been monitoring this student's monthly moon phases by isolating him in the chamber as requested. He has posed no threat to anyone nor shown any signs of turning. He has also been self-medicating with my bane of wolf elixir to help suppress the urges."

"So you see, dear child. This were-human is hardly unsanctioned. We know about his particular oddities. There is very little that goes on at our school that we don't know about," the gold raven speaker announced.

"Oh, so you know *everything* about the person standing before us?" Everly challenged.

"Yes, he has been under our charge since his parents were killed. We've raised him since he was a foundling. We have not taken his curse lightly."

"Oh," Everly chuckled. "Silly me. If that is Ian Holmes, then who is this?" Everly pulled back the griever's hood that was standing next to her.

Ian's fists were clenched, his jaw ticking as he couldn't

contain his anger. With the fluidity of a wolf, he leaped from the balcony and moved to confront the imposter standing in the middle of the room.

"What the grimm?" the MC muttered. "How about that?"

The fake Ian tried to run but was blocked by none other than Hunter, who was the one who closed the door, locking them both in.

Hunter grabbed the fake Ian by the shoulder. There was a high-pitched screaming, and then Ian shrank, shifting into Kat Dorn with her fuchsia hair and heterochromia eyes. She blinked up at Ian, begging, "Please, Ian, tell him to let me go," in perfect imitation of Kat.

Ian gave her a shake. "Reveal your true self."

She shivered and shifted into Lacie Duvall.

"Ian," Lacie cried out. "We're friends. You wouldn't hurt me."

"Stop it." Ian went to the wall and grabbed an iron mace. He brought it up to the changeling's face, and she squirmed to avoid the iron touching her skin. "You may have pretended to be me, but you will talk under the touch of iron."

The changeling whimpered and looked around the room desperately before shifting into Holland Abernathy to plead to her brother.

"Hunter, please, it's me. Let me go. I didn't do anything."

"What the grimm! Oh no, she didn't!" Holland yelled from the podium, pulling down her white raven's mask to reveal she was impersonating the MC. "Just because I'm not allowed to come to these"—she used air quotes—"'secret meetings' does not mean you get to pretend to be me. Plus, my hair does not look like that. I, at least, use a conditioner." Holland crossed her arms in disgust that the changeling not only took on her image but did it badly.

"Eeee," the changeling cried and shifted again into a dark-haired man in a tan uniform for a fleeting second.

Ian recoiled. His breathing ragged as he stared up at the man before him. "You can't be here. You're dead."

A rush of raised voices followed. "Blasphemy! It's a ghost." And they came from the society balcony.

But the changeling took on Everly's face and mannerisms. It was disconcerting to see herself—the strawberry blonde hair, the blue eyes, pleading with her.

"This changeling," Everly called, breaking eye contact with her double. "Has been living undetected on Gravemark school grounds for quite some time." Everly turned to reprimand the changeling. "Oh, and drop my face. I've seen your true form on the bluffs."

Everly shifted again, shrinking into a girl with white skin, long, waist-length white hair, and the blackest eyes slanted just enough to make her look oddly beautiful.

"Now, that's better, isn't it?" Everly said. "What are you called?"

"No, not my true name." She stood impossibly still, her body willowy and thin; she barely hit five feet, but Everly knew not to let looks fool her. She was as deadly and vicious as the fairies. "But you can call me Cass." Her eyes filled with unshed tears.

"Okay, I'm a little lost." Holland held her hand up. "How did you know, and no one else figured it out?"

"Hiding in plain sight," Everly said. "But there were two things that gave it away. Ian, you said it yourself during my training. What are the weaknesses of changelings?"

"Constant need for sweets." His eyes widened when he started to put it together.

"It became easy to figure out who the changeling was by how much candy, sugar, and sugary drinks they were consuming, and she couldn't quite recall exact conversations from earlier."

Everly held up her hands and wiggled. "The second was fingerprinting. I've learned from the journals that changelings can replicate others but can't mimic the finite details of a person's fingerprints. They couldn't possibly get those right."

"Smart," Ian said. He gave her a nod of encouragement, and she thought she saw a hint of pride there.

Everly blushed and continued. "Cass was taking turns impersonating people, trying to get to know everyone so she could eventually take their place permanently. With the help of Kat"—Everly gestured to another cloaked figure who raised her hand, pulling down her hood to reveal a flood of fuchsia hair and a calculated grin—"I checked the video cameras, noted times when I knew I was away, and found inconsistencies where I would sometimes see Lacie in the hall and the class-room—the same with Holland. There would frequently be two of a person because the changeling couldn't always know their schedule, so they needed to switch with someone permanently. Luring us to the lake party was their way of getting us away from school. In the hopes of causing strife, arguments, and getting one of us alone."

"That means Thomas didn't say I looked like a fat toad... You did!" Holland exclaimed, pointing down at the changeling.

Cass nodded.

"Why I'm going to kill you—" Holland was about to climb down from the balcony to beat the changeling to a pulp, but Kat held her back.

"Why?" Gold Raven asked.

"I wanted to be a griever." Cass pulled against Ian's grip. "It wasn't anything more than what you are doing to our kind. Putting them to sleep in the oubliette. The girl named Maddie wouldn't have been harmed; she would have just slept."

"For eternity," Ian growled.

"You do the same to my kind," Cass challenged back. "I would have—how do you say it? Repaid with same. We would be equal."

A murmur went through the Grimm Society as they were confronted with their ethical judgment. Even Everly had to hand it to her; how could she fault someone who just wanted to belong, and she did it by doing the same thing the grievers had done to her kind for centuries? She was starting to get won over.

"Both of my parents are there." She pointed to the oubliette. "Taken years ago. I have no parents because of grievers." Cass raised her chin, her voice confident. "I am a foundling. Foundlings belong at Gravemark!"

Kat started to clap loudly in agreement. Hunter released Cass's shoulder and nodded. Even Ian didn't seem as angry. Everyone looked up to the Grimm Society to see what would happen.

"So, did you, Cass, murder those people?" the golden raven asked.

"No." Everly took a deep sigh and turned toward Ian. "I'm sorry, Ian. I have to tell them the truth."

Ian went rigid. His eyes turned dark and glassy with unshed tears.

"You can't keep hiding the truth."

Everly came down the side stairs and stood before Ian; she touched his arm, feeling the cloak's fabric.

He nodded. "Okay." He wiped his nose but backed away from Everly as if she had the plague and he wanted nothing to do with her.

There was a weighted silence.

"Ian Holmes's parents were killed in a grimm attack when Ian was eight. He's been a foundling here ever since."

"Correct," a silver raven answered.

Everly said softly. She pulled out the framed photo she had taken from her house and held it before Cass. She tapped the picture again, pointing to her father, Everick Hart. "Cass, would you be willing to help me out? Can you turn into this man right here? My father. Everick Hart."

"C-can't," Cass stuttered. "I can only change into someone I've seen and had time to study and hear their voice."

"But you turned into someone tonight, this man?" Everly pointed to a different person in the photo.

"Because I've seen him."

"This man right here?" Everly asked again, pointing to the person next to Everick.

Cass's head bobbed frantically. "Yes, yes. I can." She shifted easily into the image of the forest ranger as she had seen him that night. His whole tan uniform, even down to his green wool-blend jacket and the missing patch on the arm. Everly held up her phone and moved to match it to the arm where the patch was torn off. "Perfect match. I think we know who the rogue werewolf is."

"But he's dead," the male silver mask said.

"Now, what is one of the main rules of changelings?" Everly shot back.

He didn't reply.

Instead, the golden-masked leader of the Grimm Society spoke up, "They can't shift or impersonate dead people."

Everly let the silence weigh heavily in the air. "Exactly." She turned to Ian. "You are Ranger Eugene Danville's son. Your father is the werewolf responsible for killing those victims. But you suspected it the moment we found the cabin. How?"

Ian shifted uncomfortably. "I recognized his scent. I didn't believe it at first until I saw the silver cage. Then I knew. He had been alive all these years, hiding and living in the woods. And never once contacted me. It hurt. It didn't make sense."

"That's why you broke into my house and stole the patch. You found it because you sniffed it out. You were going to track him down. Weren't you?" She jabbed Ian in the chest.

"Yes."

"Alone." She jabbed him a second time. "And if need be, kill him."

"Yes." He blinked and looked away in shame.

"Don't you know that breaks the number-one rule of being a griever?" Everly reached for his hand, lifted his head, and those blue eyes met hers. "You taught me that. You never hunt alone."

"I was ashamed," he said. "If my father was a murderer, I had to ask him why. What drove him over the edge? How could he go so long and then start killing innocent people?" He sniffed as he struggled internally with his emotions. "I needed to see him face-to-face and determine if that was my future. I needed to know why he abandoned me. He was my only family."

"That's not true," Everly spoke up. "Your family is here." She touched her chest and gestured to Holland, Hunter, Everly, and Kat.

Even Cass nodded enthusiastically, tapping her chest. "Yes, family."

Hunter spoke up. "Yeah, we're family, and family fight"— he looked over at Everly—"but we always stick together." He grabbed Ian and threw his arm around his shoulders. Holland immediately dropped her white mask on the podium and ran down to pull Ian, Hunter, and Everly into a big bear hug. "Come on, Kat," Holland called over her shoulder. "Get your butt down here."

Kat came down the steps a bit more reluctantly. She leaned

into the hug with awkward pats but was quickly pulled into the group by Holland.

Everly felt a warm tingling brush against her arm and looked down to see that Cass had inserted herself right in the middle of the hug and was smiling. Her whole pure white body started to glow with joy at the love. At first, Ian recoiled, but then he relaxed and placed his hand on her head. Cass began to blink like the fairies.

"It seems you caused quite the commotion," Hunter said. "It may take more meetings before they agree on the path moving forward."

"What do we do now?" Everly looked up at the society, waiting for their ruling. But the chamber was in an uproar. Voices were yelling loudly, speaking over one another.

"Well." Ian took a deep breath and looked between their small group. "Let's go find my dad." He cracked his knuckles, and his face was grim. "I have quite a few questions for him."

CHAPTER 31

"Is this the right place?" Hunter asked as he pulled up in the Jeep behind the cabin.

"It is," Ian said. His face was solemn as he went back and opened the trunk.

Hunter and Ian discussed the weapons. Ian reached for the poison bullets. Hunter stopped him. "I can't let you. You do not want his death on your conscience for the rest of your life."

Ian's head dropped, and he took a deep breath. "I already have my mother's."

Everly smacked Ian in the arm. "What did I tell you? You are not to blame for that night."

"What happened?" Hunter asked.

Everly decided to fill him in after reading further in her mother's journals. "It was the night his parents died. On a camping trip, Ian was lured by a level three into the forest. His parents went after him, and it didn't end well. He was used as bait. His mother died, and his father killed the grimm with bare hands."

"It was his first cold-blooded kill since being cursed." Ian's breath was ragged. "That was the thing that initiated the change in him. Wounded, my father ran into the forest, leaving me alone. I had thought he had died, like my mother."

"But he didn't," Hunter added, holding up a wicked-looking rifle. "Werewolves are impossible to kill without taking off the head or a silver bullet to the heart."

Ian looked sickly.

"Sorry, man, just stating facts," Hunter said sheepishly.

"That's why Ian wanted the wolfsbane poison; a high enough dose would kill the werewolf but possibly not trigger his curse. Poison is a passive way of killing."

"I didn't want to burden you with my family problems." Ian took a deep breath.

"You don't have to. I'm here, and it's only between us. No one else knows we're here." Hunter gestured to the empty parking lot.

"Are you telling me this is an unsanctioned reaping?" Everly said, gasping for effect.

"I didn't want anyone else, outside of this circle, to know about... my affliction." His voice trailed off. "Hunter and I decided to leave Kat and Holland out of this."

"Yes!" Everly did a fist pump. "My second unsanctioned reaping, and I made the cut."

"No," Hunter snapped and then pointed toward his vehicle. "You guard the car."

"The car?" Ian and Everly said in unison.

"Oh, come on." Everly stomped her foot. "This is my case; let me see it through."

"No, you're in trouble because you kept everything from me. You stay." Hunter was in no mood to argue. He sounded like her dad when he was trying to ground her.

Everly threw her hands in the air and looked at Ian. "Are you going to let him talk to me this way? You're my mentor."

"Oh, I'm your mentor again? Since when? Since it's

suddenly convenient? Or let's not forget that we are here to capture my father?"

Everly bit her lip and gave a wide grin. "But you wouldn't even know he was alive if it wasn't for me wanting to investigate the cabin."

"On second thought. I agree with Hunter. Stay in the car." Ian took a club and another duffel full of weapons and headed with Hunter into the cabin. When they found nothing, they moved to the cellar before heading into the woods.

"I don't see any tracks," Hunter said.

"Oh, just use the patch," Everly grumbled. Ian looked at her, and she put her hands on her hips. "That's why you stole it from me in the first place. You would come out here and use the scent to track the werewolf alone without us."

His ears turned red. "How did you know... I was a werewolf when I tried so hard to hide it?"

Everly crossed her arms. "It was all the day drinking. I thought it was something else, but I learned in a journal that you are drinking diluted wolfsbane." Her voice softened. "You've been poisoning yourself to make sure you never turn."

"What the grimm, Ian? Tell me you weren't." Hunter looked shocked.

"Not to mention, you found the evidence I had buried in the wall and sniffed it out. The final clue was when you tripped over the footstool and you left blood. It tested as not human."

"I didn't even know that," Ian said.

"Birdie says you owe her new pots—pink ones—and next time you need herbs for poisons, just ask."

Ian nodded. "Now, get in the car, Everly."

Everly crawled into the front seat and locked the doors. She watched as Ian pulled out the patch and breathed it in. He scented the air and gestured for him and Hunter to head east.

She watched as they disappeared into the woods. She hated not being able to see them.

"See anything?" she asked Corvis, who was sitting in a tree keeping watch.

"Nope," he said, turning his head and looking around. "We should play a game. I spy with my little eye."

"No," Everly shot out. Her heart immediately started to hurt. "Not that one."

"Fine." Corvis was upset, and he ruffled his feathers.

Everly started to fan herself as she was left in the car for thirty minutes. It was hot, and she really doubted that he was going to come back to this cabin.

Then she heard it. The unmistakable sound of a gunshot echoed off the side of the mountain. Then a second and third shot rang out.

"No!" Everly got out of the car to listen, but the woods were silent. Did they find the werewolf? Did those shots mean they injured him?

"Corvis," Everly called.

"Do you want me to check it out?"

"Would you, please?"

Without waiting, Corvis took off, and Everly prayed everything was all right. That Hunter and Ian were safe.

She paced in front of the car, her ears listening for the sound of Ian and Hunter returning. Should she ignore their warning and go after them? She'd give them fifteen minutes and then head out. Rules or no rules. She could occupy herself for another fifteen minutes.

Everly drummed her fingers along the car's hood while processing everything. Something bothered her about Eugene Danville having been alive for these last ten years. Where had he been? More than likely, he was hopping between the various ranger stations, except for this one. It looked like it had been used to lock himself up every full moon.

She was missing something important, and she needed to take another look at the cellar. Everly walked down and let her eyes focus in the near darkness. She entered the cell and stepped inside, closing the door halfway, worried she would lock herself inside. Closing her eyes, she tried to imagine being a werewolf, going wild in this cage, afraid to touch the bars. The bars burned her hands, scraping her claws against the cement floor and waiting for the hours of the complete moon phase to pass, and waiting until the lock was opened.

Her eyes flew open as she looked at the lock—the key.

"A second person!" Everly breathed out. Ms. Bellcamp was the person who monitored Ian during a full moon. Someone had to lock Eugene away and let him out—an accomplice to the murders.

Everly started to run up cellar stairs as the crunch of gravel announced a second vehicle pulling up. She ducked at the last few steps and crouched in the cellar, looking around the side of the house and under bushes. A black unmarked police car pulled up next to the Jeep.

The static of the radio came over the speaker. "Just arrived in the general location of shots fired. Ten-four."

Everly breathed a sigh of relief, stood up, and waved as Sergeant Mitchell exited the car. He was looking around the grounds carefully, his hand on his holster.

"Everly, what are you doing here?" Mitchell whispered.

"Sergeant Mitchell, I'm so glad you're here. I believe that Shelly Miller and Rocky Cordone were not killed in a freak wild animal accident. I don't know how to explain it, but they were murdered, and it has to do with a witness—" Everly stopped speaking when Mitchell pulled his gun from the holster and aimed at her face.

"Why don't you ever learn?" Mitchell sneered. "Your family is always sticking their nose where it doesn't belong. But you just aren't smart enough." He moved to the rear tire well of the Jeep and pulled out a tracker.

"What are you doing?"

"You already know; you go to that school of freaks. You know what I keep in that cellar."

"Why?" Everly asked.

"I used to run the county's biggest underground dog-fighting ring. I trained the best killers and then encountered an injured wolf. Payday for a guy like me. All I had to do was heal him and train him. Except he wasn't a wolf—not really. That was an interesting surprise the first time he shifted. He became my biggest moneymaker. Undefeatable in the arena. But then my old girlfriend decided to turn me in. I couldn't let that happen when all she had was her word against mine. So I had to get rid of her and her nosy lawyer. Almost got away with it, but you...You're just like your father. I knew when Eugene saw you and let you go on that night. I knew it would only be a matter of time. You distracted him, and he lost the other girl. She got away, but not for long. I knew what kind of school you went to. I did a stakeout and never saw her leave, but you did. I put a tracker in your friend's car, and you led me right to her."

Everly's heart hammered in her chest. "No, you lie."

"Didn't you like my photo? I tried to warn you to drop the case as a favor to your dad. As soon as I tracked you here"—he pointed to the Jeep and the cabin—"I knew it was time to clean up all loose ends. Including that girl Maddie."

"But she didn't see anything, I swear."

Mitchell raised his eyebrows in disbelief. "You immediately went to the police station the next day after visiting the Dorian facility."

"But I didn't turn you in; I didn't know."

"You identified the Kwik Mart boy. You were closing in, Everly. Now, I have to return to that looney bin, flash my badge, and clean up that mess too."

"Please, believe me, she didn't see anything."

Mitchell gestured with the gun to the cellar. "Turn around, now!"

Everly turned around and reached into her crossbody bag, grabbing her keys. She spun and heard yelling as she sprayed Mitchell in the eyes with her pepper spray. He screamed, and she tried to run, but she was hit in the head with the butt of the gun, and everything went black.

CHAPTER 32

Her head was spinning, and there was a burning sensation in her eyes and nose. Everly coughed and sat up, taking in that she was locked in the silver cage, the cellar door closed.

She coughed again and covered her eyes, and embers started falling from the cabin above her. Seconds later, part of the floor above her collapsed, and smoke filled the cellar.

"No!" She pulled her shirt over her nose to help her breathe as she tried not to panic.

"Help!" Everly yelled, but yelling required her to breathe in the toxic fumes. A roar from above her told her that the cabin was already in flames, and it wouldn't be much longer before the place might collapse in on her. The only saving grace she had was that smoke rose, and she was in the lowest part of the cabin.

Think, Everly, she told herself and immediately reached into her crossbody bag. Her phone was gone. But not the black lockpick kit that looked like a makeup bag.

Grabbing the pins and wrench, she pressed her body against the hot bars and started to work on the lock from behind. It was a different exercise she hadn't practiced before, but the exhilaration made her hands flow and move quickly, and she felt the pins move. Seconds later, she was free.

She ran for the stairs and tried to push open the wooden doors, but they were closed. She pushed up again using her back, and the doors held firm. Looking through the crack, she saw a chain looped through the doors and another padlock.

Running out of options and air, Everly started to pound on the door with her fists and yell.

"Help!" she cried out, hammering as hard as possible.

Gunshots followed, and Everly froze, terrified. Did Hunter and Ian return and get shot by Sergeant Mitchell?

Her eyes were burning, and tears were streaming down her face. The cellar was filling with more smoke, and she struggled to breathe when she only wanted to stay awake.

"Everly! Are you down there?" Ian yelled, yanking on the doors.

"Ian," she cried, tears filling her eyes that someone was there. She started to cough. "Ian, I'm here."

There was the smallest gap where she could see a thread of light between the doors. Everly slid her fingers through.

"I'll get you out. I promise." Ian grunted as he pulled with all his might, but he couldn't break the chains.

"They're too thick," Everly said weakly. "The key, find the key."

"We don't have time." Ian leaned close to try and see her. "The whole cabin is about to collapse in flames."

"Go," Everly said. "Just go."

Her head started to feel fuzzy, and she slumped onto the top step. Her vision faded as she began to black out.

"Everly!" Ian yelled. "Answer me!"

A scream turned into a guttural roar as the doors were ripped off the hinges and flew through the air. Everly was bathed in the fading light as a terrifying sight loomed over her.

A wolf man. Part Ian, part wolf. He tapped partway into the wolf side of him. His eyes were deadly. His breathing was ragged, and his lips were pulled back as he snarled. She could almost see his wolf with her griever sight, like a glowing halo outside his body. His uniform shirt ripped and exposed a muscled chest, and his fingers gripped the doorframe, leaving deep indentations in the wood. He had torn the three-inch chain like it was paper links.

She should have been terrified when he reached down and pulled her up into his arms.

"No, you shouldn't have saved me. It wasn't worth tapping into your wolf side. The curse. It's too dangerous," she said weakly. "Playing with fire."

Ian couldn't speak; he ran, carrying her like she weighed nothing.

There were bloody scratches on his chin and chest and a few swollen areas on his arms that would bruise later—battle wounds, she guessed, from his father.

She couldn't help but notice that she was pressed against his naked chest, and her palm touched the muscles as he ran.

"See, you do look better with a shirt off," Everly muttered.

A choked half grunt, half laugh followed as Ian carried her farther away from the burning cabin, just off the main drive where Hunter waited.

Ian put Everly down on the grass and collapsed to his knees, his head hung low, and he fell forward on his hands, panting as he tried to control his emotions. Slowly he forced the wolf side of him away.

"Ian." Hunter was shocked at his transformation. "What did you do?"

"What needed to be done." He looked at Hunter, his jaw clenched, and a silent message passed between them, and Hunter nodded in understanding.

"Sergeant Mitchell," Everly coughed out. "He was in on it."

"Stevens took care of him." Hunter pointed across the road toward Officer Stevens and the second patrol car. Beyond the car, she could see a gasoline canister and the body of Sergeant Mitchell lying face down.

Officer Stevens, his face pale, a gun still in his hands, was using his radio to call for help.

"How did you get here in time?" Everly asked, looking between the two.

Hunter pointed to Corvis. "Your omen came for us and brought us here."

"Thanks." She started coughing again. And in the distance, she could hear the fire trucks drawing near.

"Ian, she needs help, and I don't think you should be seen right now," Hunter said.

Ian glanced down at his half-naked body, covered with claw marks and blood. He nodded. "I got it. Take care of her. She's my responsibility."

"I will," Hunter promised.

Ian slunk into the shadows of the evening, and Hunter picked up Everly and carried her through the woods to the fire truck and the ambulance behind it.

"Here!" Hunter yelled. "I need help."

Everly was shuffled between medics and given an oxygen mask to help her breathe. Hunter stayed by her side at the back of the ambulance bumper. His arm wrapped around her protectively. Everly felt herself leaning into his side for strength and comfort.

"Can you talk?" Officer Stevens came with his notebook to interview Everly. His eyes were red and bloodshot, possibly from the smoke, possibly from crying at having to shoot his commanding officer.

Everly nodded. "How did you know to come here?" She started the interview before he even got a question out.

Stevens grinned. "I followed the same leads you did. Once you identified Eric Mulligan, I interviewed his coworker at the Kwik Mart. It turns out I wasn't the first to interview him. He marked the cabin on a map, and I radioed it in. Except, I didn't get here first. Mitchell did and…" Stevens took a deep breath, struggling with what was coming next. "I saw him dousing the cabin in gasoline. When I confronted him, he denied doing anything wrong. Said it was condemned and a hazard as a distillery. Needed to be disposed of."

Stevens wiped at his brown eyes. They were filled with tears. "I argued about destroying evidence, and then I saw it."

"Saw what?" she asked.

Stevens pulled out a set of keys, with a Gravemark key chain and a pink can of pepper spray. "It was on the ground. I recognized your keys from our interview. Then I put two and two together. I asked where you were, and he denied seeing you. Then I heard you crying for help from the cellar. There was only one reason to burn a house. I pulled my gun. Mitchell fired first and missed—I didn't."

Hunter hugged Everly as Stevens looked away and coughed.

"I just don't know how you got out of the cellar." Stevens rubbed the back of his neck.

"I saved her." Hunter pulled Everly closer.

"But the doors, man." Stevens pointed to the heavy wood pieces lying ten feet from the cellar. "They were ripped from the hinges."

Hunter coughed to cover up and try to think of something. "They were old, and when you are desperate to save someone you care about—you can do anything."

Everly felt her heart flutter; she reached for the oxygen

mask again to help her think straight. Stevens walked away to answer more questions from Sergeant Garret.

Hunter gently rubbed a blanket over her shoulders, and Everly pulled the mask away.

"What happened to Ranger Danville?" she whispered. "I saw how badly Ian was beaten up."

Hunter's knuckles turned white, and he took a deep breath. "He was pretty far gone to the wolf side. There wasn't any turning back."

"Did Ian have to—" Everly couldn't bear the thought of him having to kill his dad.

"No, when we tracked Eugene down, he was already on death's door. Shot by a silver bullet. I'm pretty sure Sergeant Mitchell was cleaning up his mess and all loose ends regarding the court case. The wounds Ian sustained were from trying to get close to his dad. Eugene was too far gone to the wolf and didn't recognize anyone." Hunter paused. "But Ian wouldn't give up. He fought and held him down, talking to him and bringing him back to his human self for his last moments of lucidity."

Everly felt tears falling down her cheeks as the story brought back her memories of the last moments with her dad.

"But he was able to get closure—to say goodbye."

"That's good." Everly quickly recounted everything she learned from Mitchell. The dog fighting, capturing a werewolf. How he would force Eugene to make the witnesses and anyone that crossed him disappear.

"How do you force a werewolf to do anything?" Hunter said.

"Lock them up in a silver cage long enough. They will do almost anything—Stockholm syndrome at its worst. But Eugene let me go. He could have killed me that night, but he let me go."

"He did one good thing among the bad. That doesn't make

him a saint, Everly. He still murdered three people and who knows how many others at Mitchell's whim."

"But why did he return and damage my car?"

"I don't know, but I'm guessing it's because you went back. He wanted to scare you into leaving before Mitchell learned your name and forced him to hurt you. He didn't know the person he was looking for, Maddie, was captured by the fairies. He was still hunting a girl."

Just then, the cabin roof collapsed, and they both jumped. Firefighters and trucks were lining the access road and trying to keep the fire from spreading toward the preserve.

They both turned to watch the night light up with red and embers floating into the sky. Everly was sitting on the ambulance bumper. Hunter reached for her hand, and they clasped fingers, threading them through each other's like they had been doing it all their life.

He released her hand and stood over her, grasping her shoulders. She looked up into his handsome face.

"Everly I—when we returned to the cabin and saw it in flames. I thought you were gone." His green eyes met hers, and she was falling hard. "I don't know what I'd do if I lost you." He took her chin in his fingers and lifted her face to meet his.

"You didn't lose me," she whispered. "I'm right here."

"Everly, I—" His lips parted, and he leaned forward to kiss her.

Everly closed her eyes and inhaled as the lightest touch brushed against her bottom lip. Her heart fluttered; she leaned forward to meet Hunter in a kiss.

A phone rang, piercing the silence and her heart.

Hunter pulled back as if snapped into the present. His eyes were dilated, and he looked around as the sound continued to punctuate the night. He let go of her face and wiped his hands on his pants. Hunter was irritated as he pulled out the phone, and his face fell. He stepped away from her as he was overcome with guilt as Aimee Stillwell's name appeared on the screen.

"It's okay, you should answer it. Aimee's probably worried about you."

Hunter's face was flushed as she watched him go from desire to frustration, but the one that tore at her heart the most? *Guilt.*

"I'm sorry, Everly. I never meant—"

"Answer it," she commanded.

Hunter moved away to take the call. Everly stepped away from the ambulance to watch the building burn.

There were so many unanswered questions. *Why didn't Eugene go back for Ian? Was he ashamed?*

Everly walked toward Stevens, who was leaning against the bumper of his police cruiser. Another officer had taken his service pistol away, and he looked like he had seen a ghost.

"Can I tell you something in confidence?" Stevens whispered.

"Sure?" Everly moved to lean against the trunk with him.

"I think I'm going crazy?" he rushed out.

"Why do you think that?" she asked.

"I saw." He shook his head. "After I killed Mitchell, I swear I saw a monster."

"A monster," Everly breathed out.

"Yeah, it was carrying you into the woods; it was like a half-man, half-wolf thing."

"You must be mistaken; that was Hunter."

"No, it was someone else or something else."

Everly's mind started to rush through the possibilities; then she looked up at Stevens's young face. "How old are you?"

He blushed. "Twenty."

"Really? I thought you were older."

"I graduated high school two years early and then enrolled

in college before joining the police academy." Stevens stared off into the night. "But what has that to do with anything? I swear, I'm not making it up."

A raven fluttered through the night, causing Stevens to duck down in surprise. What looked like a slow-falling black ember fell in front of Stevens. He frowned and reached out to brush it with his finger as it turned to ash.

"That looked like a feather, and was that a raven I just saw?"

Everly started to laugh as she realized what was happening. "The unkindness has just marked you."

"The what?"

"I think we will be seeing more of each other very soon." Everly got up and moved to stand by Hunter's Jeep. "And no, I don't think you're crazy. Just don't tell anyone at the department what you saw."

Stevens looked confused as Everly moved to catch up with Hunter, and he hung up the phone.

"That was Aimee." He ran his hands over his face. "She was in tears and just confessed to destroying your dorm room. Why didn't you tell me?"

"I don't stoop that low," Everly said softly. "She was angry with me, and she dealt with it, and I will deal with her later. But for now, I want to go home."

"Gravemark?" he asked.

"No, my home. I want a shower and a nap."

EPILOGUE

Everly washed her hair three times and still couldn't get the smell of smoke from it. Her clothes went right into the garbage. She wrapped a fluffy pink towel around her hair and headed to her room, where her window was open, and Corvis was sitting on the ledge.

"Thank you for bringing help."

"I returned to tell you that Mitchell shot the werewolf, but he already had you in the basement and was starting the fire. I had to fly fast to get Ian and Hunter."

Everly sighed. "It's a good thing you fly so fast. Thank you, Corvis. For everything you did these last few days."

Corvis puffed up his chest. "Does that mean you'll extend my TV privileges?"

"Sure." Everly laughed and then grew solemn. "How is Ian, do you know?"

Corvis tilted his head. "He is recovering with the help of the real Dr. Madsen. There seems to be no permanent damage for his half shift to save you."

"What of the changeling?" she asked.

"The society is still deciding what to do with her."

"You mean to put her in the oubliette?"

"No." Corvis hopped over to her nightstand and started picking through her jewelry box. "A changeling at Gravemark can be quite helpful to the society if she behaves. They are thinking of enrolling her." Corvis lifted a ring and moved it to the side. "Also, know that the headmistress is awarding you full-griever status and high marks for your work in discovering both the grimm killer and the changeling. The license is already on your desk at school."

"You snooped, didn't you?" Everly said. She unrolled her towel and began to brush out her wet hair. "I like that you are as obsessed with gossip as Holland."

"Knowledge is power, and as your omen, I want to help you to the best of my abilities." He picked up a bracelet. "Can I have this?"

"No, put it back," Everly commanded.

"Did you also know that Hunter and Aimee broke up?" Corvis looked at her, and she swore the raven smiled.

"No, when? It's only been a few hours since the fire."

"During the phone call, after she confessed. Hunter told her it was unacceptable, and they needed a break."

Everly's heart started to race in her chest. She closed her eyes and almost felt Hunter's lips press against hers in that almost kiss. Was that her first kiss? Did it even count? Then she opened her eyes to see her photo wall and the image of her and Holland hugging.

Everly's heart broke, and she quickly shoved aside and buried her feelings. She couldn't hurt Holland like that. She would have to be the strong one to resist temptation.

Speaking of temptation, she couldn't get Ian's bare chest out of her mind. Everly flopped over on her bed, buried her head into her pillow, and screamed.

She was still screaming when Corvis spoke up.

"You have company."

Everly lifted her head, looked at her open bedroom door, and saw it was empty. Birdie was replanting her pots downstairs, and Summer was up in the attic playing the ukulele. Everly could hear the out-of-tune strings strumming along.

"Where?" She turned to her open window to see another raven sitting patiently with a letter.

Everly gingerly took the papers and opened them up to read the notice from the

Grimm Society.

This time, there were only two words on the paper, and it was unsigned.

Well done.

Everly smelled the paper and immediately got hints of vanilla, lemongrass, and...

She crushed the paper in a ball and tossed it into the trash.

A knock came at the door.

"Come in," Everly said.

Birdie came in with a wistful smile on her face. "Heard the news from a little birdie." She grinned at Corvis.

Everly couldn't hide her smile.

"Well, I guess it's time to give you this then." She reached into her pocket, produced two keys, and handed them to Everly. "You've proven you're ready."

Everly stared at the key in confusion.

"It's the key to outbuilding, where your father kept his cases, solved and unsolved. The second key is to the desk. You might find some interesting things in there."

Everly didn't wait. She jumped out of bed, kissed Birdie on the head, and ran out to the back building in her bathrobe. Corvis took the shortcut out the window.

Her fingers struggled with the key, and then she was in;

flipping the lights on, she walked to the back office, her grandpa's, her father's, and now hers. She went to the desk, unlocked the bottom filing drawer, and pulled out the first file.

She quickly read the case file and couldn't stop grinning, already ready to take the following case on.

"What?" Corvis asked. "What did you find?"

"Sea monsters!" Everly's voice rose in excitement. She laid down the file folder to look at the photos of a small town on the bay, a fishing village with a problem.

"But I hate sushi," Corvis whined.

THE GRIMM SOCIETY #2

COMING DECEMBER 2023

Chanda Hahn is a NYT & USA Today Bestselling author of The Unfortunate Fairy Tale series. She uses her experience as a children's pastor, children's librarian and bookseller to write compelling and popular fiction for teens. She was born in Seattle, WA, grew up in Nebraska, and currently resides in Waukesha, WI, with her husband and their twin children; Aiden and Ashley.

Visit Chanda Hahn's website to learn more about her other forthcoming books.
www.chandahahn.com